SWORD
AND THE PYTHIA

A
NOVEL
BY

BALTAZAR BOLADO

C. L. B.
A. F. B.
S. L. F. B.

NOVELS IN SINGULARITY

BBI Publications

PROLOGUE Umbilicus

I will pour out of my Spirit upon all flesh: and your sons and your daughters shall prophesy, and your young men shall see visions, and your old men shall dream dreams: And I will shew wonders in heaven above, and signs in the earth beneath; blood, and fire, and vapor of smoke.

—Acts 17-0 KJV

The man was long-haired and hairy-skinned. High Priest of the Nazarites, Othniel deKharouf, stood upon Mount Parnassus and looked down at the perdition below—a bottomless pit out of which a mysterious vapor and fire escaped.

Comparable to a wound, the pit cut into the earth's skin, savagely wounding the rock of the mountain. Its spiritual bottomless, not visible to human eyes, prevailed outside of earthly dimensions.

Within deKharouf's spirit, a war raged. Bloodshot eyes, bursting in torment, relinquished to ruddy, inflamed skin. His long flowing hair, like a banner blowing in the tempest, swirled in the malicious whirlwind blasting out of the fiery pit.

Regarding the darkened heavens, deKharouf stood upon the mountain and wrestled against God. "I am a man!" His shout, mighty in texture, did not penetrate the vapor spilling out of the chasm. "You are the Almighty God!"

The mighty winds evanesced, as if in acknowledgment of his declaration.

Peace entered deKharouf's soul, the calmness of the winds seemingly bringing composure to his spirit. The reprieve lasted a short time, before the agony returned to his troubled heart.

Another mighty windstorm surged through the mountain, hitting him directly. At the same time, lightning flashed across the dark clouds. After the atmospheric outburst, torrential rain punished the never-ending pit, from wherein a spiritual beast and four mighty angels stirred.

Pointing an accusatory finger at the black firmament, deKharouf yelled, "All of my life I've served you! But in my spirit, I declare before your throne that I will stop this prophecy!"

For many years, his war with the Almighty consumed him. A spiritual battle deKharouf refused to surrender.

As the vapor extended beyond the chasm and climbed up the mountain, even as it spread across the lowness of the valley, deKharouf's cries reached into heaven. "I will stop the son of Zeus! I am but a man! But I will stop the four angels who will rise out of the bottomless pit!"

Vapor and the Scarlet Colored Beast

At the dawn of the perdition, a star fell from the heights. Some fifty kilometers northwest of Thebes, the earth shuddered and quaked in aftershocks. After the shaking, a chasm appeared at the foot of the mountain.

The umbilicus pushed down until it fell into a pit without end. A titanic spiritual reservoir lay in its void. Abundant smoke arose from its depths and fire came out if it.

Inside the pit was a prisoner: a great scarlet colored beast. The beast began to breathe again, then to prophecy and command.

In the ancient times, the goats and the goat people were the first to see the chasm spewing forth hot vapor. The goat people were the first to feel the breath of the beast, and hear echo of the ancient prophecies foretelling his return.

After the oracular resonance, the vapor moved north and south bringing forth, into their fatherland, the *Heraclaidae* from the north wielding their swords of iron, and the *Temenidae* from the south brandishing their royal blades. The vapor rose out of the hole in the earth—a spiritual smoke brimming with destruction—intoxicating the selected people.

Death came from the sacred lot existing under the dreadful view of twin-peaked Parnassus. Here great earthquakes shook the planet at strange times and sweet gases came out of the gorges and rocks. Among the rocks and gases, at *rocky Pytho,* the Heraclaidae came to hear the voice and will of their god.

Soon after, the royal instrument of the perdition—rising from the imperial dynasties of the Temenidae—moved northward to sit upon the throne of death at *Pella.*

Hell soon followed.

Chapter 1 If You're in Hell

Set me as a seal upon thine heart, as a seal upon thine arm:
for love is strong as death.

—Solomon 8:6 KJV

Uziel Basra, a mighty Nazarite warrior, also stood upon the height of the peak to look down at the perdition.

The winds blew through the mountain. The umbilicus opened, pushing its fire over the earth.

I cannot lose you now!

Oh my love, I am dead without you.

For so long I've loved you.

Basra knew the history of the umbilicus, the story drummed into him from a young age.

As the gusts of the fire blew all around him, he recited his oath. The oath replaced the vow he declared to God, long ago.

From out of the umbilicus the beast will come.

I will slay him.

If you are in Hell, my beloved, then I'll enter its gates to save you.

1.2

"No!" The sound exploded out of Uziel Basra.

"I sent her out at dawn," said High Priest deKharouf. "She's gone." Reaching into his mantle, he held out a light pink envelope. "She told me to give you this."

Basra's hand shot out and snatched the envelope. He recognized her fragrance on the paper.

Rosewood, jasmine, lilacs—her favorite scents. Now she's gone.

Gently, he opened the covering, careful not to tear the ends of the paper.

My wonderful, Uziel,

I'm sorry I couldn't say goodbye to you. High Priest deKharouf felt it best this way. It hurt me so inside to leave you, my love.

Uziel, don't try to find me. It will endanger our nazar.

Set me as a seal upon your heart, until we see each other again.

Your only love,

Ariella Muloc

"Her nazar," Uziel said softly, without looking up, "what is it?"

"I cannot tell you."

"You will tell me."

"No," deKharouf declared, "I will not."

Uziel moved toward the priest.

The priest stood unmoving.

"Master deKharouf," whispered Basra, "did you send her to *Siwa,* or did you send her east to acquire the path of the four angels?"

In a voice meant to calm, deKharouf said, "I sent her to fulfill her *waid.* A promise cannot be broken."

Out of control, Basra gripped deKharouf by the shoulder and placed him up against the wall. "You're my Master. Because of you, I am prepared to fulfill all of my vows." He shook his head and gripped the priest's shoulder tighter. "Don't talk to me about promises that can't be broken."

Without flinching, deKharouf said, in a steady voice, "I sent her…to fulfill her promise…as I will send you to fulfill yours. If there are consequences, I care not."

1.3

"Ariella, I'll love you forever" came his solemn promise to his best friend, the love of his love.

"I believe you," she whispered. "But time's an enemy that can't be defeated."

"You're my treasure? I'll love you beyond time."

They lay in the Atacama Desert surrounded by the dryness of the ground.

"You've loved me how long, my darling?"

He pressed her close to his chest. His hand passed over each wrinkle around her eyes.

"Eighty years…" he tenderly said. "I've loved you for more than eighty years."

The dry mountain crests over the desert looked down at the amazing sight of the friends.

"What do the geoglyphs tell you?"

He lifted her head gently and looked into her eyes. "The geoglyphs tell the story of our love."

Her eyes twinkled. Finally, she laid her head back on his chest and whispered, "But I'm an old woman."

He gently pressed her tighter to his chest. "All I see is your beauty. I see you now as I did the first time I laid eyes on you."

"We shouldn't have translated here. We're only supposed to use our spiritual authority to accomplish the Kingdom's business."

"Ssshhh," he touched her lips. "We are about the Kingdom's business. We are the Kingdom's riches."

Quietness moved over the desert.

After a long while, she said, "I'm ninety-two, you're ninety-six. I don't think we're treasures anymore."

They did not appear to be in their nineties. To the world around them, they were a young couple deeply in love.

"You'll always be my treasure," Basra said, gently.

Once more, she lifted her head off his chest and looked wistfully at him. "He's forgotten about us, my love. My dearest Uziel, he doesn't remember our passions. We're only useful to him until we fulfill our sacred oaths."

"You're wrong, my beloved," Uziel defiantly shook his head. "He hasn't forgotten about our love. After we fulfill our promises, he'll allow us to be husband and wife. To become one."

"But Uziel, we wanted children, a family."

"Remember *Abram* and *Sarai*," he quickly responded. "Recall when they started their family. I will always love you. Even after all these years. I've loved you faithfully. I'll love you forever. Always."

1.4

Uziel Basra discerned the potent figure of the *hosioi* a mile away.

They detected me, he surmised. *I have no choice but to fight.*

Discernment was a spiritual gift, able to pierce through darkness and fog and perceive entities and places long distances away, in some cases, even across the world.

The spiritual vapor of the hosioi hung in the air, preventing Basra from discerning the enemy.

The vapor's too thick.

At that instant, the weight of the spiritual weapon pounded him to the ground and he suffered the sweltering heat of the Rig-e Jenn Desert, as he writhed in pain.

The hosioi travel in numbers of five.

Driving his body to the side, Basra narrowly avoided the next strike of the hosioi.

In his haste to make the killing strike, the hosioi came out of the protective vapor. The mistake imperceptible, for a split second he stood defenseless.

Using just his eyes, Basra drove his spiritual violence into the hosioi warrior's organs, killing the man instantly.

There's four more. Where are they?

The heat of the Rig-e Jenn restored him, momentarily. Basra fed off the desert elements.

The second and third hosioi appeared out of the vapor rapidly. Their weapons clashed against Basra's armor.

Within the whirlwind of his spiritual ferocity, Basra's transcendent sword ripped apart flesh and blood and cut into the spirit, dismembering the otherworldly killers.

Two left. They're the sentries of the elixir.

The fourth hosioi was much stronger than the previous three. In silence, he emerged from out of the vapor.

Too late, Basra reacted.

The hosioi combatant's *sarissa* caught Basra on the side of his breastplate. Even though the killing strike missed its intended mark, Basra went airborne, landing to one side of a sand dune.

Lying on his back, more dead than alive, Basra focused on the backdrop of the mountains in the distance. In a burst of energy, he *translated* miles away.

In reaction, the vapor reacquired him and returned him to the dry desert.

This time the sharpness of the sarissa cut him in his left leg and his blood poured out into the salt and sand. In pain, Basra managed to use the edge of his sword to catch the spear, breaking its point and leaving the mighty hosioi attacker defenseless. Driving his sword into the evil spirit within the hosioi, he disembodied the man, leaving nothing but entrails in the desert sand.

The sarissa of the fifth hosioi pierced Basra on the other leg, opening a long gash from his knee to just below his groin.

He crumbled to the sand.

Because of the clean strike, the hosioi went off balance. Fighting to recover, he braced before delivering the killing blow.

It was all the time Basra needed. He concentrated his energy to translate.

Perceiving Basra's energy, the hosioi hurriedly thrust his spear.

As the sarissa began to cut into his flesh, Basra succeeded in translating out of the corporal dimension. Exploding through the dimension of time, he sensed his body enter into the limitless quality of eternity. Moving through the perfect light of eternity, he felt the weightlessness of space translate beneath him.

Now positioned behind the hosioi, Basra drew his sword.

Before the sword pierced him through the heart, the hosioi perceived his destruction.

Basra stood over the five corpses of the hosioi in the desert hotness, the perfect spiritual warrior of God.

Struggling to overcome the thickness of the vapor, he moved his spiritual sight across the desolate land.

Where are you, my love?

Basra looked down at the dying hosioi. Kneeling next to the high priest, he put his mouth close to his ear. "Where is she?" he whispered, coldly.

The hosioi coughed up blood and remained silent.

"Tell me." Basra placed his hand over the open wound of the fallen warrior. "You're the overseer of these four. You know who I am. You know I have the power to heal you. I'll heal you," he whispered, slowly, "so I can torture you."

"*Fae ena kouva skata,*" replied the hosioi, nearing his last breath.

Pulling back calmly, Basra gave a dismissive contemplation to the fallen priest. "No," answered Basra, "I don't think I will."

Rising to his feet, his spiritual sight discerned what the hosioi wouldn't tell him. He pulled back in surprise. "The priestess didn't come," he proclaimed.

If the priestess isn't traveling with them, then Ariella isn't here.

Stepping away from the dying man, Basra breathed in the desert heat, rapidly processing the events as they transpired.

They're not the defenders of the priestess.

Viciously turning back to the overseer, he once more knelt next to the doomed hosioi. Searching through the man's Doric chiton, he quickly located the small flask.

Getting to his feet, he looked down at the motionless overseer. "I'll let you die now," he said.

Minutes later the hosioi overseer took his last breath.

Promptly, to avoid having the trail of his movements detected, Basra disposed of the physical remains of the five hosioi.

Finishing his labor, he took one last look around and, in the twinkling of an eye, translated out of the desert.

1.5

"Master deKharouf, please."

The priest noticed Uziel's eyes possessed vulnerability in them.

"Master deKharouf," declared Uziel. "I swear my oath to fulfill this nazar, and recover Ariella."

Chapter 2 The Great Horn

And as I was considering, behold, an he-goat came from the west on the face of the whole earth, and touched not the ground: and the goat had a notable horn between his eyes.

—Daniel 8: 5 KJV

Sunshine covered the city in the early afternoon.

Professor Ezekiel Arrhidaeus and a small party of soldiers entered an antechamber where was preserved a golden larnax containing the silver utensils, the golden wreath of 180 oak leaves, thirty-six acorns, and the cleaned bones of an ancient king.

For over twenty-seven years Arrhidaeus had dug in search of the hidden treasure.

The bones are the treasure. Genetic mapping will prove my work hasn't been in vain.

"Professor!" called out a supervisor, "there's a hall! It could be the entrance!"

"Can we be certain these are the remains we are seeking?" asked another supervisor.

Arrhidaeus fought to stay calm, his attention riveted on the golden larnax. A slight tremble in his fingers betrayed him.

"Look Professor! The star!"

Arrhidaeus ran his hand across the golden trunk and over the prominent starburst identifying the royal bloodline of the bones inside.

The diggings, a parliamentary directive funded by the Macedonian Government, led him to the tombs of the Macedonian kings. The amount of funds and resources allocated to the diggings astonished Arrhidaeus.

"What's the problem with the government's participation?" asked Hector Lagos, his longtime assistant. "We should be thrilled we've gained contributors who aren't sluggish. Have you forgotten the many other digs where we needed to steal our funding before we asked and begged?"

"Many parts of this dig haven't followed the normal arrangement digs are subject to," replied Arrhidaeus. "You don't find that peculiar?"

"Yes," Lagos quickly replied, "I do. But Professor I think we need to take advantage of our good fortune, not question it."

As Arrhidaeus examined the starburst on the exterior of the golden larnax and the golden grave crown, Lagos entered the imperial hall, an offshoot of the *Royal Tomb II, at Vergina.*

"Why is it here?" Arrhidaeus whispered.

"I speculate it was moved from Egypt to make certain it wasn't disturbed by grave robbers, or diggers like us."

"Yes, but why?"

"So another larnax could take its place, perhaps long after the creation of the tombs," replied Lagos.

"Precisely," concurred Arrhidaeus. "What better way to hide it," he went on, "then to relegate it to an antechamber." It was a statement not a question. "We'll finish the preservation of record and then transport the larnax and all of the artifacts to the lab. We'll look inside then."

The deliberateness of the process wounded Arrhidaeus. It took all of his strength to stop and not open the gold box. To distract himself, he went about the tedious procedure of cataloging every detail in the room.

2.2

The two men worked in the empty lab.

Inside the larnax were the bones.

Looking at Arrhidaeus, Lagos nodded slowly. "We agree then? Begin the genetic testing?"

Arrhidaeus imagined the media circus sure to surround his declaration; the countless second-guessers and doubters who would materialize to attempt to disapprove his findings.

"Will you announce these bones as the remains we've spent our entire careers searching for?"

Ezekiel Arrhidaeus remained motionless. The lab became a vacuum as he answered, "Yes, these are the remains we've sought after. I'm convinced of it." He turned dramatically. "These are the bones of Alexander the Great of Macedon."

Chapter 3 Will You Be My Mom?

"I love you."

High Priestess Rhea turned to look at him. "I love you too, my son." The woman gave him a warm smile.

Out of the overcast day, the scent of rain filled the room.

Sitting on the edge of the bed, the boy asked, "Will you be my mom?" Recognizing his error, Uziel added, "My real mom, I mean."

Putting down the basket full of arugula and cabbage, she rushed to him. Holding him close to her, she ran her hands through his dark hair. "Oh Uziel, my sweet gift from God, everyone has only one father and one mother. They can't be replaced. I promise you…I will always be your second mother."

Holding her tightly, Basra asked, "My mom, what was her name?"

"Hannah."

"Before she died, she left me here?"

The priestess held him closer. "Yes, she was consumed by cancer."

"God judged her?"

Rhea looked away as she spoke. Sadness came over her. "No one told you. You discerned what happened."

A lectern stood near the bed. On it rested an old book containing the law.

"Please tell me…why God judged my mom."

As much as she wanted to answer him, Rhea continued to hold him tightly in silence.

3.2

Through the years, the priestess remained true to her word. Basra recalled her dedication to his upbringing, including her presence through some of the most profound moments of his life.

"I think about her all the time, Momma. But I don't know how to tell her. Every time I try to talk to her, my words get messed up."

On the verge of manhood, Uziel turned sixteen. He'd been trying to talk to Ariella for almost a year. It took all of his courage to share his feelings with Rhea.

The priestess silently waited, allowing him the chance to continue.

"I've been trying to do as you said, and tell her honestly how I feel, but she's so beautiful. Her hair's long and wavy, like the ocean. And she smells like honey, and her face reminds me of…Hubb's wool."

Hubb was the name of the little lamb he'd raised as a boy.

Priestess Rhea waited until he finished before responding. "Your thoughts are pure, Uziel. There's nothing wrong with you. If it's true, love will wait."

Uziel turned to Rhea. "Momma, have you ever loved anyone like I love Ariella?"

Chapter 4 Voveo Vovi Votum

When thou shalt vow a vow unto the Lord thy God, thou shalt not slack to pay it: for the Lord thy God will surely require it of thee; and it would be sin in thee.

—Deuteronomy 23: 21 KJV

I'm hungry. I'm thirsty. I'm weak.

Uziel Basra hadn't eaten any food or drank any liquids in forty days and forty nights.

He bowed his head low to the ground. The front of the robe opened, exposing a strong chest and revealing his body healing from the battle in the desert. In the Turkish heat, he recited his vows.

"This is my body. This is my blood. I commit my spirit to you."

The oath lightly touched the walls of the empty room and bounced back to fill his ears. "Prepare your servant," Uziel petitioned, raising his hand to his chest in contrition.

The ground, hard underneath his aching knees, pushed against his rigid and tight muscles. He'd been on bruised knees before the ancient altar for twenty-eight straight days and his body and mind were tired.

The late afternoon sun filtered through the single window as Uziel shifted his weight until the blood flow returned to his lower parts.

A door opened and a priest entered. Placing his hand on the kneeling man's shoulder, the priest whispered close to his ear, "You'll be in need of much nourishment."

Uziel, in a transcendent state, slowly rose to his feet.

Exhibiting surprising strength, the priest steadied Uziel as they moved through the door.

4.2

The priests carefully nursed him back to health and prepared him.

Slowly, Uziel's diet increased from bread and water, to chargrilled chicken, and salads composed of *hummus and şalgam.*

Seven days later his health had returned.

"Eat some *tantuni* and *cezerye,*" said the priest, having returned from Tarsus. "The *olah,* the *hatat,* and the *shelamim* are prepared."

Uziel ate.

"The five hosioi you intercepted, forty-seven days ago," said the priest, "carried the elixir and an accelerant."

Uziel, weakened from the long fast, held up his hand. "Don't compromise yourself, Priest Enoch."

The priest continued without hesitation. "They were carrying chromosomes capped by telomeres, absent of oncogenesis transformation."

"Immortal cells," Basra said in a low voice.

"Precisely," replied Priest Enoch.

"The elixir's regulating the normal restraints on cellular proliferation?"

Priest Enoch paused slightly. "It's difficult to tell. While testing, I confirmed the gene accelerant we've detected in the previous elixir samples."

"Your conclusions confirm the cells overcame the *Hayflick Limit?*"

"Most certainly."

The men went silent.

Out of the silence, Uziel said, "Thank you, Priest Enoch. I realize you're jeopardizing your relationship with High Priest deKharouf by sharing this information with me."

"How so, my son?"

"He does not approve of my decision to serve two masters—my God, and my emotional attachment to Ariella."

"No need to concern yourself about such affairs, my son. You see, it was High Priest deKharouf who directed me to give you this information."

4.3

High Priest deKharouf stood before the Great Altar of the Nazarites—the Table of the Lord—and tilted his head back.

The perpetual fire burned upon the stone altar in perfect love and vicious anger.

"It's time to swear the oath." Emotion saturated the priest's voice. "Time is no more. It is finished."

The ram, the ewe, and the lamb highlighted the prepared sacrifices carried over by the priests of the temple. The temple courtyard ceremonially displayed the dishes and utensils dedicated to the act of ransom. To appease the deity, the priests offered a generous tribute of grain offerings, followed by gifts of drink and beverage.

The *mikveh* completed, Uziel entered the expansive courtyard bordered by the seven priests.

High Priest deKharouf held up the sharpened blade, glistening in the sunset.

Uziel spoke in the voice of the spirit. "My body is the temple, my blood is the nourishment, my strength is my purity, and my love is my life. All other oaths are void. I am reborn and renewed to my vows. I cannot die until their fulfillment. Anoint me, Master, to purge the past and achieve the future."

The God of Consuming Fire knows my heart.

First, the blade removed the bottom tips of his locks. Methodically, the high priest also removed certain locks and curls. Minutes later, much of Uziel's dark wavy hair, full of the vibrancy of life, lay discarded on the cold ground.

Shivering in the early Turkish evening, Uziel walked up the three steps and bowed before the prepared altar.

"Collect the hair," commanded deKharouf.

The priests collected the hair and placed it on the fiery coals to one side of the consecrated slab. The smoke elevated into the air.

"Thread the seven locks," called out the high priest.

The priests laced the seven locks and arranged them according to the stellar arrangement.

In the night, Uziel stood with seven distinct locks.

"Until the fulfillment of your oath, your hair must not be cut," commanded deKharouf. "Swear to purge the iniquitous past and the principalities of the air."

"I swear my vow," Uziel replied.

As the sun set, the ceremony ended and the priests began to file back into the sanctuary. Only the high priest and Uziel remained in front of the altar.

The high priest opened the holy scroll.

Cool evening air permeated Uziel's blood and entered into his marrow.

"The four angels are released from the bottomless pit," announced High Priest deKharouf. "The seed of perdition, kept and preserved two thousand three hundred and thirty-seven years, awaits at the chosen temple of conception."

Uziel waited to perceive the translation.

"The chosen Pythia can replicate the image of the man, and his number." The priest anointed Uziel's head, the oil running down the locks of his hair.

Uziel kept his face near the sacred ground, paralyzed by the unquenchable, merciless Fire. "I am the blameless sacrifice of the Almighty," he declared. "Command my arm."

The priest placed his hand upon the dampened head of the mighty warrior. "According to divine law," deKharouf proclaimed, "the princes of the power of the air in Siwa have dominion of the ground. Fulfill your nazar. Overcome their dominion and stop the replication of the beast."

Chapter 5 Phoenix Dactylifera

"Allah il Allah!" he sings his psalm,
"On the Indian Sea, by the isles of balm;
thanks to Allah who gives the palm!"

—John Greenleaf Whittier

"Akhenaten, do not hurry. The fruit is in the rutab stage," said Phoe Ptahhotep to his nephew. "Patience."

Fourteen-year-old Akhenaten squeezed the dark reddish-brown drupes in his hand. "Yes, Uncle, I'll be patient."

Even though technology reduced the labor of cultivation, Phoe chose to preserve certain family traditions passed down from generation to generation. Each season found him in the field, sharing family trade secrets no longer considered necessary by modern industry.

"Do you remember why you cannot hurry the fruit?"

"Yes, because of the eternal *tree of life*."

"Precisely. Each season of growth is a whisper from the god." Dramatically, Phoe Ptahhotep gripped his nephew's shoulder. "The god refuses to be rushed. Our purpose began long ago when the *prophētai* divined the message of the vapor. The fruit of the tree of life preserves the cell. After the birth of the beast, there will be an image of the beast."

"Uncle, you speak in riddles."

"The beast who ascends out of the vapor will soon speak clearly. We will cultivate the fruit. In time, its seed will preserve the image."

Akhenaten cocked his head to one side. "The men who collect the fruit of the tree of life, are they the speakers of the god?"

"The *prophētai* speak the words of the god. Their labor cultivates the fruit. In turn, the harvest brings forth the *hosioi*."

"The hosioi," whispered Akhenaten. "What do they do?"

Phoe gripped his nephew's shoulder tighter. "They are the slayers out of the vapor. They perform the will of the god. They guard the *Castalian Spring* and are the sentinels of the *Kassotis*. From the ancient times until now, they are the sentries of the *omphalos*."

Akhenaten stopped to study his uncle intently. "Since my childhood, you've promised one day to teach me how to prepare the elixir."

Phoe turned away. Looking up at the palm, he closed his eyes. Across the Siwa Oasis, a sudden cool breeze brushed across the ground.

"Uncle?"

"Do you realize what you're asking of me?" Phoe asked.

Akhenaten held his uncle's scrutiny. "It's our purpose to tend to the tree and prepare the *elixir*. It's the will of the god that I do my part. Yes, I know what I'm asking of you."

After a long silence, Phoe released a tired breath. "Very well," he said, quietly.

Chapter 6 It Wasn't Human

And it came to pass that night, that the angel of the LORD went out, and smote in the camp of the Assyrians an hundred fourscore and five thousand: and when they arose early in the morning, behold, they were all dead corpses.

—2nd Kings 19: 35 KJV

In the Afghan darkness, like a bolt of lightning, the deadly warrior appeared out of the thick vapor and flashed through the night. Then—in a split second—he appeared behind a wall of mountains, on the left flank of the Afghan force.

The unearthly speed of the movement caused shock along the Afghan front and rear positions, instigating an overreaction. Irregular gunfire erupted, kicking up rock and old sand everywhere, going through and around the streaking flash.

Uncontrollable yelling ensued.

What the hell? No human can move that fast!

"Watch our nine!" yelled out Britney Shafer, first lieutenant commanding the platoon-sized Quick Reaction Force (QRF), posted near the right of the Afghan Group.

"Sergeant B!" yelled out one of the soldiers. "Whiskey Tango Foxtrot! The foot mobile went right through Haji fire. They hit it! It didn't fuck'n care!"

Sergeant Huck Bentley, outfitted in full battle rattle, coolly followed the flash of light. "Keep 'em zipped up!" he commanded, repositioning to get a better vantage point.

Shafer's QRF, linked to a forward Reconnaissance Group, attached to the 12th ANA Commando Battalion, possessed a seasoned core. The soldiers obeyed their sergeant's orders. Not a shot came from the Reaction Force platoon.

Bentley kept fixed eyes on the streaking image as it disappeared behind another wall of mountains directly behind the QRF. "Check six!" Bentley called out, his voice even. In the same breath, he commanded, "Cleared hot!"

Shafer didn't countermand. "Stay frosty!" she yelled out, quickly calculating every second in her mind. *We're outside the wire, but we've got over a thousand hadjies covering our wing,* she reasoned, fighting to calm her nerves. "We're just playing in the sandbox!"

More gunfire bursts came from the peripheral of the commando recon group, followed by more screams.

"Slackman, put the SAW on our nine! Set up a kill box!" Bentley coolly barked out commands.

Heavy bombing sounded across the night. The Afghan Commando Group released mortar fire where they'd last observed the ghostly figure, pounding the surrounding mountains behind them.

A cold chill ran up Shafer's spine as the night exploded from the brightness of the mortar shells hitting their target.

Three mortar rounds, within a span of seconds, struck the eerie image of the warrior.

Shock came over Shafer's face.

The wraithlike figure ran through the concussion field without losing any speed.

No effect? Nothing? Shafer questioned the reality around her.

"Lay down suppression fire!" directed Bentley.

Moments later, the platoon unleashed full-on fire directly on the phantom warrior's position, their powerful weapons hitting their target.

The unearthly combatant suffered no effect, continuing on his deadly rampage.

It isn't possible! It looks like a human soldier…

More screams filled the night as the chilling warrior once more cut into the Afghan Commando Battalion.

"Platoon—fall back!" Lieutenant Shafer screamed into her headset, swinging her arms wildly over the roar of the battlefield.

Dangerously, in haphazard fashion, the QRF rapidly began to extract itself from the location.

"Maintain your platoon stations as you move!"

Bentley's command relaxed the platoon. Regaining its composure, the QRF drew back in a more controlled manner. Minutes later, the QRF took up a defensive position at an elevated location near the foot of the mountain.

Looking down into the valley, Shafer and her platoon witnessed the carnage.

The killing thing in the night, a devil using hellish weaponry, shredded the Afghan Commando Battalion, leaving a trail of inconceivable death.

"Go hot!" Bentley called out.

Promptly, the QRF cut loose, releasing concentrated violence along the Afghan rear position, striking the warrior attacking the Afghan Battalion.

Feeling the weight of firepower, the apparition broke off the attack. Within seconds, the attacker retreated toward the heavy vapor swirling across the distant mountains.

A dreadful silence descended upon the night.

6.2

Matt "Topper" Highcliff knew a good lead when he saw one. Rarely did he come across information amounting to anything suitable to grab a lead, or a respectable news grab, unless the battalion commander, Lieutenant Colonel Edgar "Dynamo" Walker, gave the go ahead.

"It's the best way to deal with embedded journalists, Highcliff," Walker often lectured. "We can't let you guys run all over, spilling your guts on everything you see. It's to protect you as much as us. You don't want to be under a 'blackout' do you?"

When he got the email from First Lieutenant Britney Shafer, the threat of blackout didn't enter his mind as he scheduled an interview without letting the arrogant son-of-a-bitch colonel know.

Two days later, he arrived at the unusually quiet FOB Mehtar Lam. The early summer sun blazed hot behind the mountains.

Following a small contingent of troops into the DFAC, he noticed Lieutenant Shafer sitting in a far corner of the mess hall. Even though she wore dark sunglasses, Highcliff felt her eyes on him as he sat down.

"Laghman Province still requires vigilance so the faster we get this over with, the better," she said, evenly.

He nodded, slightly, as he set down his backpack and removed his laptop, a notepad, and a tablet.

Without deliberation, Shafer cleared her throat and spoke in a low voice. "I've seen a lot of shit out here, so I don't spook easy. What I'm about to tell you stays between us."

"I'm a journalist. You know I'll keep your identity out of it."

"No, I don't know that." Shafer still hadn't removed her shades. "Embedded journalists aren't always trusted out here," she said, disparagingly.

"Why are you willing to tell me anything?" Highcliff asked, forcefully. Experience told him the closer to death a soldier felt, the more chance information would be disclosed.

Something definitely happened to shake up the first Lieutenant.

Deliberately, Shafer removed her sunglasses. "Because I—" A long breath gave way to silence. "You can't write about this. Not yet, anyway."

She hadn't asked him if he was "wired."

I'm a journalist, goddammit. I won't tell her.

"Mind if I take notes?"

Shafer didn't object as Highcliff scribbled something on his notepad.

Fidgeting with her glasses, Lieutenant Shafer spoke quietly, without emotion. "The battalion… We got called back, you know. We hadn't come back full strength since we gave up FOB Mehtar Lam two years ago."

"You're back now?"

Shafer shook her head. "Not exactly. Lima Lima Mike Foxtrot. You know."

Highcliff didn't say anything.

"Afghan forces observed strange shit in the mountains before they got hit. They requested an Incident Assessment Team to investigate possible civilian casualties. ISAF Joint Command thought it'd be a good idea if the 4th kicked up some dust. Five days later Division called us to Laghman Province."

"Yeah, I heard. The insurgents killed thirty-eight Afghan soldiers and—"

Shafer's appearance stopped him in midsentence.

"What hit the Afghan forces wasn't a soldier. Not a human soldier, anyway."

Highcliff locked eyes with the lieutenant. "A soldier? You mean soldiers, don't you?"

Lieutenant Shafer's eyes didn't shift, as they bore into his. Cautiously, she continued. "At fifteen minutes to balls...our satellites... followed its movements. It was here...it was there...it was nowhere and everywhere. Our UAVs," she shook her head. "Our sensors..."

Sensing a major story, Highcliff leaned forward. "Why do you say it wasn't human?"

Shafer flashed anger but maintained her composure. "Don't talk to me like some juicy girl split tail," she sneered. "I don't need a trigger puller to wipe my ass. That fucking thing..." She shook her head slowly, putting her shades back on to cover her eyes. "It went through a thousand Afghan soldiers like they weren't even there."

"Those are the kill numbers?"

Shafer didn't answer.

"That thing?"

"Yeah," Shafer nodded, slightly.

"What do you mean?"

"Like I said: It wasn't human," she answered, lowering her head. "At least, not like anything human I've ever seen."

Highcliff leaned back and studied the soldier. "First Lieutenant?"

Shafer sat unmoving. She didn't respond.

"First Lieutenant?" Highcliff said, louder than before.

Shafer lifted her head.

Again, Highcliff sensed her eyes on him through the shades. He spoke in a calculated tone. "If I hold off on this story, can you tell me what happened out there?"

Chapter 7 Love at First Sight

When Othniel deKharouf first saw Rhea Korban, it was love at first sight.

Bound to God through sacred promise, their oaths usurped all other commitments, needs, and wants. They were both Nazarites, dedicated to God. Their nazars extended to their last breath on earth.

In his vicious character deKharouf dared to explore his heart and spirit for answers.

Rhea's beauty gripped him day and night. A fierce warrior chiseled out of steel and stone, hardened by grueling daily training, the mere sight of her left him weak, unable to rationalize his environment. Her voice reduced him like a river cutting through a mountain.

Like the promise of a fresh dawn, her appearance in his life awakened him to the time of love.

Every day, angels ministered to deKharouf. Equally, conflict gored him.

A man in motion—spiritually, and physically—the enormous pressure threatened to destroy him.

In time, he reached a breaking point.

Chapter 8 I'll Love You Forever

"You're beautiful."

"Thank you, Uziel." Ariella blushed.

In the summer hotness, they lay in a wheat field in the early evening and held each other after a warm rain.

It was many years ago, but Uziel remembered the night well.

We were young. I loved you. We still believed then.

"I remember when I first saw you."

She smiled. "I was twelve, you were sixteen."

"Yeah. Four years ago."

"I didn't realize."

"It seems like yesterday."

She smiled again, her eyes twinkling.

"You were quiet."

"I was just a girl," she said, through another smile.

"Now you're a woman."

They both went quiet, looking up at the night sky.

"I love you."

She rolled over and propped herself up on an elbow. "Uziel, you mustn't."

"I don't care anymore. You're it for me. He'll release us after we've fulfilled our oaths."

Yearning filled Rhea, her body awakening to the implication of his words. "Oh, darling," she moaned. "Do you suppose that one day we can love each other?"

First came the caressing, clumsy at first, then more refined.

"Uziel…we can't." Confusion made her voice sound far away.

Uziel sensed her weakness. When she lost all strength to stop him, he stopped. Full of lust, he said, "It'll be okay if we do it. God will understand." In his physical weakness, he resisted the will of his spirit.

Trembling excitedly, Ariella broke away from Uziel's embrace. In a burst of energy, she got up and ran away into the cool darkness.

Far into the night, beyond the tree line, Uziel chased her. A full moon lit their path. Over ten miles he chased her. Underneath the moonlight, he finally caught her.

A woman in the heat of summer, her hunger insatiable, a growing lust pushed into her. Her body, driven by a hormonal urgency, overcame her spirit. Unable to control herself, she reached out into the night, her kiss landing full on his lips.

Down to the ground they fell.

He reached for her breasts.

In the same movement, she rolled away. Back on her feet, she ran beyond the countryside until she came to a lake, five more miles distant.

Moonlight bounced off the water. She swam in its rawness.

Uziel dove in and swam toward her.

"Don't come any closer," Ariella called out.

He took her in his arms. Floating in the water, he planted his kiss on her lips, lustful, hard, and concentrated. Intoxicated by her scent, he didn't sense the blow until contact.

Ariella lashed out and caught him on the side of the chest.

He lost his breath and fell back into the water.

Before he went under, she saved him, and pulled him to shore.

Under the stars, they lay in each other's arms.

When he recovered his breath, Basra called out to her. "Ariella, you're all I think about."

Again, she ran away, shielded only by the night air.

This continued until the sunrise.

"They'll think we did something." She touched his lips with her fingertips.

"But they'll know we didn't…because my hymen isn't broken."

"Ariella," he whispered. "I'll love you forever."

"I'll love you forever too, my wonderful Uziel."

"We'll love into eternity," he declared, in the morning sunlight.

"Only in our spirits," she whispered in pain.

Chapter 9 Whiz Kids

*It would be inconceivable for us to do [our] work if we didn't make people
excited and uncomfortable with the things that we do at the same time.*

—Regina Dugan

"DoD wants us to reopen Project S," said Lysander Wilson.

Onmus Praetor stopped working on his laptop, his head lowered viewing
the computer screen. "Who's the next dummy we're gonna put in the lead
position over the whiz kids?"

Lysander Wilson shook his head. "No clue."

"Put the prophet in charge."

Wilson went completely still as he ran the idea in his head. "Why?"

"We've got money to burn, and we've gotta move fast. What better way
to get results than to put a fanatic in charge?"

"It could backfire. If the team's too radical, we won't be able to find the
head."

Maps of the Middle East, Russia, China, and Europe took up much of the
walls in the office where the men sat. The circular desk, each end's oblong
wings unique in contrast to the square shaped office, was cluttered with charts
and graphs.

"Who do you think it should be?"

Wilson put down the chart he'd been studying before answering. "The historian might be a good fit, personality wise, but his intelligence might get in the way. The pathologist, maybe."

Praetor's nervous eyes shifted. "I think someone beat us in the development of the super soldier." A trace of perspiration bled from his temple. "The need for speed outweighs the consequence of error. You went over the same data I did. We were created to prevent this sort of thing from happening." Praetor paused to cough and wipe the perspiration away from his neck before resuming. "It would be disastrous if an enemy surprised the United States on the battlefield. The military reports coming out of Afghanistan don't fit the military norms. Without question, there's a vastly superior soldier out there and if we don't get a handle on this, and right quick, we'll fail in satisfying the purpose of our existence."

Wilson sat stone-faced. His silence, to a certain degree, supported Praetor's conclusion.

"We gotta determine who and what hit those Afghan soldiers." Praetor declared.

Wilson turned his coffee cup in his hands before taking a sip. "The Russians maybe?" he whispered. "Maybe the Chinese. Or, the damn Germans. We'll explore every lead, Onmus. The Madam wants all stops pulled on this."

The *Madam* referenced the iron skirt woman in charge of DARPA.

Praetor tried to fight off his agitation. "Maybe it's the Iranians…or the fucking Syrians."

Wilson nodded stiffly and said under his breath, "If we name a project, we go all the way. Identification, Study and Research, everything."

When he didn't finish, Praetor asked, "And the third?"

"We leave it to the hunter-killers."

Praetor looked down. "Outline the trail."

Wilson got up and walked to the graphic war map. When he pushed a button, the map lit up and zeroed in on the Middle East. Blips came up in various regions of the map. "The activity mostly involves Turkey, Syria, Iraq, and Egypt, right now. We think Macedon, as well, but the activity there isn't so well known."

"They're suppressing the info?"

"Possibly." Wilson returned to his desk. "DoD wants our study to support Grey Fox 99. They consider the super soldier a major threat to our interests in the region, and the entire world. I agree."

Chapter 10 Rocky Pytho

…all the treasure in rocky Pytho, beyond Apollo's marble threshold, is not worth life itself.

—Homer, *The Iliad*, Book IX

Vapor came out of the chasm in the ground.

Writhing in the grips of passion, the Pythia's lithe body twisted violently on the tripod assembled over the crater. Perspiration soaked the diviner's body, her long, flowing hair blowing in the wind. Her feminine beauty—striking and pure—glowed in the soft radiance of the mysterious smoke emanating from the fissure in the earth.

Encircled by the gas and smoke, the aroma of the sacrifice nearly strangled the Pythia, her peplos wilting in the vapor as she opened parched lips to speak. "Sck…augh…tilu…oim…nrt…" Guttural echoes bounced off the ancient stone.

In the shadows of the broken temple chamber the five hosioi stood around the *adyton,* frenziedly recording the Pythia's utterances and prattle. From the hosioi, the Pythia's wide-ranging, encrypted sounds were passed on to the other six dark figures standing to one side of the assembly—the *prophētai.*

Dressed in long robes made out of goatskin and goat hair, the shadowy cleric spoke intensely in hushed voices. As the babble came out of the Pythia, the prophētai re-spoke her words in the old tongue.

Dorian dialect, mixed with the earliest Macedonian tongue, formed the morphological base from which came the translation of the Pythia's answer to the question put before her.

In the ancient tongue of the Argeadae, a language all but lost through the ages of time, the prophētai divined. "I have counted the vastness of the numbered sands of the sea, even the infinite mysteries of the heavens. I am the reason the earth trembles below the Euphrates. I am Apollo."

One of the hosioi raised his head—the slightest of movements. The posture of the priest expressed reverence.

From the gibberish, a *prophētēs* divined in a loud voice. "The date, the vessel, and the seed are readied."

At the declaration of the prophētēs, the Oracle writhed and convulsed. As the vapor darkened around her, the Pythia pulled her head back and moaned from her depths. From the prevailing wails arose the ravings of the divination as she shook in her tripod.

The ruins of the temple trembled, as the Pythia's moans cascaded down the slopes of Mount Parnassus and lingered amongst the surrounding treetops. Across the high mountains, the earth shook, pulled here and there from the pressure of the Kerna and Delphic faults.

Working tirelessly, the hosioi and the prophētai successfully deciphered the prophetic utterance, revealing the clear secrets of the god.

In the late night, the ceremony ended and the ruins atop the heights of Parnassus went silent. Three of the hosioi lifted the cataleptic Pythia off the tripod and carried her away in the darkness, leaving the six prophētai and the remaining two hosioi to go over the prophecy of the god.

Chapter 11 Train Wreck

Blessed is he that readeth, and they that hear the words of this prophecy, and keep those things which are written therein: for the time is at hand.

—Revelation 1: 3 KJV

Scrambling for answers, DoD turned to the DARPA Whiz Kid team to explore the strange recent battlefield events taking place across the world.

Sitting around the oval table, Geoffrey "Wizard" Merlin, a genetic engineer, Ronald "Cat" Tomlin, a kinesiologist, Adam "Anatomia" Corliss, a pathologist, Erwin "Rommel" Lisps von Hessen, a military historian, and Daniel "Prophet" Nabil, a Professor of New Testament Interpretation, made up the team.

Like a nonfunctional appendage on a deformed body, Nabil did not fit the pattern and fluidity of the team.

"They request my field of study to lead Project S." The statement from Daniel Nabil stopped the movements of the four other men.

Lisps von Hessen raised his hand. "Hold on a second. Your field of study? What bearing can your field of study have on this project?"

"They called his field of study when they named the project," replied Adam Corliss, before Nabil could respond.

"I'm no Bible thumper, but I've got an uncle who gets into that shi— stuff," Tomlin cut in, his eyes narrowing as he spoke. "And some of the images are crazy. There's a lot of metaphors. They can't possibly be taken literally. Besides, like Rommel asked: What the hell does his field of study have to do with any of this?"

"I agree with both of you. But I'm not an apparition," replied Nabil. "Someone happens to think I can help in this, somehow. Let me correct you. Eschatology is literal and flawless and doesn't need interpretation." Professor Nabil took a swig from his water bottle. "Of course, this isn't the view of the church, or sanctioned by my college. Many times, a certain group will offer an interpretation of a Biblical scripture or prophecy rather than take it literally. If the interpretation is contrary to another group's, it'll cause anger and create misunderstanding."

Tomlin help up his hand. "Just a second there, Moses—"

"Name's Daniel," corrected Nabil.

"Fine, Daniel," Tomlin agreed. "But your academic title is New Testament Interpretation."

Nabil slowly nodded. "As I said: my college doesn't sanction my view of translation over interpretation."

"Look," started Tomlin, "next thing you'll say is God told you to collect our money to build a Ferris wheel, or God told you you're better than all of us ordinary chums and you're allowed to fuck as many women as your balls can handle, or—"

Nabil shook his head. "I'm not a televangelist, I don't want your damn money, and I fuck only one woman—my wife."

The room went quiet.

Out of the quiet, Tomlin said, "To put your field of study as the central subject matter doesn't make sense. Hell, your entire field of study comprises a bunch of metaphors, unproven in our time. We need facts...not metaphors."

"There are no metaphors in eschatology. Bible prophecy is literal," declared Nabil.

Corliss shook his head. "With all respect, Daniel, the book of Revelation is full of imagery. If the images aren't metaphors, what are they?"

"They're literal spiritual images," Nabil answered. "You asked me a direct question. I'll answer it. The images in Revelation, and used throughout prophecy, are images as seen through spiritual eyesight."

Tomlin started to say something, thought better of it, and remained quiet.

Nabil continued. "Spiritual sight sees the world in true reality. Physical eyesight can't. Because of this, physical eyesight gives us a distorted view of reality. Only through spiritual sight can we see the actual world around us."

Hessen shook his head. "No one understands Bible prophecy. Everyone's got their own interpretation and no one agrees with each other."

Nabil looked down quietly before responding. "Let me ask you all: Why do you think DARPA put me on the team?"

All the team members sat in silence.

"Exactly," declared Nabil. "I'm here because they believe I'm the dumbest and craziest one of the bunch."

The men on the team, not expecting such brutal honesty, weren't sure how to respond.

Nabil nodded, "I think they're spot on. So do all of you. Let's give them what the hell they want. They expect this train to derail really quick. Let's not disappoint them."

Nods of approval and looks of respect went across the group.

Leaning forward, elbows on the table, Nabil began. "They don't want me try to figure out my role and interject my knowledge into the project and group. All of you, yes—not me. Obviously, they want me to speak about my area of knowledge, period. More than that, they want it to be the principal part of the project."

Tomlin gradually leaned back in his chair, lost in thought.

Nabil cleared his throat. Like a thunderclap, he said, "I know why I was put on the team. This super soldier incident in Afghanistan, I think I may be able to shed light on it."

"Go ahead," responded Corliss. "Enlighten us."

"I will," Nabil nodded. "But I—we—need more facts and data."

Hessen, following the direction of the group, said, "If you're right, then we've got a lot to catch up on."

"Yeah, we do."

Geoffrey "Wizard" Merlin, genetic engineer, possessing a precise and clear mind, father of four, prided himself on being the quiet leader of the team. Scratching his chin, his voice cut through the energy in the room. "Okay, everybody got a clear picture of what's going on here?"

The entire team acknowledged the question with a yes or a nod of the head.

"All right then. Everybody get on board this train wreck."

Merlin turned and bore his eyes into and through Nabil. "Listen to me closely, Prophet. Your field of study can take control of this project, but only if, and as long as, it leads us into the right ditch. The minute we discover you're a waste of our time, we'll throw you and your field of study so far away from this team you'll need a spaceship to come into work. Got it?"

No one in the room stirred.

"Good then," Merlin said, cautiously. "Let's get this train wreck started."

Chapter 12 Latter Rain Harvest

Be patient therefore, brethren, unto the coming of the Lord. Behold, the husbandman waiteth for the precious fruit of the earth, and hath long patience for it, until he receive the early and latter rain.

—James 5: 7 KJV

Bathed in the spring sunlight, the oasis glistened like a jewel half buried in the desert sand. The pleasant weather promised to extend into the upcoming festival period.

The festivals *Ramadan, Eid al Fitr*, and *Eid el Adha* gave precedence of a cultural importance, while the tribal level status of the *Siyaha Festival*, united and reconciled the population.

A man dressed in a white *galabeya* stood examining a date. A woman, dressed in the traditional *tarfottet*—an azure embroidered garment covering her entire body, and a Siwa veil—stood next to the man. Except for her eyes, visible through a small opening, the thick black cloth completely concealed the woman's face.

Rarely did the women in Siwa leave their homes. However, because of the prominence of the date as an agricultural product in the region, women often assisted in the family business, if a shortage of men in the particular tribe made it necessary.

"Sir, if I may be so presumptuous," said the man in the galabeya, in *Wiwi*, the ancient Berber language. "I guarantee you will be delighted with the quality of the seed." He extended a sample of the fruit to the businessman.

The businessman, dressed immaculately in a Brioni Wool Two-Piece Suit, looked European. Possessing an American flair in marketing and a strong aptitude for communication, the frequency of his recent Siwa Oasis visits seemed to indicate the probability he'd soon be offering terms. "I'll need to visit your grove again," the businessman said, speaking the native tongue fluently.

Ptahhotep, the proprietor and caretaker of the grove, nodded his head. "Whenever you decide to come, your presence will honor us."

Dactylus.

The date, the fruit of the palm—like the fingers of a hand—grips eternity in its clutches, bringing timeless sustenance to the people in the desert. Not the same as the expression meaning "a time"—the fruit's alluring, oblong fruitlet holds hands with those who embrace its luscious piquancy.

"Expect me in the following month. I'll observe the progress of the fruit," the man said. "We can meet then to discuss the finalization of our predetermined arrangement."

"As you wish, sir."

12.2

The following month, at the prescribed time, the businessman sat in Phoe Ptahhotep's small, ordinary office.

The businessman, fashionably dressed, radiated a strange energy. Phoe Ptahhotep swept his vision over the man's lean body, under the finely tailored business suit. As in their previous discussions, he tried to hide his confusion about the mysterious stranger.

This man possesses the sharpness of an executive but moves with a deadly smoothness.

"Was your journey pleasant?" Ptahhotep asked, in the Berber language.

"Yes," answered the executive, in English, flashing a quick smile.

"I'm happy to hear that." Phoe Ptahhotep turned to a young man sitting to one side of the desk. "My nephew, Akhenaten, will join us. He's been involved with the business all of his life. He started in the groves and is indispensable throughout every stage of our process. Many times, I conclude he understands our concepts better than I do. He will be your main contact, as I no longer participate in the business as much as I once did. It's one of the many blessings of having such an astute partner."

The executive extended his hand. "The name's Samuel Nemaeus, I'm pleased to meet you."

Akhenaten appreciated the power of the handshake. It contradicted the man's business demeanor.

"My uncle's too kind," the young man responded in cautious English. "I will never acquire the knowledge to surpass his expertise."

"Uncles should be proud of their nephew's exploits," concluded the executive.

"So," sighed Akhenaten, "we offer a sizable business arrangement to allow commodity prospectors the ability to make a clear judgment of the crop."

Samuel Nemaeus politely lifted a finger in respectful protest. "As I mentioned to your uncle, I represent Karpos Peristera Incorporated. We wish to purchase in large scale. I'm not a prospector; I'm here to buy. We're most interested in your *Aghurmi Amasis cultivations*—trees, seed, and crop."

Clearing his throat, Akhenaten said, "I believe there's been a misunderstanding, sir. That particular brand is privately contracted to another company, exclusively. I'm sorry." Akhenaten twisted the old looking ring around his forefinger tensely. "However, we have a popular *Ghazaal* brand."

Slowly Nemaeus leaned back in his chair. "Of course, we're prepared to offer a sizable security to harvest the Aghurmi crop."

The young man glanced at his uncle.

Phoe Ptahhotep kept his head bowed and his body still.

To deflect some of the young man's agitation, the executive said, "There are festival organizers who will help me establish the market and I don't want to jeopardize the opportunity by a shortage of supply."

The young man deliberately leaned forward. "I see. Your company wishes to acquire rights to the production harvest?"

"I'm quite certain a buyout can be negotiated, unless, of course, you're not interested in a significantly larger turnover margin."

Ptahhotep adjusted his tie. "Well, of course we are. However, a quarter of the harvest is under obligation." After a slight hesitation, the young man carefully constructed an inquiry. "How much of a margin does your firm commit to, sir?"

"A four hundred percent upturn."

"Well," Akhenaten Ptahhotep stammered, "please understand." He paused to collect his thoughts. "We've already made arrangements."

The executive deliberated intently.

"What my nephew's trying to say," broke in Phoe Ptahhotep, calmly, in flawless English, "is that our prior business commitments do not allow us to accept your offer." Betraying his simple bearing, the man's sharp eloquence continued. "Our covenants have existed generations. It may be difficult to understand, but we cannot terminate our previous agreements. I'm sorry."

It was the only time that Ptahhotep had spoken in English to the businessman.

12.3

Date. An appointment. A fixed period in time.

Like the date fruit, there are folds and crevices in the fabric of time. A prophecy closely intertwines within these deep pleats and intricate crevices, isolating precise future events and magnifying their details.

The dates and times give intensification to the eschatological culmination. The mystery of a prophecy becomes visible only in the fullness of its maturity. Every facet of the prophecy grows independent, locked in its origin until time reveals its forecast.

Out of the soil, the fruit date grows.

Each season of growth reveals prophecy's dates, bringing revelation to the tribulation mystery.

A prophetic date parallels the fruit date, the seasons of the date divulging the fabric of prophecy.

12.4

New, crisp furniture filled the comfortable office. The swirl of the freshly brewed coffee pushed through the air-conditioned coolness. A kentia palm occupied a corner of the room.

Akhenaten Ptahhotep went through his open briefcase, rifling through the abundant paperwork inside.

"Please forgive me, Mister Miller, but up until now my uncle shielded me from any direct business relations regarding the Aghurmi Amasis cultivations. He kept the identity of your company secret to me. I look forward to learning more about your company, as well as its parent corporation, SHU International." Unlike his uncle, the younger man spoke English regularly, albeit retaining a Berber harshness. His courteous manners softened the ruggedness of the Berber severity.

Camden Miller took a deep breath. "Your uncle isn't as assertive in his business demeanor. His office is humble and his communication simple."

The young man didn't reply.

Crossing his legs carefully, Miller cleared his throat. "Our enterprises originated in the London area, in local European commodities. As our ventures flourished, we decided our vision shouldn't remain so narrow. Soon after we delved into new commodities and reached out to different venues we were acquired by our parent company."

SHU International, a commodities brokerage firm grew and developed into a vast trading conglomerate over the course of seven decades. Its ties were widespread in northern Africa, the location of the company's birth in 1946, and it held established connections across the Middle East.

According to SHU International's directory, Camden Miller started as a company field sales representative in the late seventies. When SHU International swallowed up the smaller satellite, Argead Dates retained its status and operated under its original identity and business appellation. His field position retained, Miller concentrated his efforts on the company's one particular commodity, succeeding in developing a clientele base that furthered SHU's massive growth. His climb to an executive position, in the otherwise predominantly Arab corporation, came soon after. A rumor ascended within the executive ranks claiming he wasn't a total outsider, pointing to reports asserting his mother to be of Imazighen descent.

After SHU International's take over, Argead Dates discarded the original plan to distribute dates in modest amounts and began to develop a more compelling plan. The parent company's growth, prompted Argead Dates to likewise grew. Its selling operations spanned the globe and the company moved beyond the broker stage to launch its own buy and sell operations.

Disregarding Camden Miller's disparaging manner, Akhenaten Ptahhotep announced, "I am happy to take over our family dealings with you."

Camden Miller paused slightly. "Your uncle won't be along?"

"If you like, I can certainly call him," the young man answered. "But I hope you and I can talk business."

Miller arose from the sofa and walked to the window. Looking out into the arid region, beyond the oasis, he softly said, "I see." Returning to his seat, he crossed his leg and measured the young man carefully. "You know who I am?"

"Of course, sir."

"You're also aware my name isn't Camden Miller."

"Yes, sir," the young man replied quietly.

"Very well." Miller nodded his head.

"We can begin then?" asked the young man.

Without further hesitation, Miller said, "Tell me about him."

"He approached us two weeks ago. He wasn't just interested in our harvest, he made overtures to four other tribes I'm aware of."

There were ten existing tribes.

"Did he reference the firm he represented?"

"Yes." The young man picked up the handcrafted *Egyptian Hookah* sitting on his desk. "Honor me?" he asked, extending it to Miller.

As Miller breathed in the *shisha,* the young man continued. "Yes, he said he represented Karpos Peristera Incorporated and sought after the wholeness of our seasonal harvest. He expressed interest in the last day seasons—*the latter rain harvest.*"

Miller grunted in reply.

"Master," whispered the young Ptahhotep, "he knew things."

In a powerful voice, Miller commanded, "Let him buy the harvest."

The young man sat stunned. "Master, I don't understand."

"Your uncle doesn't question my commands." An edge came through Miller's voice.

The young Ptahhotep lowered his head. "Please forgive me."

"Speak your mind."

Ptahhotep spoke slowly, choosing his words cautiously. "You command us to give away the final season of the tree of life after generations of my family have cultivated the immortal seed?"

"Who told you this is the tree of life's final season?"

"Well, I…" Ptahhotep stuttered over his words. "I shouldn't have assumed," he finished.

In an unusual display of liberality, Miller extended the hookah to the young man.

Ptahhotep gripped the multi-stemmed instrument. Deliberately he inhaled the shisha.

"Your grandfathers, your uncle, your father, and now you, have served faithfully," Miller said. "We will not forget your dedication. You will now cultivate a greater harvest not grown from the soil."

Ptahhotep remained silent.

"The Ptahhotep name will be remembered into eternity. Your reward in paradise will be to govern 80,000 servants and seventy-two *houris,* and live in a dome composed of pearls, aquamarine, and rubies."

Akhenaten Ptahhotep fixed his vision on Miller. "I do not require…" The young man stopped to reevaluate his words. "I realize the god of rocky Pytho is not the god of my *Ibāḍī* fathers. He does not need to make such promises to me. I serve him without expectation of reward."

Miller slowly nodded, paying close attention to the man's words. "You are wise to think in such ways. Our ancient covenant elevates the hearts and minds of its servants."

Ptahhotep set the hookah down, captivated by the man's words.

Before breathing in more shisha, Miller calmly said, "If you remain faithful, the god of rocky Pytho will open to you the gates of Olympus and the riches of the gods."

12.5

Camden Miller, Executive Director of Growth and Expansion at Argead Dates, was privy to the fullness of SHU International's expansion and development plan. His additional position as SHU's Chief Global Strategist didn't make sense to many.

He recalled how Sevilo De'Esanatasos, CEO of SHU, arranged to see him the day after SHU acquired Argead Dates, twenty years earlier.

"Camden, you cannot be listed in the company's directory as anything more than a consultant," De'Esanatasos explained to him. "You realize why, don't you?"

"Of course."

"I charged SHU to acquire Argead Dates so we could accomplish this one project."

"You desire expansion," interjected Miller.

De'Esanatasos nodded quickly. "Growth orchestrated through the use of a dual set of markers. Expansion driven by more than purely economic considerations. Money will take care of itself. Secondly, the expansion must be primarily centered on precise geographical locations, not global ascendency."

"What locations did you wish to concentrate on?"

"I want to purchase control of the production of Dates in the five thousand hectares of cultivated land in and around Siwa," De'Esanatasos replied.

"The oasis?"

"Correct."

SHU International's long history of success provided it the financial luxury of implementing such an unprofitable plan.

"Which tribes are the targets?"

"All of them," replied De'Esanatasos. "We'll seek to gain control of the cultivated land around Siwa. Not to purchase production rights, but to acquisition the land. Production won't be the main objective."

"They'll resist," stated Miller.

"Yes, they will. But not until we procure enough land to establish a district around necessary environs."

"What vicinities?"

"I surmise you know the answer to your question."

"I do. I just want to hear you say it."

De'Esanatasos told him. "One last thing," he said, raising a hand. "I read through your history. Tell me your name—your birth name."

"I surmise you already know."

"I do. I just want to hear you say it."

Miller told him.

Chapter 13 Buy and Sell

And he causeth all, both small and great, rich and poor, free and bond,
to receive a mark in their right hand, or in their foreheads: And that
no man might buy or sell, save he that had the mark, or the name of the beast,
or the number of his name.

—Revelation 13: 16, 17 KJV

The phone buzzed in the office of the Greek Minister of Finance.

"Yes," answered Philip Kritolaos.

"Sir," the secretary's voice sounded, "it's a call from the governor. Are you available?"

The governor!

A governmental appointee, referred to as the governor, was the chief officer of the Bank of Greece. Kritolaos didn't pick up the phone immediately.

It's not the governor. It's 6:12 p.m. on Friday.

"Hello?" He restrained his voice, slightly.

"Professor Kritolaos?"

The voice. It's him.

No one referred to him as Professor. "Yes, you've reached Minister of Finance Kritolaos."

The voice spoke in a layered tone of insolence. "I am Tyrimmas Archelaus."

The professor's hand trembled as he gripped the phone tighter. As in the two previous calls, the voice on the other end spoke in Greek. He detected a slight trace of a *Slavic* accent.

"I hadn't heard from you all this time," Kritolaos stammered. "I thought things were resolved."

"Resolved, Professor? Resolved in what way?"

"Disregard my words, Mister Archelaus."

A pause ensued, and then, in a slow methodical way, the voice on the other end spoke again. "Sovereign default is the next step."

Terror gripped the minister of finance. After all the work he'd put into Greece's economic recovery, he detested the idea of a default. "But we're moving into a primary surplus. Unquestionably, there are other options."

"No, Professor. We must weaken Greece further."

The voice on the phone—measured, icy—cut into the defenseless areas of Kritolaos.

"The purpose and conclusion of the other defaults will push Greece further to the edge of the abyss. When they reinstate the *drachma*, we'll drive up the *denar*."

"I don't understand. Please allow me to—"

"Enough!"

Kritolaos dared not attempt to speak over the man's voice.

"The god Apollo has prophesied!" The man's voice cut deeper into the Finance Minister's soul. "Two thousand three hundred, and thirty-seven years have passed, and the prophecy of Apollo has gone unfulfilled. Now all the nations of the world will shudder at his divination. Greece has once more become the center of the world! You are the vessel the god has put in place to accomplish his will. You will not obstruct his prophecy!"

"I submit to his will," Kritolaos whispered in dread.

"We have billions of euros to exploit! We will not lose this opportunity! You will procure the euros on behalf of Macedon, and Greece will be left to blame for their economic downfall."

Kritolaos experienced utter powerlessness. He remained silent.

When he'd been Professor of Economics at FON Univerzitet his destiny materialized dramatically. In college, certain faceless, nameless men and women had taken control of his choices and direction in life. Although they never contacted him face-to-face, he'd never found the strength to say no to the commands they dispensed.

Even now, thirty-five years after college, he couldn't resist their commands.

They control my afterlife too.

As an educated man, he'd been raised an atheist. Yet, strangely, he still feared the gods of his ancestors and was terrified of their retribution if he disobeyed them.

Hades, Apollo, Zeus—I will yield to your power. I will kneel before your greatness.

"We cannot allow the Greek economy to become strong enough to return to the markets," Archelaus declared.

Hope drained out of Kritolaos. *Raising money on international bond markets could revive Greece from the dead.*

"The work is done, Kritolaos," said Archelaus. "It is finished. Do as the god commands."

Chapter 14 Yahweh's Slayers—Apollo's Killers

Son of man, prophesy, and say, Thus saith the LORD; A sword is sharpened, and it is furbished, to give it into the hand of the slayer.

—Ezekiel 21: 11 KJV

Pinching the bridge of his nose, Merlin reached down and took a circular shaped device out of a small box and put it on the table.

"What do you got there?" Tomlin asked.

"It's an *etymological configurator*." Merlin arranged the controls of the device as he spoke. "It's DARPA's latest and greatest. I've been using it the past few days."

Hessen's eyes were steady on Merlin. "Using it to do what?"

"The inception of this latest phase of Project Superman came from the recording of an interview conducted by an embedded journalist with 27th Brigade Support Battalion, of the 1st Cavalry Division, in Afghanistan. The interview centered on the incident we're studying presently, involving the 4th Brigade Combat Team. I entered the recording of the interview into the machine. The machine than took the words and created images from them."

"Who's the journalist?" asked Hessen.

Merlin referred to his notes. "His name's Matthew Highcliff."

"Who did he interview?" Hessen persisted, stoically.

"A First Lieutenant Britney Shafer," answered Merlin, as he prepared the machine.

"Are you going to play the recording?"

"Certainly, but first…"

The lights dimmed and a screen lowered.

"The machine rendered an image from the words in the recording," said Merlin.

On the screen appeared the eerie image of a man with long hair, rough beard, and a sword protruding out of his mouth. Strangely, a lightning bolt flashed out from the man's eyes.

The letter "E" flashed across the front of the white robe of a man seen rushing at the long-haired man, in an apparent battle posture.

Quickly the room lights returned and Merlin asked, to no one in particular, "Does this make any sense?"

Without hesitation, Nabil answered, "It's a Nazarite engaged in battle with an Essene squaddie."

All attention riveted on him.

"Go on." Merlin demanded.

"The sword coming out of the Nazarite's mouth—it's the inspired Word of God. The Essenes dispute the wholeness of the Word, as declared by the Nazarites. They believe there's more to God's Word and insist the Nazarites corrupt the truth." Nabil lowered his voice. "Both sides fight a war to the death to possess the truth."

"What's a Nazarite?" broke in Corliss.

"A spiritual warrior of Elah, who's sworn an oath of separation and service to uphold the law of God to the death."

"Talk clearer. Who's Elah?"

"Elah is an ancient name of God in Aramaic."

Tomlin gave Nabil a look of careful scrutiny. "And the Essenes?"

Nabil measured his response. "They're spiritual warriors of God."

"The Essenes are like the Nazarites?" asked Tomlin.

"They share many similarities," replied Nabil.

"An assumed person of God fights against another assumed person of God to possess the truth?" Tomlin bristled. "Jesus! What the fuck's wrong with them? Religion's about love and goodwill. They've turned it into a fuck'n warzone."

"It's not about religion," corrected Nabil.

"Let's stay on track," cut in Merlin.

The lights dimmed. On the screen appeared the image of a man in a long *ephaptis,* bearing a cryptic "E" on his chest, emerging out of a thick, mysterious vapor, armed with a long spear.

"What you see before you is a hosioi," called out Nabil, his voice even and emotionless.

"Another religious freak, spreading the assumed word of God?" asked Tomlin.

"No," answered Nabil, softly, "a religious freak—as you put it—spreading the assumed word of another god."

"Explain," commanded Merlin.

"The hosioi are the five guardians who defend the Oracle and the *eidos* to the death—they're Apollo's killers."

The lights came on.

Merlin appeared irritated. "Prophet, maybe it's best if we go about this in an alternate method. Let me finish the display and then we can explore its relevance and meaning."

The next series of pictures of the slideshow presented the likeness of immeasurable rage and violence. A mighty man stood over a full-grown lion, ripping apart its jaws. More pictures displaying mightier acts of ferocity followed. Then came a final series of photos showing a man—his eyes gouged out and seemingly helpless—pushing apart what appeared to be two support pillars.

The lights returned.

Merlin turned to Nabil. "Okay, give us the specifics."

"The Nazarites are mighty men and women. The machine concentrated on one of the mightiest—Samson." Nabil rubbed his jaw before continuing. "Like the ancient Jews, the ancient Greeks chronicled the exploits of their mighty men: Heracles, Achilles, Odysseus, Perseus. The mightiest of these warriors were the hosioi, a guild organized within the lines of the *pentakis,* whose sole purpose for existing is to guard the Temple of Delphi. In eschatology, the Nazarites and the hosioi are destined to fight a war to insure the fulfillment of their deity's prophecy."

"Prophecy?" Hessen leaned forward. "What prophecy?"

"The God of the Bible uttered many prophecies," answered Nabil. "So did Apollo."

"What does the God of the Bible have to do with Apollo?" Corliss began. "Are you suggesting the prophecies of God and Apollo are related?" Turning to the other men, he slightly threw up his hands and shook his head. "This isn't the right ditch."

Nabil didn't reply.

Merlin pushed aside his laptop. "Not so fast." He rubbed his eyes. "Explain the 'E' in the images."

"There's much dispute on the subject. Plutarch's essay on the 'E' references Plato's *Sophist* and *Philebus,* claiming two different supreme principles. In the same way, he announces the 'E' has two distinct meanings, one being an earthly, physical, meaning, and the other being infinitely spiritual. He concludes the letter is an appeal—a cry raised in awe and worship to the god—throughout all eternity."

"Hold on," demanded Corliss. "The ancient warriors you're talking about existed a long time ago."

"The Nazarites and the hosioi aren't ancient. They exist today."

Corliss remained skeptical. "Is this what you meant by shedding light on the Afghan incident?"

"If I'm correct in my judgment, eschatology has everything to do with Project Superman."

"How so?"

Nabil ran his eyes over each man. "This project's named Superman," he answered softly. "Well, the Nazarites and the hosioi…are supermen."

Chapter 15 How Long, Oh Great God?

LORD, how long shall the wicked, how long shall the wicked triumph?

—Psalm 94: 3 KJV

High Priest deKharouf stood in torment before the Great Altar. His voice came out in hoarseness. "How long, oh great God, will you sit idle and allow the enemy to do whatever he desires?"

The Fire upon the Great Altar remained calm, barely flickering.

"Do not become angry," pleaded the priest, his voice rising to a feverish pitch. "But I cannot allow the image of the beast to stand and defile the pureness of the holy temple. Neither will I permit the abomination of desolation to desecrate the Holy of Holies."

In reaction to his words, the Fire upon the Great Altar flamed over violently.

"Let it be me who incurs your wrath. I submit my spirit to you." The priest raised his hands to the heavens. "Punish me for trying to stop the enemies of the Kingdom!"

The mighty Fire scorched the edges of the stone and rock.

"I dare to speak to you in righteousness!" called out deKharouf. "I war against the prophecies of the Little Horn! I am responsible!"

The flames of the Fire blasted out from the altar.

"I am your faithful servant. I will answer your voice, oh great God!" the high priest called out.

Climbing upon the Great Altar, without hesitation deKharouf stepped forward into the Fire!

The blaze engulfed him, surrounding his entire body!

Standing within the hot flames, the consuming Fire did not devour deKharouf. Instead of burning, the Fire whispered counsel to deKharouf.

"Speak Oh Lord God," whispered deKharouf, in the midst of the Fire. "Speak to me, a new creation born of spirit and truth."

Kneeling in the Fire, deKharouf cried out, "I am one of the stones, proclaimed by the Baptist. I kneel in the Holy of Holies and seek your guidance."

The Fire turned a violent white.

"Almighty God! You are too strong. Flesh and blood cannot withstand you who has the power to destroy spirit!" Bowing his head, deKharouf went still. Throwing his head back, he released an indignant yell into eternity. "Do not do to Uziel and Ariella what you've done to Rhea and me!"

Exhaustion overtook deKharouf. He collapsed in a heap within the Fire.

After a time, the angel of the Lord appeared in the flames. Reaching down, the angel kindly lifted deKharouf's motionless body and carried him away into the night.

The angel and deKharouf translated atop Greater Ararat.

There, hidden from the world below, the angel laid deKharouf upon a thick bed of oiled vine roots, softened by wine and sun.

Blowing across the mountain, a cold wind struck the priest's skin. Exhausted and cold, he again lost consciousness.

As deKharouf drifted into a fitful sleep, the angel heated a cluster of stones. The fiery coals warmed deKharouf.

Upon the burning stones, the angel made a loaf of bread. Sometime later, the angel touched deKharouf on the shoulder. "Arise, and eat," he commanded.

Groggily, the priest sat up. In front of him, on a flat rock, the angel arranged the freshly prepared loaf of bread and a jar of chilled water.

Hunger overtook him and deKharouf ate every morsel. When he finished he rose to his feet.

The angel departed, leaving deKharouf alone.

Standing upon the high peak of Mount Ararat, the priest looked down upon the dark Turkish countryside. Lifting his head, he scrutinized the moonlit sky.

Reaching up to the sky, as if he intended to pull God down off his throne, he whispered, "Please…don't do this to them."

Chapter 16 Grey Fox 99

Roger Daniels and Will Johnson of Intelligence Support Activity (ISA) stopped by Colonel Lasker's office.

"I'm Lieutenant Daniels. This is Sergeant Johnson. We're here to see the colonel."

Colonel Lasker's secretary glanced up from her desk. Three times in the past month she'd seen the men. Although not gruff, she sensed an uncompromising resolve underneath their surface. It made her uneasy.

"It's an urgent matter," Daniels added, quietly.

Seconds later, the men were sitting in Colonel Lasker's office.

Numerous military decorations on the wall highlighted Colonel Lasker's mahogany desk. On the right side of the desk a standard containing the US flag and an unidentified division title stood, while on the other side of the office sat miscellaneous file cabinets and a liquor cupboard. In contrast, a clear jar of candy occupied the edge of the desk.

These were all the items the room contained.

Daniels and Johnson were part of ISA's Field Operations Group (FOG) classified as Grey Fox 99. For the past ten years, GF99's field task operational oversight was limited to peripheral and isolated command.

Essentially, GF99 existed as a separate entity unto itself. It didn't receive orders from any military command structure, neither did it answer to any presidential office. It reported its activities on an "as needed" schedule, mostly maintaining the reporting schedule to procure "black funds" from Special Capabilities Office.

"We found 1612, sir," Daniels said, in a low voice.

ID number 1612 designated the specimen number tracked by GF99, on behalf of Project S.

Apprehension gripped the senior officer. He leaned back in his chair. "Where?"

"Syria. Near Lake Jabboul."

"When?"

"Yesterday. We confirmed the kills."

"How many?"

"Eleven."

"What else?"

Daniels shifted in his seat. "An IED detonated near a checkpoint. He went right through it."

Colonel Ivan Lasker pinched the bridge of his nose and closed his eyes, the better to push blood into his cheeks. Since the reinstatement of Project S, he'd resumed his close contact with DARPA's Defense Sciences Office (DSO). Across multiple offices, DARPA's assistance to DoD on Project S centered heavily in the areas of consulting and technical development. "Where'd he come from?"

"Zimbabwe, Angola," answered Daniels. "We lost him for a while. He turned up in Uzbekistan. In each location, the field team reported abnormal physical feats, and bodies turned up wherever he moved. From Uzbekistan, he jumped to…an oasis in Egypt. Four months later, we detected him south of Bagdad."

"Our subject's been busy. Where's he now?"

"We think he's back in the Egyptian oasis."

"What's the extraction forecast?" Lasker's carefully measured tone disguised his cautiousness.

"If we use heavy weaponry, there's a fifty-fifty chance of success. The problem'll be placing a team in the area without being exposed."

Grabbing the clear candy jar, the colonel pulled one out and popped it in his mouth. The sweetness helped him think. "Here's the call: We're assembling *Task Force 88* and other tactical teams right now. We'll keep intelligence on him."

"What's the first step?"

"We need to determine his supply network, and remove it." The colonel's features fluctuated slightly.

"Throughout the field activity, we need a bionetwork expert and an environmental science architect to help us better understand the supply chain and the logistical disposition. It won't be easy to remove. Let me show you."

Daniels got up and began making notes on a large grid map fastened to the wall. Seconds later, satellite imagery appeared on a screen next to the grid map. "Observe the activity surrounding our subject."

Lasker got up and pointed to a specific image on the satellite screen and asked, "What the hell is that?"

Johnson got up from his chair and stood next to Daniels. "That, sir, is a flock of ravens."

"And what the hell are they doing?"

Johnson blurted out, "We've observed them extensively. They bring food…to ID 1612."

The colonel turned in astonishment. "Good God. He trained them to do that?"

Daniels shook his head. "We don't believe the activity's coordinated. But it occurred at multiple sites. The wildlife experts you're assembling will confirm our intel."

Lasker slowly sat back down, followed by Johnson and Daniels.

Daniels drew in a guarded breath. "There's more, sir. FOG units confirmed most of the data. The Activity deciphered a great deal of strange happenings in and around the areas of interest where we've studied 1612. Weather manipulation, element alteration—"

"Stop right there, Lieutenant," Lasker interrupted. Clearing his throat, he firmly said, "Observe your headings. Leave The Activity to their field discovery." Leveling his vision on both men, he finished by saying, "When the time comes, I'll disclose The Activity's operations."

After the colonel's instructions, Daniels resumed his discovery briefing. "Colonel, Intel Headings report a super soldier specimen—they mark it *'code 3S.'* Sir, Grey Fox needs some particulars."

Silently, Lasker considering the man's request.

"Colonel, the Banner Series documents the subject walking on water to ford a river." To emphasize what he'd just said, Daniels repeated, "Walking on water, sir."

The colonel's eyes became eerily calm. Slowly, he leaned back in his high-backed chair. "The Activity's intel of ID 1612—the walking on water and other physical exploits—are true. All of it." The words came out as a whisper.

Daniels and Johnson sat riveted, unable to respond.

"Our *table of contents* doesn't have to confirm or deny the intel," Lasker went on. "Concentrate our objective to gathering all sat images and assembling field info, without drawing attention." After a slight pause, Lasker resumed. "Over the years, we've collected organic material of 1612. We're compiling a database to compare to the recent material gathered. From there we can create a CONOPS."

"Recent material…from other targets?" asked Daniels.

Lasker's expression slightly contorted as he turned away in thought. An edge accentuated his tone. "ID 1612 is one bad ass motherfucker. But he isn't the only one. We're detecting a lot of strange shit coming from certain global hot spots. I need you to build a team of hunter-killers. We need the best of the best."

The delicate matter of assembling a hunter-killer team—meshing the dynamic personalities into a cohesive killing unit—mandated extreme application. Following a brief delay, Daniels squared his shoulders, and, with absolute confidence, said, "I need a Shadow, a Sentinel, and thirteen killers. Get me those, and me and Johnson will kill the son-of-a-bitch for you."

Chapter 17 Unwinnable War

"I've come to reason with you." Elijah Basra presented an imposing figure. Standing at the edge of the ancient Turkish villa courtyard, his long, windswept hair contrasted with his rugged garments. Weathered and vigorous, his skin radiated like the sun.

Without acknowledging him, Othniel deKharouf went about the business of preparing the daily sacrifice. He detested Elijah Basra and bristled in anger that the outcast priest dared to interrupt him while he prepared the temple.

"I'm speaking to you, priest."

Basra's tone, although even and nonthreatening, further infuriated deKharouf. Putting down the sacred utensils, he considered Basra. "You were instructed not to come here."

"Only if Uziel was here," corrected Basra.

Returning to his task, deKharouf said, "There's no time for this."

"We speak here, or before the Fire," insisted Basra.

"About what?"

Basra stepped closer to the priest. His elegant lengthy robe and traditional priestly garb heightened the rage he exhibited. "Stop your insanity, deKharouf." Basra shook his head in disgust. "You can't win this insane war!"

"How would you know what's winnable?" lashed out deKharouf. "You've rebelled and turned away from the sacred utensils of the temple. Stop moralizing my nazar."

In anger, Basra entered further into the courtyard. "Your nazar? It isn't your nazar anymore!"

Returning to the details of preparing the sacrifice, deKharouf rebuffed him. "Leave me. My duties require my attention."

Deciding against the futility of trying to persuade the priest, Basra backed away slowly. "I will walk up and down in the midst of the Stones of Fire. I will stand against your insanity."

No response came from deKharouf.

"You can't go against the Almighty and win, deKharouf! His prophecies are final! If you wish to continue, I care not. But leave my son out of it!"

Chapter 18 "Where Are the Bones, Tyrimmas?"

I came to see a king, not a row of corpses.

—Suetonius, Divus Augustus, paragraph 16

"Professor Ezekiel Arrhidaeus."

"Yes?"

"I am Tyrimmas Archelaus."

Professor Arrhidaeus recognized the voice. Six weeks prior, the same voice had contacted the excavation team and instructed the diggers on how to reach the antechamber, where they'd located the golden larnax and the scrubbed bones.

"Yes."

"You confirmed the bones are the ones we sought?"

"Yes," replied the professor.

"I'm on my way to your office."

18.2

"Your appointment over the archaeological project will remain." Archelaus boldly stood in the middle of the office. "It'll be for the benefit of the public and the financiers. Your operational control will no longer be obligatory. This has been clarified to you, correct?"

In the mind of Professor Arrhidaeus, Tyrimmas Archelaus's features were magnetic—strong brow, stately jaw lines, piercing eyes—all of the physical qualities Arrhidaeus imagined a god would assume if he took physical form.

"Professor! I need your full attention!"

Arrhidaeus came out of his frozen captivation. "My apologies. Yes, Goran Lukic informed me of this but—"

"Contact Lukic as to the finality of the diggings," the man resumed, ignoring all of his comments except the apology. "Tell him to preserve the site. We may need to return to it."

Archelaus was one of the men and women who had controlled his life since birth. Throughout his life, the communications—ordinarily absent of faces or names—subjugated him. After years of conditioning, he succumbed to their mastery over him.

To see their faces or know their names would be the end of me. If I learned their identities, I would not live to see the next sunrise. Into eternity, I'd be subject to the wrath of the god.

He trembled all along his spine.

He now understood the strangeness of the archaeological operations. From the unusual funding originating from anonymous sources, to the absence of the myriad of specialists who normally accompanied the process of archaeological excavations, to the nonexistence of the usual scientific and journalistic curiosity—all made sense to him now.

Then, the actuality of the site puzzled him. The workers and the volunteers had not been sourced from the normal pool. It seemed to him the workers on the dig were not there due to their scientific strengths, but rather for their abilities to keep the site isolated and private.

The heavy presence of military personnel at the diggings left him further disturbed.

Other oddities troubled him. Such as, the minimal satellite imagery before commencing the diggings, the foreknowledge of the site, and—most shocking of all—the concentrated focus of the dig without the usual preliminary, scientific foundation.

"If I list an end time to the archaeological diggings," Professor Arrhidaeus stammered, "it'll jeopardize the scientific—"

"Don't trouble yourself, Professor."

The abruptness of the man's command stunned him. Nonetheless, the academic, scholastic energy gained from discovering the bones of the great Macedonian King poured out of him. "The world deserves to know this incredible discovery!"

Tyrimmas Archelaus considered the seated professor in the same manner a parent would an openly defiant child. "Your position has no relevance to the excavation. This is a governmental dig. Academia is subordinate. You've procured the bones, the number one objective of the excavation. Leave the rest of the operation to others. Is this clear?"

Arrhidaeus bowed his head in obedience. "It will be as you say," he answered, softly.

"The government will appropriate the bones," declared Archelaus. "Council Minister Agelas Storic's office will instruct the soldier company to escort the bones to an unnamed repository in Skopje. The company commander will tag the remains for parliamentary extradition." In deep thought, the man clasped his hands together behind his back. "The bureaucratic trail will be sufficient to cover the remains in governmental formalities. In a matter of hours, all trace of the bones will be lost."

"Lost?" Mesmerized by the man standing in his office, the professor slowly came out of his dullness. "How? Historians believe the bones of Alexander never made it out of Egypt's border. That the funeral procession was intercepted by Ptolemy."

Archelaus perceived the man's pronounced struggle and inner turmoil. Moving closer to the desk, he said, "Historical record is correct, Professor. At the time of the destruction of the tombs of the Ptolemies, we relocated the bones to the valley of the Macedonian Kings."

His face pale, his voice hoarse, Arrhidaeus cried out, "I beg you. Share the historical meaning of the bones to the world."

"I assure you, Professor, we do not intend to keep the bones secret forever. In good time—we will reveal them to the whole earth."

18.3

Evening came and Council Minister Storic labored at his handcrafted desk in his office. Tyrimmas Archelaus stood in front of him boldly.

"Where are the bones, Tyrimmas?"

"They're being kept at Army HQ. There's no possibility disturbance or amputation can occur."

The men spoke in precise Macedonian.

Archelaus walked to the window and looked down ten stories to the moving traffic below. "I'm bringing in more soldiers and strategists. There's a unit of fifty specialized troops coming from Kabul to take over the transfer operation. Introducing Macedonian soldiers across five countries will draw the attention of the Nazarites."

Council Minister Storic reacted in shock. "You want to draw the attention of the Nazarites?"

Archelaus moved back to stand in front of the desk. "My foreign affairs schedule corresponds with the transfer of the bones. Commission the hosioi and a bodyguard troupe to the repository to protect the bones, not me. I'll assume command over the operation, and deputize the hosioi as my ministry staff."

Storic's features clouded over. "Master, there's great risk using the ground route. Things could go wrong. Please allow additional troops to see to your safety."

"Do you trust me," asked Archelaus, earnestly.

"You are my god. I trust you with my soul."

"Separate and transport the material in multiple operations," commanded Archelaus.

"Yes, Master," agreed Council Minister Storic.

"The Great-Horned Macedonian King wished to be buried at Siwa Oasis." Archelaus grimaced. "Those ignorant of the king did not understand his meaning. He spoke not of a corporeal burial, but a genetic one."

18.4

Site Director Goran Lukic's intense personality appeared to be in a constant adrenaline blast. Dedicated to the specifics of the archaeological objectives, Professor Ezekiel Arrhidaeus did not foresee him receptive to culminating the diggings.

The following morning, arriving at the excavation site before the dawn— a time when he knew Lukic customarily prepared for the day's activities—the professor broke the news to him.

Surprisingly to Arrhidaeus, the site director accepted the news of the expiry of the site diggings without question. Lukic actually displayed an upbeat spirit upon learning the news. "Ezekiel, I am honored to be part of this historic archaeological expedition. Please join me in a morning toast."

In the cool sunrise, the champagne came as a jolt. The ancient ground spread out before the men as they raised glasses to toast the findings of the dig.

Chapter 19 Oath of Life

Hidden atop the majestic mountain, the Mediterranean breezes swept back Ariella Muloc's long flowing hair, revealing her beautiful features.

In the warm night, the chief Pythia and her four deputations were bathing in the Castalian Spring. The hosioi *pentakis* stood guard nearby.

In the air drifted an ancient melody to Ariella's ears.

The Pythia and her four lower subjects sang with old emotion.

"Be submissive to the spiritual elements," she remembered High Priestess Rhea's instructions in her mind. "Your nazar will be threatened if you're detected."

Careful to avoid detection by the *Oreads*—nymphs positioned by the god to guard the pathways into the mountain—Ariella translated atop Mount Parnassus.

It was a necessary risk.

Although the vapor could possibly detect her translation, she considered it even more dangerous to try to go through the god's defenses physically to gain a position atop of Parnassus.

Not by might, nor by power, but by my Spirit.

She trusted God.

Avoiding detection, she hid within a group of laurel trees and a clump of conifers, sensing the movements upon the mountain.

"The Pythia is isolated from the outside world so she can remain an instrument of divination," Rhea repeatedly instructed her. "For her, time stands still. This gives you a chance to discern her movements. But never forget: The hosioi will offer their souls to keep her isolated."

Ariella's lovely eyes widened. "This means she moves slowly." Almost instantly, her eyes narrowed. "Apollo, and the subjects of Apollo, cannot translate?"

The spiritual gift of translation—the ability to ascend above the four-dimensional *Planck length* of the structure of time—was a gift of the Holy Spirit.

Rhea shook her head. "They cannot. Only by the ministry of the Lord can the Nazarites use the spiritual technology of translation."

"And the Pythia won't use modern transportation?" questioned Ariella.

"That's right, child." Rhea answered.

Rhea was 151 years old.

Ariella was ninety-two years old.

Deep in the night, the Pythia and her four subjects concluded their singing. They emerged out of the cleansing spring and began their prepared diet: bay laurel leaves, fresh fruit, and *Kykeon*.

As Ariella followed their movements, she sensed the sweet fragrance of the god who ruled over the Oracle.

A heavy sweetness clung to her nostrils.

19.2

In the dark night, upon the mountain, Ariella remembered the ceremony of her nazar.

High Priest deKharouf raised the old flask and poured the oil over the head of the kneeling Ariella.

"Swear the oath of life, to the death of your flesh," commanded the priest.

Without hesitation, Ariella called out softly, "I am promised to God. I am His blameless oblation. My soul and my flesh are His to use. I vow to my death to keep my waid."

The priest stopped pouring the oil over her head. "Hold out your wrists," commanded deKharouf.

Ariella did so.

Anointing her forehead and her wrists, the priest declared, "I anoint you servant of the Lord Almighty. I promise you a slave to God."

Her head bowed, Ariella said, "Tell me my nazar, Master. I am a slave to God."

"You're nazar is…to the end of the *Planck length* of the oasis. Do you understand your *waid*?"

Ariella lifted her head. Her eyes looked into the eyes of the High Priest. "But Master," she said, "*Elah* has prophesied the rise of the beast. How can my nazar…"

When Ariella's voice trailed off, deKharouf did not fill in the silence.

"Master? My nazar…" Struggling with the high priest's meaning, Ariella blurted out, "The prophecies of the Almighty demand the Pythia reach the oasis."

19.3

Before the sunrise, the hosioi and the prophētai led the Pythia and her four subjects down Mount Parnassus.

Waiting until they were far enough away to not be able to detect her, Ariella translated into the midst of the countryside. Thereafter, she followed their trail into the horizon.

"The trail of the hosioi and the Pythia will be revealed to them by the prophētai." The voice of Master deKharouf came back to her. "Do not forget. The trail of the prophētai leads to the trail of Alexander."

"The trail of Alexander?"

Drawing closer to the kneeling woman, deKharouf said, "It is the trail of blood and death."

Chapter 20 Abomination of Desolation

When ye therefore shall see the abomination of desolation, spoken of by Daniel the prophet, stand in the holy place, (whoso readeth, let him understand:) Then let them which be in Judaea flee into the mountains. For then shall be great tribulation, such as was not since the beginning of the world to this time, no, nor ever shall be.

—Matthew 24: 15-22 KJV

The image of the abomination of desolation will stand in the Holy of Holies, and bring desecration to humanity. The image of the abomination will dare to defy the separation of life from death and supernal immortality from earthly transience.

Those who acquire the power to give life to the image of the abomination dare to stand against the Almighty and attempt to be like the Highest.

They are mighty angels, released from a boundless pit, willing to make war on life itself, in their quest to rule the incalculability of immortality.

The location where they will begin their quest revealed to the image of abomination long ago, in an oasis in the middle of a sea of sand and lifelessness.

The time when the abomination will be fulfilled is a mystery to all but the most learned. By knowing the time and place of the mystery, the learned—if they so wish—will have occasion to try to prevent the prophecy of the abomination.

Chapter 21 Consecration

This is the law of the Nazarite who hath vowed, and of his offering unto the LORD for his separation, according to the vow which he vowed, so he must do after the law of his separation.

—Numbers 6: 21 KJV

High Priest deKharouf observed the woman approach the temple. Laurel leaves embroidered the fabric of her simple gown.

Reflecting on the day, nearly ninety-six years earlier, deKharouf remembered his disgust. The implication of the laurel leaf embroidery sickened him, but he said nothing.

She's not here for herself, he reasoned. *She's here to save her child.*

Kneeling before him, the woman lowered her head in the spirit of humility, and held up the boy in the warm morning sun.

"Holy man," she said, in a humble voice. "I need to know he will be used by the Almighty."

The priest stood unmoving. "Woman, God uses all to do his work."

In fear, the woman lowered herself closer to the ground. Holding the baby to her breast, she reached out and, in a bold move, clutched the priest's robe tightly. "Oh please, righteous man of Elah, let us be as the dogs eating the crumbs that fall from the holy table."

The high priest proclaimed unwaveringly, "Be aware, even dogs, in their ignorance, are not immune to the laws and commandments of the Almighty."

In contrition, the woman lowered herself even closer to the ground. In an act of debasement, she crawled forward and kissed the holy man's feet. "Let the mighty God punish me," the woman whispered. "But not the child."

Anger trickled out of deKharouf.

She's not the Pythia anymore. She's a dying woman making endowment for her progeny.

The woman's sobs lifted into the heavens, the scent of her tears a sweet aroma wafting into the nostrils of mercy.

Soon after, disturbed by his mother's anguish, the infant's cries joined the woman's heavy laments.

Groaning within himself, the priest reached down and touched the woman's head. In a voice of power, he said, "Rise woman. Bring your child."

He walked boldly toward the temple entrance, the woman in tow.

The closer they came to the temple's doorways, the more terrified the woman became, holding the child closer to her bosom.

Perceiving the woman's growing fear, deKharouf stopped.

Once again, the woman fell to the ground and bowed her head in absolute submission. "Master, I cannot enter the holiness. I'm defiled."

Again, deKharouf took pity on her. Walking back to her, he once more touched her head. "You may enter in my company. You and the child may enter the presence of the Almighty Fire."

Slowly raising her head, the woman looked from the temple to the priest in unbelief.

"Come, enter into the temple of forgiveness, you who are weary and heavy-laden, and the Almighty will give you rest."

Back on her feet, the woman brushed the tears away from her face and followed.

Precious stones and acacia wood combined to adorn the temple's interior. Concealed within the extravagance, toward the front of the sanctuary stood an ancient altar. Simplistic in construction and lowly in appearance, the altar's *supreme golden ratio* gave way to a perfect golden ratio manifesting infinitely within its dimensions. From the altar's sacred dimensions, the creation of a stone urn, made of plain rock, sat at its equidistance.

Upon the ancient urn—absent of all embellishment—burned the Eternal Consciousness of the Almighty.

Slowly, deKharouf led the woman to the simple altar. "Stop." he commanded.

Instantly, the woman stopped and stood before the Divine Fire.

Kneeling before the unsophisticated bench, deKharouf lowered himself in reverence and humility.

The woman, still fearful of the temple's holiness, also lowered herself before the Almighty Flame.

"Woman, remove your shoes," commanded the high priest, without turning around. "Come forward. Do not gaze upon the Fire of the Almighty."

Keeping her head lowered, the woman advanced toward the Flame on her hands and knees, still holding the baby.

On the altar's stone, burning gold through its height, the fire's strange purple streaks throbbed across its length.

"Speak before the Altar of the Almighty," commanded deKharouf.

In a broken and tired voice, the woman cried out, "Oh, Mighty God, I'm dying. The doctors find my breasts empty of milk, but full of sarcoma. Almighty God, I know you can heal me, but my time on earth is over. On behalf of my baby, I wish to dedicate him to you, oh Lord. To use as you wish."

The holy place where the altar stood became bright as the fire flamed outward and overflowed. Its intensity engulfed the simple altar.

The fire came closer to the woman and the child.

Feeling the intense heat, the woman began to lift her head.

"Do not move, woman!" deKharouf viciously commanded.

Keeping her head lowered, in fear, the woman drew back. "Please oh Mighty God! Do not burn my child!"

The voice of the priest thundered through the altar chamber. "Be still before the Almighty Fire!"

Frozen by the priest's thunderous command, the woman stopped, her body trembling from her head to her toes.

The mighty Fire burned stronger, warming the cold stone floor.

The high priest walked up to the woman. He held out his arms. "Give me the child," he commanded.

Not daring to lift her head, the woman offered up the child to the priest.

"Lord of Hosts," called out the priest, lifting the baby up to the temple's magnificent ceiling. "Allow the child of this humble servant to reside in your all-consuming Spirit."

Immediately, deKharouf placed the baby directly on the hot coals!

The Fire waxed fiercer and surrounded the baby.

The baby did not cry.

The Fire did not burn the baby.

Chapter 22 Spiritual Warfare

For we wrestle not against flesh and blood, but against principalities, against powers, against the rulers of the darkness of this world, against spiritual wickedness in high places.

—Ephesians 6:12 KJV

In a twinkling of an eye—infinitely faster than a flash of lightning across the sky—he translated to the Delphic Oracle.

Faster than an electrical impulse within a synapse of the brain, faster than the speed of light, Uziel moved from where he'd been—a neatly ordered manor in the Turkish countryside—to the place of the Oracle, without the passing of cosmic *Planck length and time.* Across the distance, overcoming the barrier of human consciousness and earthly reality, Uziel translated from the temple, where he'd undergone his preparation, to Delphi.

He walked along the *Sacred Way.* Ancient steps leading to the proclaimed center of the universe were mostly empty.

As he emerged out of the whirlwind, he caught her scent in the quiet dusk.

My darling Ariella, I miss your honeyed fragrance.

He translated to the navel of the world to discern the *timetable of the path.* His body moved through the spiritual whirlwind.

Covered in a priest's robe, the sheepskin warmed him in the mountain coolness.

If I can discover the route of the priestess, I will find you, my love.

In the still air, the sweet fragrance of the god clung to the ancient stones. He took a heavy breath, the perfume clinging to his nostrils. In the honeyed smell, he discovered movements in the darkness. The stones spoke a hardened language, revealing to him the images of the prophetess and the priests of the god.

They've departed. The stones are cold and there's only a trace of the fragrant incense.

His emotional turmoil left him dizzy. He tracked the route they travelled. He discerned some of their words. More than this, he discerned the spiritual power of the angel who prevailed over the ruins.

Unconstrained, the stench of the evil spiritual forces emerging from the bottomless prison, reeked throughout the mountain.

From the otherworldly residue of the god's emancipation, Basra perceived the trail of the priestly caravan.

Continuing up the stone path, Basra stood in the midst of the desolate adyton, the presence of the god vapor still lingered among the ceremonial remains.

He trembled in rage.

Hurt her and I will drag you down from the heights of Olympus and throw you into the lake of fire.

Hurt my beloved and I swear I will destroy you.

22.2

Across the sky, he translated, caught up in the clouds that led him into the wilderness, past the war-ravaged hell of Aleppo. Losing all sense of earthly existence, the translation left him dumbfounded.

Deep in the night, the angel of the Lord appeared to him in a vision.

Uziel, Uziel, what are you doing here?

Basra lowered before the angel of the Lord, unable to answer.

Uziel, why are you here?

Shielding his eyes from the brightness of the angel, Uziel softly answered, "I search for my love."

I am your first love, Uziel, answered the angel. *Did you forget?*

"No," he shivered from the coldness moving across the desert. "I haven't forgotten." In a pleading voice, he cried out, "We're promised to each other."

Wait here, Uziel, commanded the angel of the Lord. *Await my word in the desert.*

The angel charged him not to enter any towns or villages in the district, commanding him to subsist only on the comestibles and raw materials the land provided.

Basra waited.

He came to a stop in the dryness, underneath an abundance of concentrated sunlight. The aridity crept into his sinews, pulverizing and afflicting him.

Eight days later, his provisions nearly exhausted, he suffered three days and nights dreaming of Ariella. In his weakness, the angel comforted him.

On the twelfth day, he awakened hungry, thirsty, and feeble. In the morning, he meditated by a calm stream. In the evening, the rivulet lifted into the air and watered his spirit. The following afternoon, he positioned himself by the dry brush and reached out to seize the flight of the locust. By late afternoon, his belt sack bulged full of flying creatures.

Nightfall found him in the nook of a sand depression. A fire warmed him and he maintained it carefully, making sure the smoke and smell did not give away his position.

The locust cooked in the fire; the anticipation of their taste awakened him to his hunger. Opening the skin hipflask hooked to his belt, he collected the syrupy honey in his fingers and brought it to his tongue. Like a child, he savored the sweetness.

Basra remembered his forty-seven days and nights of preparation. The Turkish countryside flashed across his mind and recollected in his heart.

The Aleppo dryness injured him like a violent enemy. Preparing himself for another long night of thirst, the honey tasted sweet and the crunch of the locust made him even thirstier, leaving him barren and gasping. Late into the night, the thirst in his body pursued his life.

Then, in the stillness of the interval, the desert parted and released the dampness of its deep. Water flowed over the sand and puddled all around him.

He drank its liquid salvation.

His thirst quenched, he slept soundly in the peace of the Aleppo heat.

22.3

In the year 1936, three months after his sixteenth birthday, he first laid eyes on her. Four years older than her, he discerned the gentleness of her flowering youth. Coming to him in dreams and visions, her magnificent aura caused the exploding world of war and hate around them to fade away.

Only after two years did the Holy Spirit permit him to approach her. By then, he'd flourished into his eighteenth year.

Like a mighty gale, pubescence thrust the storm of his manhood toward her womanliness. For the first time, he experienced lust.

"Hi."

"Hi." She warmly smiled.

"What's your name?"

"Ariella."

He tried to tell her how lovely her name sounded in his ears, instead he stood there like a stone. He wished to tell her the many ways her beauty pleased his eyes, but his mouth refused to form the words and he remained mute.

"I'm Uziel," he burst out.

Her eyes were brown, a woman of the Mediterranean, feminine and pure.

Recognizing her virginity, he marveled at her exquisiteness.

Ariella felt his energy weaken her defenses. In her mind, she recalled the wisdom of her Grandma Mott, instructing her in the ways of women. "A woman reassures and encourages the man she selects. Only encourages."

She played with her hair, entangling it through her fingers. A series of tingles went up her spine and her knees weakened.

Virtue left Uziel. Some of his spiritual energy entered Ariella, and her purity held him inside of her knowledge. Thoughts collided inside his mind.

"You're the most beautiful woman I've ever seen in my life," he blurted out.

Although only fourteen, in her young mind and body Ariella comprehended as a woman. She wasn't sure how to respond, so she stood in the sun and waited.

"When I see you, I'm inspired," Uziel said. "I see who you are, inside."

Ariella stood straighter. She arched her back, slightly, and said, "Thank you, Uziel. Your words are kind." A smile elegantly framed her mouth.

In his soul, eternity passed in seconds. Realizing her encouragement, he asked, firmly, "Can we walk together?"

Slightly blushing, she lowered her head. "Yes. I'd like that."

22.4

The Nazarite vow pulverized him to dust every second of the day. A carnal spell, cultivated by his eyes, entered his flesh. The enchantment shocked him and before he realized, its allure reached into the dormant places of his body and awakened the fat and the muscle.

His daydreams became night visions leaving him sweaty and unfulfilled. Unable to resist their summons, the physical hunger grew stronger and more evident. Nothing curbed his wants, nor suppressed his needs. In the nights, he clung to a hope that somehow, he would find a way to partake of the carnal spell.

Persistent and sweet, his petitions burst out from his abandoned humanity. Only after he called upon God did guilt emerge out of his weakness and steal his peace.

I've never felt guilty before.

His conscience persecuted him, leaving him lonely but unrepentant. Indeed, her breasts were the semblance of an altar and he willingly knelt before their indestructible stone and rock. Never before had an image of lust estranged him from his vows and he felt a wave of guilt convince him of the wrong in pursuing Ariella.

It punished him without end.

22.5

"I'd like to be your friend."

Two years and eight months after he first laid eyes on her, he made his first overture.

Her eyes widened. She slowly reached for his hand and shuddered.

Their feelings were a violent act against their vows. They both dreamed of their union together.

"Friends," she smiled.

Squeezing her hand, he said, "Friends."

They walked together, talking about things only friends can talk about. They spoke of hopes and secrets sheltered in their hearts.

"We're the same, you and I. Our ways, our devotions."

She melted before his words, as if her completeness depended upon them. A revelation came to her and she experienced the full consciousness of her womanhood. She loved him instantly. "Yes, Uziel, we're the same. Your words are like water to my soul."

22.6

The desert encircled him. He perceived the devils moving in the night. Disembodied entities, they did not possess the spiritual weaponries to match his power.

He destroyed them all.

As Uziel struggled against the enemies in the night, he became weak in his night dreams. He recalled the command of the angel of the Lord: "Go into the desert and wait upon my word. Do not be discovered."

Pushing out into the air, he detected the potency of a malicious cherub and immediately pulled back into the physical. He possessed the power and authority to destroy a devil. A cherub, on the other hand, could only be bound and imprisoned.

Assuming the appearance of a Turkmen villager, Uziel evaded all spiritual conflict, spending the night in a quiet pasture east of Aleppo.

Using the ancient north Syrian dialect of Arabic—a transitional dialect sandwiched between Syrian and Mesopotamian Arabic—he conversed with a small group of villagers concerning the path of the locusts he'd encountered the days prior.

Thirst became unrelenting.

Uziel resigned himself to another dry night and even thirstier day.

The next night he resumed his search for the principalities dominating the air in the region.

"Be careful," came the voice of High Priest deKharouf, in his mind. "Your enemies in the vapor are expansive and powerful and can detect when your spiritual sight searches the air and ground. You mustn't allow them to draw you into spiritual battle until the appointed time."

The air burned frantic and the number of devils and evil spirits increased to more than a hundred. Uziel realized the cherub who headed the force no longer inhabited the area and the vacancy freed him to operate without concern of restriction.

I cannot permit them to escape and report my whereabouts.

The battle proved to be ferocious but short. He cut through the fiends' defenses and routed them entirely, destroying all of them.

Immediately following the battle, Basra translated to a position thirty-five kilometers eastward, near Lake Jabboul.

I dare not translate further, he reasoned.

Lake Jabboul's cool, salted water solved one problem, leaving only hunger as his main concern. Locusts didn't migrate through his new surroundings.

Humility caused Uziel to lower his flesh to the ground. In the solitude beside the lake, he imagined himself underneath the full canopy of an olive tree, or near the richness of a pistachio tree.

Instead, he found an Aleppo Pine.

In the hopes of avoiding detection, Basra decided against building a fire. Wrapping himself in light sheep's wool, he deadened his physical senses against the earthly environment. Retreating to his spiritual refuge—a transcendent cave buried deep in the universe's viscera—he watched the light give way to dark and night covered him. Only the sound of the lake water reminded him of his physical connection to the planet.

Morning came and sunlight revealed three ravens perched atop the solitary pine. On the ground below them, Basra saw the bread and flesh.

Afterwards, conformed to the direction of his spiritual guardians, he lowered himself to the lake's edge and drank. Instantly, spiritual energy transformed the lake's salt water into fresh water, reviving him. Drinking his full, he lowered his skin hipflask and filled it.

Well-fed and his thirst quenched, Basra lay down under the pine tree and slept. Because of the substantial toll spiritual force placed on the body, much of his training and preparation concentrated on his physical conditioning.

Notwithstanding his great physical condition, it still took Basra much rest to recover from his sufferings.

The next day the ravens brought him more nourishment. He consumed all the food they brought, wasting none of it.

As the day before, he transformed the salt water of the lake into fresh water. After drinking, he filled his hipflask.

A week later still found him by the lake.

22.7

Dreams of Ariella warmed him.

Desert cold awakened him.

He recalled a time nine years after he first laid eyes on her, in the year 1945.

He'd served five years in the world war bloodbath, having returned from Anzio a few months earlier.

He still loved her.

As the world healed, so did Uziel.

The memory of her touch stirred his heart, leading him to a special place and a long-awaited nuptial kiss.

As their love matured, their powerful destinies continually pulled them apart. In the end, their love desperately pulled them back together.

"I prayed for you every night."

He nodded slightly. "Yes, I felt your faith. It kept me safe. I saw too much death around me. Your faith kept mine strong."

Taking in a deep breath, he inhaled Ariella's fragrance of mauve and incense, swallowing every part of her scent.

"You mean everything to me," he breathed into her ear and stroked her hair. "I missed seeing your eyes and touching your smile."

Ariella arched her back. "Uziel, we mustn't."

Five years apart did not kill their emotions.

Dreams and images of her, like a river, dripped into a massive cavern leading to his ocean. He held her tighter. "Every day I thought about you," he said, as he kissed her. "Every night I begged him for your hand."

In his night pleadings, his needs overwhelmed his righteousness.

"He never answered my pleas," Uziel said. "I won't let you go again." His affirmation bled into the ground they stood on.

Her eyes grew wider. "What did he say?"

Eternity—a vacuum he'd often considered—comforted him, even though his youth could not fully perceive it. By the earnestness of his adoration, he observed the vastness of infinity.

"What did he say?" she repeated.

Dark thoughts entered his mind. Somberly, in the back of his heart, he wondered if his devotion would ever reside within the enigmatic places of a woman's secret.

Chapter 23 SCI Library Superman

Lysander Wilson and Onmus Praetor sat at the head of the table of the progression forum.

"As in all the teams I assemble, I need fresh perspective and extraordinary thinking," said Wilson, adjusting his eyeglasses. "Each of you bring a different point of view to the team."

"We're having trouble seeing where that point of view comes from," spoke up Corliss. "Lysander, how can we make this work with a religious fanatic gumming up the whole thing?"

To his credit, Daniel Nabil didn't react.

Wilson mulled over the man's words before responding. "What we're about to show all of you just got sent over to us from Sensitive Compartmented Information (SCI) Facility A. It should explain some of the reasoning to you on why Mister Nabil—all of you, in fact—were recruited to this team. I remind you: you've all been given 'SCI Access' to this information."

The room went still.

"You were all given high-level clearance to work on Project Superman."

Wilson looked over the faces of the men as he adjusted his glasses. "Kill the lights," he called out.

The lights went out and a large screen lowered from the ceiling. Soon after, images emerged on the screen.

"In the past fifty-two years, since its inception, DIA (Defense Intelligence Agency) accumulated innumerable military reports describing inexplicable battlefield events, and mysterious combat zone phenomena. These reports, labeled and classified in 'SCI Libraries,' are vast. They're broken down into major and minor categories. One major SCI category is titled: Superman."

On the screen, the images—some sourced from military satellites, some from battleground footage, and some in the form of classified files—exploded before the men's eyes.

The screen displayed thermal-infrared imaging of a human figure moving at an accelerated rate of speed.

Ronald Tomlin, the kinesiologist, leaned forward in his chair, viewing the image on the screen in unbelief. "How fast is he moving?"

"In excess of sixty miles an hour," replied Praetor, without turning his head.

"Holy shit!" exclaimed Tomlin.

"That's fucking impossible," whispered Erwin Hessen, the military historian.

Nodding his head slowly in understanding, Nabil remained silent.

"A human can't move that fast," pronounced Tomlin. "The contractile fibers of the muscles can't handle such stress. The impact to the skeletal frame would be insane. He'd fall apart...literally."

Merlin opened his mouth as if to say something, then reconsidered and remained silent.

Another thermal-infrared image came over the screen. "Here we observe a subject traveling over topographical challenges and obstacles."

Adam Corliss observed the shifting and unevenness beneath the moving image of the man. "What's he running on?"

Praetor paused before answering. "Water."

Corliss and the rest of the team sat in disbelief.

Nabil didn't appear shocked.

"He's running on water in a storm," Praetor went on.

Erwin Hessen pinched the top of his nose. Prolonging his moan, as if fearful of taking the next breath, he voiced the fears of everyone on the team. "Someone—some other country—beat us in developing the super soldier. Another country has developed 'game changer' technology."

Slowly, Praetor turned and ran his vision over each man across the table. "There's more, a lot more." On the screen behind Praetor, there appeared an image of a man jumping off a precipice and landing evenly a great distance below. "Here we observe the subject moving through the ruins of the old town of Ma'rib, Yemen. He's been observed leaping from forty feet up, and higher."

Now the screen showed a man lifting a massive boulder and hurling it through a tree, the tree and the boulder crashing to the ground in pieces.

"Initially, our investigation determined close fitting equipment was responsible for the subject's incredible abilities," Wilson said. "However, as you can see from the images on the screen, this is not the case."

Tomlin considered both men. Clearing his throat, he said, "I'm a kinesiologist. What I'm seeing is biologically impossible. Subjecting the human muscle to such horrific stress, would result in extreme myorrhexis."

Two images appeared on the screen. Using his red pointer laser, Wilson referenced the picture on the left. "This image is of the subject leaping off an ancient building in *Ma'rib* in 1962 by a covert CIA surveillance team on the ground. The image next to it is of a subject two months ago by another CIA surveillance team on the ground in the *Qattara Depression* in Egypt. We enhanced the 1962 image." The modern image on the left transposed the older version on the screen. "As you can see, it appears to be the same individual."

"That's fifty years apart!" Hessen broke in.

"Fifty-one years and four months, to be exact," responded Wilson. Focusing his attention on Tomlin, before scanning the rest of the men on the team, he said, "I assembled this team to not only help us catalogue the SCI Superman Library, but to provide DoD specific architectures and mechanical designs to allow us to understand, even attempt to create a super soldier to do the *impossible* on the battlefield."

The men sat in stunned silence.

Wilson's eyes landed on Nabil, who sat unmoving, studying the images on the screen. "To this end you were put on the team, Mister Nabil. And why your subject matter is the leading study in this project."

Nabil lowered his vision.

The DARPA team came out of their shellshock.

"We'll need to compile a list of all the countries capable of fashioning this kind of technology." Merlin unemotionally brought the team to life. "Then, we need to explore R&D construction and assembly. Lastly, we need to conduct analysis of interfaces and constructive prosthetics. I am releasing all files regarding the LUKE arm developed under DARPA's Revolutionizing Prosthetics program."

The men immediately began to assemble their workstation platforms and sub teams.

After being still throughout most of the conference, Nabil finally straightened up in his seat. "We mustn't proceed from this perspective."

The men stopped their hurried work.

"What you mentioned back at the lab?" asked Merlin, quietly.

"Yes." Nabil's penetrating eyes remained glued to the large screen and the images of the super soldier. "What you see on the screen…is a Nazarite."

Chapter 24 Please…Feed Me

For he shall give his angels charge over thee, to keep thee in all thy ways. They
shall bear thee up in their hands, lest thou dash thy foot against a stone.
Thou shalt tread upon the lion and adder: the young lion and the dragon
shalt thou trample under feet.
Because he hath set his love upon me, therefore will I deliver him: I will set him
on high, because he hath known my name.

—Psalm 91 KJV

On his face, Uziel Basra slept by Lake Jabboul.

He dreamed of his childhood, a childhood filled with separation and pain. Raised by a temple order of high priests, he learned much of his mother, and little of his father.

"Do not live in the past," High Priest deKharouf often told him. "Exist today."

As Uziel dreamed, he returned to a cold morning many years ago, a few months after his eighth birthday. As he lay on the cold ground shivering in the night, he heard the words of High Priest deKharouf in his ears.

"Spirit is life, flesh is death."

Since dawn, the boy had sat at the table. Now, the late morning sunlight crept across the floor.

Looking up innocently, the boy said, "Master, I'm hungry."

Food lay untouched on the plate, long since gone cold.

Affectionately, the priest ran his hand through the boy's hair and smiled. "Then eat, my son."

The boy's expression clouded over. "How?"

Tied back tightly, the boy's hands and legs were fastened to the chair.

"It is written: 'Man shall not live on bread alone, but on every word that comes from the mouth of God,'" said the high priest gently.

"Will you feed me?"

The priest sat down next to him. "No, Son. It'll be the hands of God who will feed you."

"How, Master?"

After anointing the boy's forehead, the priest spoke a short prayer before replying. "When a man eats earthly food, he will soon hunger again. The food on this earth and the human body are imperfect and can only sustain us a short time." Leaning across the table, deKharouf kissed the top of the boy's head. "On the other hand, when the spirit of man eats spiritual food—he will hunger no more."

"But, Master—"

"Silence, Son," the priest commanded softly before continuing. "The water the Lord gives us takes away thirst forever. To be invincible, eat the food from God's table and drink the water from his well."

Closing his eyes, Basra tried to focus his spiritual force to eat the food.

I can't move my arms. How am I supposed to eat and drink?

Finally, as the sunlight dipped below the mountains and the light seeping into the room became dimmer, Uziel began to cry, overwhelmed and confused. "Master," he said. "Please feed me."

Chapter 25 Wrestle with the Almighty

Jacob was left alone; and there wrestled a man with him until the breaking of the day. And he said, I will not let thee go, except thou bless me.

—Genesis 32: 24-32 KJV

The caravan moved slowly, like the days of old.

Traveling close behind, Ariella followed the small procession as it made its way south, across the hot desert. Using rare and hidden trails, through treacherous terrain, Ariella depended on her spiritual abilities to avoid detection.

"I am to fulfill my nazar, even though God's prophecy speaks against my action?" Ariella asked deKharouf, after an extremely harsh training session in the cold of winter. The Turkish wind lashed at her skin, blowing her hair wildly. "Master deKharouf, how can we go against God in our work?"

"We are not against God," deKharouf corrected her. "When Jacob wrestled with the Almighty, did he go against God?"

"No, Master. The Almighty looked upon Jacob as a *seeker of the heavenly.*"

"We who dare to wrestle against the Almighty, are also seekers. We wrestle with the Almighty because we strive to usher the *Bride* to the *marriage of the Lamb.*"

Chapter 26 Scarlet-Colored Beast

So he carried me away in the spirit into the wilderness: and I saw a woman sit upon a scarlet colored beast, full of names of blasphemy, having seven heads and ten horns.

—Revelation 17: 1-17 KJV

"How can you make a determination without conducting further research?" asked Corliss, the pathologist.

"There are definitive pieces in eschatology," replied Nabil. "They help determine the events." He shook his head. "Without knowing these details, we can't possibly design a plan to fit the crisis we see developing. The super soldiers we're tracking and studying aren't military development from an earthly nation. In fact, they're spiritual warriors."

"Are you suggesting we develop technology to create spiritual warriors?" Tomlin, unable to apply kinesiology to the super soldier library, struggled to hide his frustration. "I think everyone can agree that's beyond DARPA's potential."

Nabil answered calmly, "No. I only mentioned the origin of the super soldier's power to shed light on the situation."

Lysander Wilson normally liked to maintain distance with the thought process of his teams. Because of the time pressure coming from DoD, he broke his rule. "We need to take a step back. You seem to be extremely sure of yourself, Prophet." Loosening his tie, he stared down the professor.

Nabil didn't blink. "Some of you may know, Bible prophecy centers on the antichrist—the *beast*. Old teachings say the beast will come in the form of a man."

Here goes.

Nabil braced himself for the men's reactions.

"In regards to traditional teachings of the beast, I don't agree with most of them. It's highly possible what I'm about to tell you will be unlike anything you've ever heard before. As I've said: Bible prophecy must be taken literally, not figuratively, nor metaphorically."

Try not to come off professorial, Nabil told himself, stopping to take a drink of water from his glass before continuing.

"In the same way, I believe Jesus' parables aren't allegorical, but factual and literal, and can only be understood by translating them, not interpreting them. I call it the *pithy maxim method.*"

"What does that mean?" Corliss asked, examining every word Nabil spoke as if he were conducting an autopsy. "I'm a professional. In pathology, I center my examinations on fact."

Wanting to avoid a confrontation, Nabil provided even more detail than he'd planned. "I respect your commitment to detail and fact in your profession," Nabil said, raising his hand in defense. "Pithy means to be concise and forcefully expressive. Think of the stem of a plant. The pith—the critical tissue in the stem—holds the plant in place and helps it get the nutrients it needs." He bowed toward Corliss. "In your area of expertise—anatomic pathology—it's the essence of the surgical specimen being examined. We all know what a maxim is. When I say, all Biblical prophecy uses the pithy maxim method, I mean prophetic meaning is translated using fact and truth, not interpreted using unscientific methods, or guessing."

All the men seemed satisfied. Only Corliss maintained his skeptical scowl.

"In Bible Prophecy," resumed Nabil, "all of the titles of the beast add further clarity to his identity and actions. *Son of Perdition, Abomination of Desolation, Little Horn*—these titles, applied to him, reveal parts of his identity."

Don't speak so fast, Nabil scolded himself. He stopped to catch his breath.

"From my translation of prophetic scripture, I've added *Great Horn* to his many titles." Nabil adjusted his glasses and ran his hand through his hair to relax. "The Great Horn was the offspring of four angels incarcerated in the bottomless pit in antiquity. The Son of Perdition, the Abomination of Desolation, the Great Horn, and the Little Horn—they're all the same person. Better yet, they're the same genetic reproduction."

Merlin sat upright in his chair. "Wait," he demanded. "What do you mean they're the same genetic reproduction? We're talking about one man?"

"According to the prophet Daniel, the Great Horn was a Macedonian king who conquered the known world within a few short years. According to the same book, the Little Horn is a Syrian of Macedonian descent. Moreover, he's not composed from human DNA alone; he isn't totally human."

Merlin shook his head. "The book of Daniel, in the Bible, says this?"

Nabil waited before replying. "Yes. In chapter 11: 2-27, the prophet chronicles a historical account of the past wars between the nations of Syria and Egypt. The chronicle spans thousands of years. Verses 28-45 give a prophetic account of the future wars between the two nations, in the last days. This prophecy provides the geopolitical foundation of the wars to take place. I can supply much historical proof to substantiate the scriptures." Nabil traced a path on the world map. "The wars trace throughout the regions surrounding both nations until, in the last days, they blowout across Europe, even to the Far East."

Tracking the global path Nabil charted, Tomlin blurted, "This will involve China too?"

Nabil's expression remained constant.

"And Russia?" Tomlin turned to Hessen. "Are you buying this Rommel?"

"Just these two nations will do this?" asked Hessen.

"Not exactly," answered Nabil. "There are four primary nations listed in eschatology—Macedon, Turkey, Syria, and Egypt. The prophecies assert that four mighty angels control these nations. These angels will push against the world to bring about the catastrophic events of the last days described in eschatology."

"Only these four?"

Nabil pursed his lips. "According to Biblical teaching, every nation is commanded by a mighty angel, in control of many lower angels. There are other nations critical to eschatology's timeline but, yeah, these four angels are the central focus of all the events leading toward Armageddon."

"That's your opinion," Corliss eyed Nabil evenly.

"Perhaps," acknowledged Nabil. "But right now, there's a super soldier—like no other super soldier we've ever seen—running through the very countries the Bible references. If you choose to believe it's just a coincidence, then go ahead."

Giving him a side-glance, Tomlin remained unconvinced.

Not dismayed, Nabil resumed. "These mighty angelic forces are beyond earthly comprehension. When these four angels existed in antiquity, they caused a global shift in the territorial powers of the age. Eschatology forecasts this will happen again."

"All for global domination," stated Tomlin, skeptically.

"None of this is about earthly gain," interposed Nabil. "It involves earthly events, of course, however, the ultimate objective of the four angels goes beyond global power. The earth is simply a means to an end—nothing more."

"What is the 'end' to them?" asked Corliss.

"Heaven," Nabil answered. "All of the prophetic events said to take place are for the singular purpose of gaining military access to heaven and fighting a final war against the Almighty to dominate all consciousness and existence."

"Who's the antichrist?" Hessen tilted his head to the side.

"The Bible clearly forbids conjecture as to the identity of the beast. Only because of this project will I reveal to you my thoughts on the subject." Scratching his jaw, Nabil continued. "The answer's before you. If we know one title, we know them all. The man referred to as the Great Horn in prophecy is the beast—the Son of Perdition—and all of the other designations. Daniel 8: 5 and 8: 21, tell us explicitly the rough goat is the King of Grecia, and the great horn between his eyes, the first king. There can be little question the Great Horn is Alexander the Great."

All of the air let out of the room.

"To be clearer: I refer to Alexander the Great as *Zulkarnayn,* which means *two-horned.* Verse twenty-two further cements the identity of the big horn. The four kingdoms rising after it, refer to the *Diadochi.* From the Diadochi developed the four modern nations: Macedon, Turkey, Syria, and Egypt. Out of one of these four nations will come the little horn of Daniel 8: 9-14, in the last days."

"Just a second," broke in Hessen. "If the big horn and the little horn are the same person, and if the big horn lived in antiquity and the little horn in the last days, they're separated by a couple thousand years."

"Yes," Nabil answered.

Unbelief and confusion overtook the men. "Well, how can they be separated by thousands of years and still be the same person?"

26.2

"There are eight prominent worldly kingdoms in eschatology. Some of the super soldiers we're encountering are from the eighth kingdom."

The DARPA team did not respond quickly or interrupt his exposition.

"According to eschatology, the eighth kingdom will be headed by the antichrist in the last days. It'll be the revival of the fifth kingdom listed in the eschatological timeline. Knowing the identity of the eight kingdoms allows the trail of the perdition to be calculated." Daniel Nabil's voice carried across the room. "We can't proceed from the premise we're combatting earthly technology," Nabil gently instructed. "I will tell you this—the events we're seeing will increase in dimension and scope."

"You're saying the super soldiers we're studying will get worse?" asked Corliss.

"Yes," Nabil replied.

"Who's the eighth kingdom," demanded Hessen.

"Greece," replied Nabil. "More precisely: Macedon."

Tomlin, largely quiet through much of the historical summary, spoke up. "Macedon? It's a small country."

"Yes," Nabil agreed, before running his eyes across the room. "But remember: Macedon was a small country in antiquity."

"Daniel, we've been over this," said Merlin, sharpness in his voice.

"The angel who controlled Macedon in antiquity—and today controls it again, the *Prince of Grecia*—happens to be arguably one of the most powerful angels created. The Prince of Grecia and the eighth kingdom are described in the book of Revelation as a scarlet colored beast having seven heads and ten horns. The seven heads are seven mountains—seven kingdoms. The scripture says the beast that was, and is not, even he is the eighth, and is of the seven, and goes into perdition."

"Scarlet-colored beast?" Tomlin struggled to understand.

"This is how the Prince of Grecia, and the country he controls, are seen in the spirit."

"Why are you telling us all this? How does the Biblical image of a scarlet-colored beast help us in our research and study?" Corliss adamantly questioned.

"We're studying and researching about a super soldier not of this world." Nabil pointed to the large digital map on the screen. "The soldiers we're witnessing are only the beginning. The warriors who come after will be far more powerful. Until, lastly, the world will witness the full might of the eighth kingdom…and no one will be able to stand against it."

Merlin help up his hand. "We can all adjust our ideas, Daniel. But we can't modify the world we live in. If these super soldiers are perceived by other militaries of the world to be far superior to our soldiers, the world will no longer place our military in a high position." He shook his head. "We can't allow that."

"Yes, it would disrupt our actuality as a global super power," affirmed Corliss.

Nabil looked at every team member, before returning his attention to Merlin and Corliss. "What are you saying? We can't conceivably match the firepower of any of these soldiers. Do you hear me?"

"So, what the hell do *you* propose?" questioned Hessen. "That we stand back and let these motherfuckers do whatever they please?" He brought his fist down on the table, dramatically. "We can't! We mustn't!"

Nabil, fighting a losing battle, didn't yield his position. "Can someone in this room tell me what the hell we're proposing here? These warriors are filled with the power of God, and the angels of the perdition!" He leaned forward across the table. "Are we going to war against God and angels?"

26.3

"Could a nation's military assume control of a Nazarite, or a hosioi, and use their powers for their own military purposes?"

Nabil shook his head. "No."

"How can you be certain?" Hessen asked.

"A Nazarite, a hosioi—they're not moved by political calculation, or any other worldly objective. Money, power, acceptance—they're immune to such things. Their ways, their beliefs, are far above such considerations."

"Perhaps so," said Hessen. "But to eliminate the prospect of corruption, I propose we assemble a group of research teams to investigate all past battlefield instances of super soldier engagement."

Corliss nodded. "If we set the requirements clearly, we won't get bogged down on dissimilar, unrelated facts."

"I'll group the details," agreed Tomlin. "I can compile them into Project Superman by nineteen hundred hours?"

Chapter 27 More Than Twelve Legions of Angels

Thinkest thou that I cannot now pray to my Father, and he shall presently give me more than twelve legions of angels?

—Matthew 26: 53 KJV

Uziel remembered the lessons he learned as a boy.

He remembered as a twelve-year-old standing in a Turkish wheat field under a light rain.

High Priest deKharouf stood in front of him. Without warning, the high priest struck the boy with an open hand. "Physical attack means nothing to the spiritual warrior. The spiritual warrior doesn't waste energy defending corporal tissue."

The boy's head snapped to the side. Slowly, he recovered.

"Physical weaponry—physical violence—is of no concern to the spiritual warrior. Consider Lazarus. His decomposed body rejuvenated."

Wetness from the rain soothed Uziel's innocence. "But Master, how am I to defend myself?"

"Turn your other cheek," commanded the high priest.

Reluctantly, the boy obeyed.

"Through the absence of physical response, the spiritual warrior draws upon his greatest weapon—faith. Recall the words of the Master of Masters,

Eashoa, who declared more than twelve legions of angels at his disposal."

The boy looked out into the moisture, gazing at the damp wheat spikelets.

"When you turn the other cheek, you introduce the spiritual warfare of the Nazarite. Upon spiritual ascension you're unlimited, and have dominion over the entire world." Moving closer, deKharouf leaned over the boy. "Can you see the real world around you?"

The boy squinted in the drizzle and looked out over the hills.

"What do you see?" asked the high priest.

The boy continued searching the surrounding landscape.

"Look closer," demanded deKharouf.

Uziel's face lit up. "I see…I see…Master…in the hills…I see them." The boy's expression became dark. "Who are they?"

Putting his hand on the boy's shoulder, the high priest answered, "They are the angelic warriors who are sworn to protect you."

"Protect me?"

Giving no warning, the high priest dropped into a crouch and sent a vicious punch directly at the boy's head.

Displaying extraordinary courage, the young boy didn't move, not even flinch. Clinging to his faith in the Holy Spirit, the boy committed his soul to the will of the Almighty.

Before deKharouf's punch landed, the Lord translated Uziel to the north end of the surrounding hills, amongst the spiritual entities he'd been viewing.

His translation concluded between two commanding cherubs who took up a position directly in front of him. The earth quaked and the mountain trembled from his unassailable transformation.

The excitement of his first translation left him trembling.

Youthful exuberance came over him and Uziel desired to use his spiritual powers to play. Commanding the two cherubs to accompany him, he translated over the Mediterranean Sea, and beyond, to the cold Atlantic Ocean.

From out of the enormity of the ocean's vastness, he sensed the intriguing emotions of the whale and the dolphin. Everywhere he looked and everything he thought of—on the earth and in the sky—he desired to see, touch, and feel.

Young and unlimited in power, the cherubs guided him, helping him to control his childlike energy as he shot across the heavens like a thunderbolt.

Occupying all space and time, he existed everywhere.

Guiltless and unencumbered by earthly limitations and mortality, everything he wanted materialized into matter and substance.

Somewhere between the atmospheric dust and the solar system particles, High Priest deKharouf intercepted him.

"Master, I don't want to go back," he pleaded. Pointing to the southern sky, where in the distance spread forth the Great Nebula in Carina, he said, "I want to stay here."

"In eternity?" finished deKharouf.

"I can be everywhere, at the same time. Please, Master."

"You must come back, Son," comforted the wise teacher. "We're needed on this planet."

Sadly, reluctantly, the boy followed his mentor through the universe, and then the solar system, returning to the Turkish wheat field.

The rain still fell.

Time hadn't progressed—not even one unit of Planck time—since his translation.

"So now you see and hear what the Master of Masters said others could not in Mark 8: 17-18, and the Almighty declared in Ezekiel 12: 2." Reaching out, deKharouf touched the boy's cheek. "Do you see? The Spirit healed you when you translated."

Uziel gushed full of excitement. "Master, in eternity I can do anything I want, and see everything in my dreams!"

Chapter 28 Siege of Pelium

"A lot of prophecy predates Alexander, going back to his father—Philip of Macedon—even further back to the ancient tribes before the country of Macedon rose to power. The Argeadae and the Temenidae were too perfect—too exact—to be a coincidence. Some of the events that occurred to save Greece from being destroyed by Persia," Nabil shook his head in unbelief, "the actions of Philip of Macedon to preserve the throne..." Nabil continued to shake his head, "it's mindboggling how everything occurred so precise, so tight. Even the trilogy of Socrates, Plato, and Aristotle—they came perfectly before the birth of their greatest student—the young Prince Alexander who, on his nineteenth birthday, assumed the imperial throne at Pella. Alexander reaped the benefit of their fresh teachings. All these facts, and many more..." His voice trailed away.

"The Bible says Macedon will take over the world?"

Nabil held his attention on Corliss. "It says the son of perdition will overcome specific nations and use their resources to conquer much of Europe, the Middle East, even the Far East."

"Daniel," Merlin began, "Macedon? Syria? Really? These nations aren't big enough to impact the world as your saying."

"I agree that they're small nations. But Macedon was tiny compared to Persia in antiquity."

"In an undeveloped world, I accept this. But in these modern times, a small nation can't do everything you're saying."

The team had been working non-stop for thirty-two hours and weariness clung to each man.

The doubts expressed by the members of the team were common to the reactions Nabil faced when he elucidated the prophetic translation of the book of Daniel.

"Why will the ancient trail be used again?" Corliss asked.

"The Little Horn will follow the trail of the Great Horn because of spiritual necessity."

"Spiritual necessity?" responded Corliss.

"Yes," confirmed Nabil. "The four angels who made Alexander the Great invincible twenty-three hundred years ago, were bound in the spiritual bottomless pit. When this occurred, Macedon fell from power. Now, the angels are released from their incarceration and can, once again, exert their power upon the world. The territorial dominance of these angels spans across a vast portion of the earth, from Macedon, to Egypt, from Turkey and Syria, to India."

Erwin Hessen slowly tilted his head to one side. "You're saying the Little Horn will follow the same trail as the Great Horn?"

Nabil nodded. "He won't just follow the same trail—I'm saying he *needs* to follow the trail if he's to accomplish his objectives. These four angels are incredibly powerful and he needs their power to accomplish the prophecies attributed to him."

The DARPA team tried to absorb his meaning and make sense of it.

"The Great Horn and the Little Horn are spiritual warriors." Nabil's voice dripped intensity. "Alexander the Great was a gifted general and a physical warrior. All the same, he attainted invincibility through his spiritual power. In fact, there are many events in the short life of Alexander the Great that defy all earthly explanation. Nowhere is this more evident than the Siege of Pelium. At twenty years old, Alexander assumed the throne of Macedon and took control of the army. Even though Macedon defeated many rebellious cities in Alexander's quest to stabilize the kingdom, the Illyrian tribes succeeded in surrounding the Macedonian Army. The Illyrians controlled the high ground surrounding the Plain of Pelium, where the Macedonian Army set up camp. Alexander and his army were in a precarious situation. They were outnumbered and their supplies were running low. The military outcome of the Siege of Pelium makes no sense in the physical."

The DARPA team sat engrossed.

"Alexander marched his army out into the open plain. In clear sight of the Illyrians looking down from above, he commanded his soldiers to begin conducting battle drills. When the battle drills were concluded, Alexander ordered his outnumbered phalanx forward against the Illyrians. Incredibly, even though they held the high ground, and every strategic and tactical advantage, the Illyrians turned and ran away from the Macedonian Phalanx." Nabil swept his eyes over the men in the room. "Why?" he asked. "Why would an enemy holding all military advantage run and open the pass, allowing Alexander's army to escape?"

Captivated by his narrative, the DARPA team didn't respond.

"I don't believe they were running away from the physical Macedonian Army," stated Nabil, his voice taking over the room. "I believe they saw the invincible spiritual warriors of the Macedonian Phalanx attacking them. They were terrified, so they ran."

Chapter 29 We Can Never Be

Rhea Korban lifted the carafe and poured the milk into a chalice.

Othniel will want his milk and honey when he returns.

All of her life she'd lived as a Nazarite, observing the rituals of separation and zealous commitment to God.

Kneading the honey into an ancient looking bowl and placing the wafers on a wooden tray, she worked in silence, her hands expertly placing the items. When under vow, the Nazarite diet was extreme and restrictive. When not bound by a promise, the Nazarite ate a wider variety of foods, even consuming processed meats and breads.

Not until the light of dusk entered through a lone high-perched window did she hear the movements of the high priest. Only when he'd completed his evening devotions did the priest enter the modest room.

Making his way to the prepared meal, deKharouf sat down.

Rhea sat down next to him and asked, "What did he say?"

Casting a reflective look, deKharouf didn't answer.

Fear flashed across Rhea's features. "Will he release them from their nazar?"

Reaching out, deKharouf stroked her cheek gently. "I spoke to the Fire. I told him everything."

Immediately she arose and came to him. Putting her arms around him, she held his head to her aged breasts. "Othniel, my beloved, we've served him since before our births."

Pulling back, deKharouf reached up and caressed her face. Running his hands through her silky, youthful hair, he smiled, "All this time you've been by my side."

Rhea shook her head. "But Othniel—"

He covered her mouth with his hand. "No more. Please. I know we can never be. But I can't let him do to them what he did to us. Remember," he whispered into her ear. "Remember when we declared to each other we could never share a bed, raise children, be man and wife?"

No longer feeling the years, Rhea's passion turned her into a young woman, her adoration swelled and her desire caught fire.

"I wanted us to share the things of men and women," said deKharouf. "Time, pain, death—nothing can take away my love for you."

Chapter 30 Outlawed Adoration

In the summer of his sixteenth year, they came to Saint George Monastery.

When Uziel learned about his father, he came to the realization of his origin and everything inside of him transformed.

"Who was my father?"

High Priest deKharouf stopped preparing supper. "I can't tell you."

"Because you don't know?" Having just turned sixteen, Uziel's flesh often warred against his spirit.

Pulling out the ladle from the heavy kettle, the priest scrutinized the boy's face. "I know."

The revelation aggravated Uziel. "Tell me his name and where he lives."

"I told you, I can't."

"He was a priest, like you, wasn't he?"

The Syrian heat of summer blasted throughout the portico and engulfed the monastery, before swirling in the hot kitchen air. Sweat appeared on deKharouf's forehead. Motioning to the doorway, the priest said, "Let's sit in the refectory. We can talk there in peace."

Sitting in the open eating area, empty except for a few servants serving their penitence, deKharouf bowed his head.

From the other end of the large cafeteria, a lowly servant crawled across the floor on his hands and knees and began to kiss the feet of the high priest.

Touching the head of the repentant wretch, deKharouf offered a concise blessing before beginning. "We came here to Saint George because I discerned your spiritual conflict." After a slight pause, deKharouf said, "Your father's a priest."

Uziel exclaimed, "He's a Nazarite?"

Taking his time, deKharouf said, "He resides here. In the conservation of the castle, *Krak des Chevaliers*."

Uziel arose from his seat. "I need to see him."

"First, learn the truth," stated deKharouf, quietly. "Krak des Chevaliers preserves the root of the Christian Nazarites. Where the *new stones* of Nazarites came to completeness, and first gained preeminence in battle. We're the spiritual Nazarites. We worship the Almighty in spirit and truth. We're above genealogy and lineage."

"I'm a gentile?"

"As I am. We spiritual Nazarites are sworn to oath and promise the duration of our lives. There are nazars encompassing generations. Your father loved your mother. Their love was forbidden. Your father refused to stop loving your mother, regardless of the consequences."

Late afternoon lines crept up the high walls of the old dining hall as the Nazarite priest and the boy Nazarite talked about events of long ago.

"Can you tell me my father's name?"

Without hesitation, deKharouf told him.

"Why wasn't my father allowed to love my mom?"

"Because your father's nazar pushed far beyond his life. Because his promise didn't allow him to join in union with your mother."

"I don't understand."

"Your mother, Uziel. She wasn't a Nazarite."

Chapter 31 Into the Vapor

Charity suffereth long, and is kind; charity envieth not; charity vaunteth not itself, is not puffed up, Doth not behave itself unseemly, seeketh not her own, is not easily provoked, thinketh no evil; Charity never faileth: but whether there be prophecies, they shall fail; whether there be tongues, they shall cease; whether there be knowledge, it shall vanish away.

—1 Corinthians 13: 4-8 KJV

Elijah Basra departed the Temple of the Eternal Fire in heaviness, a father desperate to remove his son from a danger he perceived to be inescapable.

His mind returned to an ageless time, long before his son's birth.

Hannah was a beautiful woman. Her long flowing hair, swirled in the sunlit Mediterranean breezes. He first saw her as she bathed in the Castalian Spring. Sent to Mount Parnassus to carry out his Nazarite duties, upon seeing her exquisiteness, his mind considered how to possess her.

In those days, she lived the life of a Pythia. Although they existed in two separate worlds and served two separate masters, Basra cared not of the consequences of the actions he contemplated in his heart.

Her allure captivated him in his spirit. Every moment of the day, he fantasized about her, his semen bubbling within him in exquisite pain. In his dreams, her breasts were like the extension of the dawn's mists in the spring, and her nipples were like the cherry buds that dangled off the crimson trees in the orchard. From out of his lusts, her vagina became a passageway into a world of softness and heat.

Instantly he transformed outside of his spiritual perfection, for the first time in his life needing fulfillment from a source outside the unspoiled energy of God's Fire. His nazar no longer most important to him—she took priority over his needs.

One spring night, shortly after sunset, he came near to her. "I love you," he said softly, unsure of the words to say or the methods of love to use.

She stood unmoving and startled, terrified to be seen near a man. "How did you get here? The hosioi?"

Basra also stood unmoving, smitten by the freshness and beauty of her soul.

She misunderstood his intentions. "Today isn't the day of the Oracle," she told him, pulling the flowing gown closer to her body. The curves of her womanhood betrayed her pious status under the moonlight.

"I didn't come to hear the divination of Apollo," he said.

"Leave," she quickly commanded. Her throat muscles threatened to scream. Strangely, she didn't. A light in her eyes twinkled in the moonlight, as if a part of her womanhood awakened. She seemed to be aware of his hunger, her pureness fighting against his lust and repudiating hers.

Basra didn't move to prevent her from screaming. If she alerted the hosioi, he'd be too weakened by lust to put up a fight.

They both became statues in the night.

"I came to see you. Not the god."

Brushing her hair back, she contemplated in the shadows. "I'm not that kind of woman."

He came closer. "I'm not that kind of man."

"What are you doing here then?"

"Because at the first sight of you, I became that kind of man."

Grasping the full meaning of his intensity, the natural flush of her skin became ruddier. Strangely, a curious look came over her. "What kind of man are you…now that you've seen me?"

Basra's piercing eyes burned into her soul. "I'm the kind of man who saw you for the first time, and loved you forever."

"You're a time controller?"

"Yes. I am the lightning from the sky. I am a son of thunder. I am a Nazarite."

She considered him thoughtfully, his spirit instantly overpowering hers.

Conquering her by the energy of his spirit, he transformed her. "You're no longer a Pythia," he commanded. "You're the love of my life. You're mine."

Standing upon the expansive mountain, she looked up into his eyes.

He owned every part of her; he dominated each cell that completed her.

Reborn into womanhood, her body burned beyond the hunger of women. Consternation spread over her. With extraordinary clarity, she admitted, "We're enemies. Your god, my god, are opposed to each other's will."

In the moist air of the night, Basra did not remove his focus from her beauty. "Your god...is not God."

An impossible encounter, they were two people from completely different worlds. Joined by their spirituality, the Nazarite placed his love inside the Pythia's spirit.

"Come closer." Hannah wrestled against the extreme deviation of a spiritual woman—sheltered from the outside world her entire life—to request a strange man to come closer.

Basra slowly came closer and stood in front of Hannah.

"I'm a Pythia," Hannah said. "I cannot love you."

"You discern my love," said Basra. "My spirit consciousness touched your spirit consciousness."

"Yes," she whispered. "Because of this I am powerless to call out, or run away, or resist you." Her whisper, crushed by emotions, revealed her subjection.

"I can never hurt you," said Basra.

"Yes," she answered, brushing away her flowing hair. "But if we cannot love each other, then why are you doing this?"

"Doing what?"

"What it is you're doing, right now. Your love is tearing my insides to pieces." At last, she managed to turn away from him, her passion spreading to the vastness of Mount Parnassus. Overcome by emotion, she uttered, "This cannot be."

Basra took her in his arms. "I desire to love you, and touch you into forever." Holding her tighter, he pressed her to his chest. "I'll love you like a goddess. Come with me."

She remained unmoving, conflicted by her sensations and her sense of duty to the god. "I can't, my dearest love." Her voice took on a different, softer texture, full of the submission of a woman in the heat of passion. "I can't leave my god."

She pushed against him, but he didn't release her.

"I'll die if I let you go. Come with me!"

His voice pleased her like the breeze, even as his desire surged through her flesh and penetrated into her complexities.

"Come with you where, darling?"

"Everywhere." He held her tighter. "Translate with me. Be everywhere with me. Let me love you into oblivion."

Not able to answer, she did the only thing that seemed natural to her. She gripped him fiercely. Oblivious to the concept of time, frozen by the immenseness of their love, only when he spoke did she break out of her swoon.

"Hannah?" he crooned into her ear.

She hadn't told him her name.

When she didn't react, he repeated, "Hannah?"

"Yes," she answered, her words barely audible, more spirit than physical.

"Come with me."

In the passing seconds, Basra saturated her womanly mystery with his spiritual power.

As a result, in her woman's heart, she perceived a glimpse of eternity and in a flash of light experienced their love affair through the portals of time. Carried away in her spirit, she discovered their love in eternity, olden, yet new.

"Oh, my darling," Hannah cried out softly, "I cannot. I am bound to the god everlastingly. Even now, I fear him watching us, judging us."

A gentle breeze surged up the mountain, caressing the leaves on the trees, kissing their skin.

Her spine tightened.

"What's wrong?" he asked, his voice heavy.

"Do you love me, my treasure?" she asked, in a voice also encumbered.

"With all my heart," he quickly assured her.

"Then *you* come with me."

"Come with you?"

"Yes. Come with me into the vapor."

Instinctively, Basra pulled back and became distant. "I can't come with you into the vapor," Basra said. "It would defile me," he concluded.

Hannah broke free from his lessened grip, moving away from him into the shadows bordering the dense vapor.

Basra weakened in his flesh from love and lust. In shameless hunger, he grabbed her arm again and pulled her to him, forcefully pressing her breasts to his chest.

"What do you want from me?" she savagely whispered. "It's you who came here. Do you expect me to give up my life without question? And you? What do you give up?"

Basra didn't reply, sensing the sinister vapor getting closer.

"I need you to love me beyond your heart," said Hannah. "With all of your mind and soul, too."

Basra let go of her. "I'll give up everything for you." He shook his head. "But my life isn't mine. My mind and soul belong to the Almighty."

In the darkness of the cold mountain of the god, the menacing fog and smoke closed in on Basra.

She was a woman. From the deepness of her secrets, she determined she couldn't live without him.

He realized, too late, what was happening.

He saw her running away into the vapor. He stood alone upon the rocky peak of the god.

All of my life I've been alone. Now, everything's changed.

I need her!

He wasn't a man of impulse or whim, such frailties dangerous to a man of his vocation. Yet, impulsiveness overtook him and he felt his legs moving without his command.

Running after her—his greatest love—he ran full speed into the vapor.

Chapter 32 Cave of My Affliction

And though the Lord give you the bread of adversity, and the water of affliction,
thine ears shall hear a word behind thee, saying, This is the way, walk ye in it,
when ye turn to the right hand, and when ye turn to the left.

—Isaiah 30: 20, 21 KJV

He lay in an abandoned cave, isolated and cold. The cave was uninhabited since before his birth.

The Almighty built the cave for my affliction.

As deKharouf sat upon the unbreakable rock, three angels stood before him. "I discerned you'd be here," he said to the angelic presence.

Dressed in elegant robes, the angels wore belts of the finest gold around their waists. Their bodies were like chrysolite, their faces shown translucent and bright, their skin gleamed like topaz, and their eyes were like flaming torches.

In his mind, he perceived their voices like the sound of a multitude.

In the silence of the empty cave, the angels ministered to him.

Looking into the brightness of their appearance, deKharouf revealed his heart to them. "Nothing's changed," he proclaimed, discerning the clarity of the angels and the purity of their spirits.

The angels spoke to his disobedient flesh, beyond the ability of words and human expression.

"No!" In righteous anger, deKharouf pointed to the angelic beings. "I judge this world to be wrong! All of it! The winepress doesn't judge this creation."

The three angels did not react, allowing him to continue.

"It judges the pre-Adamites! I say, judge the guilty—not the innocent!"

Chapter 33 Iron Sword of Heracles

The noble Temenidae have royal rule over much wealth-producing land; for it is the gift of aegis-bearing Zeus. But go in haste to the Bouteid land of many flocks, and wherever you see gleaming-horned, snow-white goats sunk in sleep, sacrifice to the gods and found the city of your state on the level ground of that land. (sic)

—Diodorus Siculus 7.16 An Oracle of Apollo to Perdiccas I

The rise of the *Temenidae* kings of Argos and the rise of the *Argeadae Macedones,* in near perfect sequential order in antiquity, was a carefully constructed chain of events.

Around 3000 BC developed the *Minoan* civilization. Through its fierce, yet peaceful culture, its great cities mastered the *Aegean.* Through the abundance of trade and commerce, *Cretan* art, commodities, and influence permeated east as far as Palestine, west through Italy, as distant as Spain, north to the city of Troy, even to the mainland.

Fusion of the Minoan and Greek inhabitants brought the dawn of a civilization of progression: the *Mycenaean.* The Minoan powered culture of trade, through measured peace, sired Europe's destruction and death: the *Helladic.*

33.2

The inscriptions of *Rameses III,* the writings of *Pliny, Homer's* poetic lines, the calculations of *Eratosthenes,* the nineteen-century excavations of *Heinrich Schliemann,* the fresh data of modern study—all prove the event of the *Trojan War.*

The Greek-speaking, war-like Mycenaeans appeared in 1700 BC. Less than two centuries later, they dominated the Aegean Sea and ruled the mainland.

In 1400 BC, a northern tribe expanded south across the *Peloponnesus,* mingling their blood alongside the *Pelasgo-Mycenaeans.* By 1250 BC, a *Creto-Pelasgo-Mycenaean-Achaean* union emerged as the new ruling tribe of the mainland. A physical people—their men tall and muscular, their women beautiful and ardent—Achaean culture ruled through militaristic law.

The fall of Troy, in 1194 BC, brought Achaean dominance to Asia.

It would not last long.

Ninety years later, the 1104 BC invasion of the *Dorians*—physically large, war-like tribes seeking new pastures for their cattle and new lands and people to conquer—pulverized and energized the Helladic gene.

As destiny willed, the advancing barbaric tribes emerged out of the European darkness composed of iron souls and iron weapons.

The Achaeans never knew what hit them.

With machinelike coldness, the cheap, hard iron swords of the Dorians slaughtered the bronze-armed Achaeans, nearly wiping away their 400 years of rich life. Only elements of the ancient civilization remained. In the *"Return of the Heraclaidae"* the Dorians—descendants of Heracles—took the Peloponnesus by heroic force.

From the Dorian blood the Temenidae kings arose.

In the savage intercourse of the age of iron, the blood of the Achaeans spilt to the ground, impregnating the soil of Greece, conceiving a new mighty people from out of the ruins of their destruction. The trial of gestation brought forth a new man-child within the old womb of Greece. Old blood mixed with new blood, barbaric and unrefined mixed with cultured and civilized, the mixed blood fused into one.

Bronze became iron.

In the outcome, a 350-year pregnancy of agony took place before the miracle of birth.

33.3

Greece fell into a dark, unprogressive pit.

The Dorians, much lower in skill and ability than the Mycenaeans before them—in the same pattern as the Mycenaeans were much lower in skill and ability than the Minoans—propelled their new culture through violence and war. Wonderful art declined to unrewarding, prosaic artifacts; organized records succumbed to obscure emptiness; writing decayed to illiteracy; finely made weapons of bronze descended to raw, primitive weapons of iron; magnificent burials deteriorated to profane cremation.

In the complexity of the developing new creation, the utter destruction of mainland Greece planted the seeds of *Hellenic culture*: the city-state formula, personal and political freedom, a shared common language, and cultural unity. The ethnic foundation—containing diametric ends of the political, military, and social spectrums—served to function as a massive laboratory, providing a wide range of scientific choice to accomplish the terrible vision.

Sparta ultimately took on the Dorian way of existence: illiterate, physical, animalistic, savage, and militaristic.

Athens retained much of the Mycenaean values: literate, cerebral, humanistic, civilized, and democratic.

Not until the mainlanders began trying to duplicate *Ionia's* ambitious culture, and elevated life style and art, did the Hellenic pregnancy move to the stage of labor.

Amidst the dreadful hurt of the induced birth pains, the old Grecian womb gave birth to Homer.

The mighty race of iron was born.

33.4

In the age of bronze, the area of the upper *Haliacmon (Aliakmon)* was known as *Maceta* and the Haliacmon valley as *Macednia*.

Dorian conquest brought chaos and death, and then more conquest. For the Aliakmon shepherds, the vanquishing came in the form of a Macedonian tribe called the *Orestae*. In the culmination of the incursion, the ground came to be known as *Orestis,* meaning *mountain-land*.

The Orestae invasion pushed the *Macetai* and *Macednoi* south into *Pieria*. Here, in the Pierian range north of Olympus, in the land called *Macedonis,* the insignificant tribal cluster found strength to survive and regroup.

A century later, the ethnics took the shape of unity.

They called themselves the *Macedones*.

Another tribe is mentioned in the *eleventh fragment of Strabo's seventh book*. Ruling over the Macedones, this tribe infused the spark of greatness into the humble blood.

The name of the ruling tribe was the *Argeadae*.

These descendants of *Areas,* son of Macedon, distinct from the Macedones of Upper Macedon, and the *Lyncestae* and the *Elimiotae* tribes, the Argeadae were part of a tribal cluster identified in history as the Macedones. Interestingly, their point of origin did not derive from the city of *Argos*, in the Peloponnese, rather, their dwelling traced to *"the Argos in Orestis."*

All the same, this link to their homeland drew the sons of *Temenus,* king of ancient Argos, to the northern crests of Maceta.

In the beginning of the seventh century, the first Temenidae ruler, Perdiccas I, seized the throne of the Argeadae Macedones.

33.5

Temenus, king of Argos, descended from Heracles, son of Zeus.

The cold words of Demosthenes against Philip of Macedon notwithstanding, the Temenidae monarch kings were descendants of Temenus, making Temenidae genealogy Argive in blood. Many events and details, including Alexander I entering the Olympic games in 504 BC—only

Greeks participated in the ancient Olympics—give proof of genealogy.

A monarchy was set up by assembly—rule by consent agreed upon by the Argeadae Macedones. By the declared right of their subjects, from 650 BC to 310 BC one family held kingship, central institution of government, and legitimacy to the throne—the Temenidae—and only in the male line.

The paramount function of the Temenidae king was to conduct relations between the god and the Argeadae Macedones.

From out of the throne of the Argeadae, there came rule and communion with the god.

From the power within one man, a mighty nation marched forth into perdition.

Chapter 34 Krak des Chevaliers

"Forever is not ours."

Rhea silently lay next to him, her head on his chest.

It was many years earlier. They were younger. Burning in the flames of their passions, their promises to each other controlled them.

"Because we will never be, I will tell you of our love, and the children we will never raise."

She pressed her head into his chest lovingly. "And our home, my love? You said it would be in the ocean."

"Yes," he replied.

It was the day before their nazars. The following day they would swear to God to refrain from all of the emotional attachments of the world, until their deaths.

"Across the winds of eternity," he said, as they lay on the bed. "I declare our life together, which we will never live. Our days will be full of laughter. Our nights will discover the perfect kiss and reveal heaven's touch."

From the height of their room, within the Tower of the King's Daughter, at *Krak des Chevaliers*, they looked out across the *Wādī al-Naṣārá* below. The castle dominated the view from all directions.

The year was 1886, and from St. George Monastery near Al Meshtayeh, on the opposite side of the valley, three miles away, they rode horseback across the countryside that surrounded the imposing castle.

In the late afternoon, true to their custom, they arrived at Krak des Chevaliers.

Leaving their horses to graze in the sun, deKharouf and Rhea walked toward the tower, a prevailing monument of the crusader knights.

In a prearrangement they followed, deKharouf unloaded the thin mattress off his horse and Rhea unloaded the sheet and bedspread. Quietly, they made their way through the arched entry and beyond a tangle of cobblestone pathways leading to their special room.

On the edge of the slope looking down to the *Valley of the Christians,* the horses, furnished fodder and spread to feed and roam, fed lazily in the bright sun. Amongst the bulwarks and collection of safeguards arrayed outside the window, the sound of chirping birds pleased their ear. Their love, forbidden as long as their sworn oath to God existed, pulled them to their secret sanctuary in the hot days of summer and the cold nights of winter.

Prior to that fateful day, they often came to the room to pledge their devotion to each other. As if sensing their rendezvous on this day was different, the chirping of the birds became softer.

"Othniel?" Rhea's lip trembled slightly.

"Yes, my love."

"What if…"

"Go on, my love. Tell me what you need to tell."

She pulled away. Bending her knees, she rocked back and forth and buried her face in their folds.

"Rhea?" called out deKharouf, trying to pull her back.

Not allowing him to pull her back, Rhea sobbed uncontrollably.

"Tell me!" deKharouf tenderly demanded, as he sat up.

Through the tears and the sobs, Rhea answered, "I'm a woman! I can't give up my womanhood as easily as you can give up your manhood! What about me, Othniel? What about my needs and desires to be a woman? A wife? A mother?"

Her cries bounced off the walls of the room. Her emotional scream silenced the birds and caused the horses in the field to raise their heads in astonishment.

Rhea turned in the bed. "Othniel?"

"Yes," he replied.

"You are a mighty man of God. You are above the power and ability of normal men. I too am a Nazarite. My abilities and power are beyond the normal female." Her tears and sobs returned. "But what if…we didn't take our oath? What if we just ran away?"

The young deKharouf turned to the side.

Turning him back to face her, Rhea cried out, "No Othniel! Don't ignore my question! Please!"

"I can't do it! I've served him my entire life. I can't betray him. Not even for you, my love."

Deep sadness materialized across Rhea's features. She rose from the bed and walked to the window, looking out across the field.

Soon after, deKharouf followed her to the window. She didn't resist when he put his arms around her.

They stood by the window, looking down at the surrounding villages.

Finally, deKharouf whispered in torment, "Rhea…we're Nazarites…because we love God. We willingly sacrifice our lives in devotion to the greatness of his light. How can we refuse him?"

Softly she turned to him.

Gently they kissed.

"Please," begged deKharouf, "if all we have is today, then let me love you forever, in my dust and ashes."

Chapter 35 Heroes and Lovers

In the year 1946, he turned twenty-six years old. Ten years after High Priest deKharouf told him about his father and mother, and their illicit love affair.

He returned to Krak des Chevaliers, a man touched by the evils of war and the intense need to reconcile past relationships and cultivate the wonders of love. Over the course of his youth into manhood, the castle took on the image of commitment, love, and family to him. As he approached from a distance, the imposing figure of the castle moved him spiritually.

"I seek the conservator," he said to a priest, doing repairs on one of the inner defense walls.

The priest turned slightly toward him. After considering him briefly, the vicar put down the trowel. Using his gifts of discernment, the holy man discovered his identity. "What is the name of the man you seek?"

"Elijah Basra."

"Yes, he's been waiting for you."

Uziel had never seen his father, nor mentioned to anyone of his intent to come to the old castle to confront him.

Using his Nazarite spiritual abilities, his father discerned his visit.

Up a section of steps, they passed through a capacious postern, which opened into a prodigious ballroom. By a row of pilasters stood a man who possessed a facial profile familiar to Uziel. High cheekbones ascended to a broad forehead. Grey-streaked auburn hair, and a matching stout chin, brought out the familiarity between both men's faces.

Without a greeting, Uziel evenly said, "You're my father."

The older man didn't flinch. "You've returned from the great war. How are you?"

"All of my life you've never once troubled yourself to know how I was. I don't see why you should start now."

"I did know about you," said the father, dismissing the accusatory tone. "I was there on the days you experienced your awful hunger. I was there on the days when you hurt because of your growing pains. I was there when you first felt love touch your heart."

The young Basra's spine stiffened.

"She's beautiful," said the older Basra. "Her name's…Ariella."

Disregarding the man's pronouncement, Uziel asked, "Why did you abandon me? Doesn't your son deserve your loyalty?"

The father perceived the deep pain of his son. "I've been with you every single day of your life. I was there on the nights when you cried yourself to sleep when Hubb died. I never missed a day or night."

The mention of Hubb stunned Uziel. "Hubb," he whispered. Only deKharouf, Rhea, Ariella, and the priests knew of Hubb, his pet lamb.

"You loved him," said Elijah Basra in sadness. "When you were happy, when you were sad… I wish I could've…held you. To share your happiness, and take away your pain. Every day and night I thought about you."

"Mother," said Uziel, "she's why I came to see you."

"Hannah," whispered Elijah Basra, turning slightly to try to prevent his son from witnessing his sorrow.

"I want to know where she's buried."

35.2

In a secret place within the Alhulu West Forest, Elijah revealed to Uziel the location where he kept his mother's remains.

"Apollo struck her with sickness and took her life away because of revenge," Elijah said, softly. "A Pythia isn't subject to choices, only obedience. Her choice was betrayal to the god."

The picturesque place where Elijah interred his wife charmed the senses. Rolling hills, churning fog above and through the forests, a tranquil rivulet eddying around the boulders cluttering the forest's edge—all seemed indicative of his unending love for her.

"I want you to know I loved your mother," Elijah announced to the contemplative Uziel. "She was the only woman I ever loved."

Uziel looked away and stared out across the scenic countryside. Turning from the unmarked grave, he took a few steps to one side to gather his emotions.

"She brought you here when you were an infant," reflected Elijah, his voice carrying over the jasmine and clump of Damask roses he'd planted and nurtured for many years at the gravesite. Elijah lowered his head to thwart the tears forming in his eyes. After a few seconds, he raised his head. "We walked along the lover's paths all around here," he said, his voice weighty and drenched with timeworn emotion. "She would tell you stories of heroes and lovers. She loved who you were destined to become."

In its descent, the sun hid behind clouds and the land assumed an opaque shade.

Holding out an old picture to his son, Elijah gave a nod of his head. "We were a family then."

Through the picture's worn creases, Uziel made out the image of a petite woman possessing delicate cheekbones. "Momma was beautiful," he proclaimed, somberly.

Slowly, delicately, Elijah returned the old photo he'd been showing his son back into a pouch within his priestly robe.

Uziel noticed the pouch sat directly over his father's heart.

The words erupted out of Elijah's grief-stricken soul. "The Almighty sent me into exile. She kept you the first year. I shared in some of those memories, but by the time you were six months old, I wasn't allowed to see you, nor touch you. When we decided to give you up to God, she brought you to the temple."

Uziel fought to suppress tears, overcome by the knowledge of his mother's torment.

"Your mother died just after you turned two. She suffered much."

Anger swelled within Uziel.

"I considered annulling my vow. I considered a lot of things," continued Elijah. "I wrestled with God many years. The wars I fought, we fought, left scars that'll never heal. Up until you turned nine years old, I remained in the wilderness. I thought God had forgotten about me. But then, the Holy Spirit led me back to the castle where we shared our love."

The sun reached the low point of its arc. Only then did they finish lamenting about lost love and tragic romance.

In the twilight, Elijah turned to his son and said, "Ariella?"

Standing to one side, Uziel quietly peered across the hill-slanted forest, viewing the sunlight as it shrunk and fell across the valley below. When Elijah's words sunk into his mind, he frowned. "What about her?"

"I know you love her. I can see it in your eyes."

"What are you getting at?"

"She's a Nazarite, as you are."

"So what?"

"Love's hard. It doesn't need to be harder." Elijah looked up through the trees at the darkened sky.

"What does that mean?"

Solemnness landed heavy on Elijah's shoulders. "Emotions process differently from the physical to the spiritual. You both exist in a dangerous world. Imperfect faith will lead to mistakes in the field of combat. It could be the difference between life and death."

"You haven't met her. You don't know her."

"No I don't," agreed Elijah.

"Then you—"

"In spiritual warfare, one split second of distraction can be fatal."

Chapter 36 The Four Musketeers

People in general, only ask advice not to follow it; or if they do follow it, it is for the sake of having someone to blame for having given it.

—Alexandre Dumas, *The Three Musketeers*

Lieutenant Daniels and Sergeant Johnson didn't build the Superman Special Mission Unit hunter-killer team under the same perimeters as other task force creations. Although Project Superman was classified as an Advanced Force Operations (AFO) mission, the fifteen soldiers comprising the SMU no longer possessed any military connection.

Essentially, the "free fall" mission meant the task force had authority to hunt and kill outside of military dominion. Much like the organization it spawned from—GF99—the Superman SMU team reported only to its highest-ranking commander: Colonel Ivan Lasker.

36.2

The four men who sat in front of the hunter-killer team were shadowy and cool.

Daniels and Johnson knew the men, having worked with them on other kill missions.

"We're the four musketeers," announced a tall, intense man with sandy brown hair and cold steel eyes, sitting next to three other men at a glass table, in a nondescript room. "We're here to brief you on the target."

The "four musketeers" were ex-CIA agents, working closely with CIA's SAD/SOG (Special Activities Division / Special Operations Group) Division. Placed in charge of paramilitary operations in the most hostile and dangerous of regions, SAD possessed a strong reputation throughout GF99. The four musketeers were instrumental in the hunt and killing of many of Grey Fox's targets.

Owen Roscom—code name "Athos"—placed his sunglasses over his sandy brown hair. To the right of him sat a thick man, whose large nose gave way to a prominent forehead.

Daniel Garvin—the number two musketeer—went by the code name: d'Artagnan.

Then came number three and four of the musketeers: Harold Dean and Kendell Perkins, whose code names, respectively, were "Aramis" and "Porthos," corresponding with Roscom's and Garvin's code names. Both men were slightly younger than the prominent men who headed their group.

Medium height and soft-spoken, Dean possessed religious zeal to match his quick wit and veiled charm.

Perkins's handsomely rugged looks, on the other hand, far surpassed his aptitude in many of the gifts and skills the other men in the group possessed. His application of data to achieve the desired outcome set him apart.

Gary "Predator" Cullum didn't blink as he declared his question to the musketeers. "Who are we here to kill?"

Daniels chomped down on his Montecristo No. 2 torpedo, as he shifted his attention to the other hunter-killers in the platoon-sized unit.

Johnson toyed with the pouch of his military tritium lensatic compass, as he stared down Cullum, neither man blinking.

Daniels set down his Montecristo. "We're all killers," he said, his words carrying through the room.

Cullum kept his vision locked directly on Johnson.

Johnson returned the favor.

"The CONOPs," Cullum asked Daniels. "Will we be in free fall?"

Daniels gave a slight nod. "No restrictions."

Johnson flicked open his compass and closed it. Without blinking, he leaned forward and whispered to Cullum, "CJSOTF will be a distant memory."

"Where's the hunt?" called out a killer behind Cullum.

"The AOR's long and wide," answered Owen Roscom. "It traverses Turkey, Syria, Lebanon, Iraq, even Egypt. We're planning to target one KZ, but mobility is critical. INTSUM (Intelligence Summary) can't get us closer to our AO."

"That's a big problem," Daniels said, softly.

"It can't be helped," responded Garvin.

Caressing his torpedo, Daniels, once again, went quiet.

"Let's go over the INTSUM reports." Perkins's icy logic—always cold in calculation—matched the precision of the hunter-killers.

An hour later, the killers finished viewing the footage from Sensitive Compartmented Information, Facility A, and reviewing the INTSUM reports and data.

Out of the silence, Cullum blurted out, "This fucker ain't human."

"The INTSUM reports say he is," retorted Perkins, firmly.

"Some of the data's old." Cullum's appearance darkened. "Why does ISA believe he's the same soldier?"

United States Army Intelligence Support Activity (USAISA) spearheaded the efforts to collect intelligence in advance of special operations missions.

"The summary lists many reasons." Dean kept his vision steady as he replied. Being the youngest musketeer, he favored a low profile. "There's no way of truly knowing if it's the same soldier until we kill him. We need a specimen to study."

"If he's the same soldier, then he's fuck'n old," Cullum went on. "He'd be eighty, maybe even ninety years old."

"How does an old man do the fuck'n shit the reports say?" asked one of the other killers.

Johnson turned slightly and gave a side-glance to the killer who asked the question. Absent of emotion, he cleared the air. "We're soldiers. We're killers."

"As you've observed, the super soldier can run over sixty miles an hour, for recorded distances of up to three miles." Roscom paused before finishing. "That we know of."

Dread and caution emerged across Cullum's visage.

Rubbing his chin in thought, Roscom said, "As you've witnessed, he can jump from incredible heights and leap across great spans."

Mindful to remain composed, Perkins added, "As the reports and libraries show, he's destroyed numerous Abrams M1A2s."

"How?" asked one of the killers.

"With his...bare hands," answered Roscom.

Cullum shook his head. "This is fucked up shit. How's that even possible?"

"This super soldier can walk on water," Perkins went ahead, not considering the reaction of the soldier. "He can go through land mines, is impervious to bullets, and resistant to bombs. All the reports are confirmed."

Daniels returned to puffing the Montecristo. Curls of cigar smoke shrouding his vision of the hunter-killers, "Anybody want out, leave now."

No one in the room moved.

"We land in the sandbox in a week," said Daniels. "We're gonna hunt him. And we're gonna kill him."

Chapter 37 Mightiest of Warriors

It is a brave act of valor to condemn death. But where life is more terrible than death, it is then the truest valor to dare to live.

—Sir Thomas Brown

Krak des Chevaliers stood as a relic from the Crusades, over a thousand years earlier. The castle suffered much decline over the years, sustaining many injuries from the wars fought in the region.

Throughout history, it served as a bastion for the soldiers of Christianity, and a fortress where the Nazarite cherished suffered through their nazars together. Remuneration for the services they provided to its upkeep.

In the middle of the spiritual warfare and the physical weakness, there came to be born the mightiest of warriors: Uziel Basra.

Chapter 38 Alhulu West Forest

*Thy lips, O my spouse, drop as the honeycomb: honey
and milk are under thy tongue.*

—Song of Solomon 4: 11 KJV

The mere scent of Hannah left him weak.

After making love under the shadow of Mount Olympus, Elijah held her underneath the splashing rain. He wanted to experience everything about her.

With his passion and lust, he told her the story of his soul.

After drinking from the *Pierian Spring*, they retreated to a soft camp by the *Pineiós River* and he made love to her again underneath the moonlight. Her womanhood poured over him like wine, her flesh offered him sustenance.

In turn, one drink of him did not satisfy her constant thirst. To savor his ardor left her in perpetual hunger.

With their hearts beating as one, they eclipsed the sunrise, as their climax upstretched beyond Olympus.

Hannah, abandoning her former life, transformed into a woman, her needs the timeless needs of women. She desired him to take possession of her deprivation and redeem her of her loneliness.

Wanting and needing more. Afraid she'd become an object in his dreams, she awakened to a deep surrender. "I need to love you forever. I need you to love me to the end of time."

Clumsily, he reached for her again, his lustful drunkenness returning.

"No," she deftly parried his advances, the woman in her demanding more from his manhood.

His voice stolen by the winds descending from Olympus's peak, he fell into a stupor.

She began to roll away from him, reaching for her purified gown. "I must go," her femininity expertly announced, pulling his masculinity out of her heat in cold deliberation.

Gently drawing her to him, Basra admitted the consequence of giving into his flesh. "I'm no longer in the thunder. I've lost eternity...to gain you. I cannot love you to the end of time, but I promise I'll love you till the end of my life."

The following day still found them by the Pineiós River.

He drank her, her body the vessel from which decanted a honeyed spring. All through the night, he quenched his thirst in her sweet waters.

Their spirits gave way to their flesh, their bodies intertwining like the roots of two trees. In their communication, they hoped to fashion new flesh and form a new creation out of their hopes.

Awakened by the dawn, Hannah's spiritual gifts perceived the growth of the seed. Unsure how to tell him, she waited until the sun reached higher in the sky and he arose to fish by the river.

"What is it?" Elijah asked, trying to read her strangeness.

Putting down the thick branch he'd fashioned into a fishing pole, he took her in his arms and held her.

Neither said a word, only the sound of the river's current interrupted the silence. Finally, when the sun reached its summit, he let go of her.

Picking up the stick, he went back to fishing. Within the hour, three fishes hung from the line. Hannah remained by his side, even when he started a fire under a group of willow trees and cooked the fish.

They ate quietly, frequently embracing.

Hannah appeared more sensitive to him and provided him warmness in the night.

"I need to tell you."

"Tell me what?"

"I felt the spark. There is a life inside of me."

Elijah put down his plate, the fish in his stomach making him sluggish. "Are you sure?"

Briefly hesitating, she nodded her head, unsure what she discovered across his features.

Unexpectedly, he reached out and put his hand over her belly.

"Thank you," she smiled warmly, "for giving me this gift."

They held hands into the night. Underneath the billions of stars, they shared another moon together.

"We are no longer betrothed, my love." Elijah buried his nostrils in her abundant hair. "We are man and wife. Our marriage is before the Almighty."

"What will we name him?" Hannah's expression revealed her vulnerabilities.

"Him?"

"Yes, my darling," she assured him. "It's a man-child in my womb."

Breaking out of his stupor, he kissed her lightly. "My son," he whispered. "Our son," he corrected.

She buried her face into his chest.

"We will name him Uziel," answered Elijah, squeezing her gently. "It's the name of my grandfather. It is a good name."

They remained by the Pineiós River ten more days, eating, drinking, loving. In the months to follow, their love grew. Often, they returned to their lover's cove, until one day Elijah detected the evil spirits sent by an angel.

"It's not safe here anymore," he told her.

Days later, he found their secret place in the *Alhulu West Forest*. "They won't find you here," he assured her, feeling her tremble under her elegant frock.

"When I'm with you, I feel safe," she said.

Elijah noticed her softer dimensions immediately. He took advantage of her sweet disposition to prepare the child in her womb. Scripture devotions in the mornings gave way to long walks in the afternoons. Prayer sessions in the cool nights seasoned their love to a spiritual pinnacle.

Chapter 39 Issus

Uziel began the path of his spiritual conquest where Alexander the Great began his physical conquest in antiquity, near *Erzin*.

Amidst the ancient ruins of Issus, in the city of *İskenderun*, in the province of *Hatay*, on the Mediterranean coast of Turkey, a concentration of angels and evil spirits blocked the spiritual passage.

The enemy spiritual force guarding the Issus entry didn't expect an assault. His ferocity cut deep into the ranks and left destruction to show its path.

"Your attack on the Issus spiritual garrison will reveal our intentions to the enemy," deKharouf's voice sounded in his mind.

In antiquity, the physical Battle of Issus gave Alexander the Great control of the entry point into the Syrian gates Likewise, the objective of the spiritual Battle of Issus sought to gain control of the gateway into the conquered otherworldly ground held by the enemy. By attacking the stronghold, the Nazarites hoped to disrupt the prophesied trail of perdition.

Pushing his angelic army against the static defenses of the Issus stronghold, Uziel's forces gained the battle initiative. An initiative they never relinquished.

Uziel's forces continued their relentless pressure, annihilating the entirety of the enemy forces. In the aftermath, Uziel and his army took the angelic princes governing the ancient ground into captivity.

Issus had fallen.

Spiritual repercussions rippled through the vapor.

Chapter 40 Zeus-Ammon

Tyrimmas Archelaus walked into the repository wherein the scrubbed bones were kept. He stood contemplating the golden larnax in silence. Running his fingers over the starburst, Archelaus scrutinized the detail of the star in awe.

Oh, great Pharaoh, all of these years you've waited patiently.

Lieutenant Colonel Hephaistos Parmenopolos, of the Macedonian Volci, walked up behind Archelaus and said, "Ten of my men came in, the other forty are guarding the perimeter."

Dressed in black uniforms, and Kevlar helmets, two of the Macedonian Special Forces soldiers guarded the doorway, while two others took up position in the far corners of the room.

"Sir, I suggest you allow me and my men to transport the bones to the next repository."

"No," whispered Archelaus. "I'll carry the bones to the next site."

"Very well, sir," responded Parmenopolos, studying the logistics of the transfer. "Sir, I'm curious about the traveling arrangements. I find it odd we won't be using Alexander the Great Airport on this delicate shipment. The next site is Berovo, one hundred seven miles from Skopje. I strongly recommend we—"

"You *will* be using Alexander the Great Airport, Lieutenant Colonel. The arrangements made are satisfactory. I, and a small contingent of your troops, will use the land route to the Berovo site."

"Am I to understand we're not here to escort you and the materials, sir?"

"There are certain comestibles in packages. You will be delivering them to Berovo."

"Comestibles, sir?"

"Correct. We wish you to transport a shipment of goods under heavy security details." Archelaus extended a shipment list to the soldier. "You will arrive before my contingent arrives. When your plane lands, instructions will be given to you as to where to deliver the shipment."

Slowly the military man went over the list. He looked up in astonishment.

"I want you to listen to me closely, Colonel."

The military man remained absolutely still, in rapt attention.

"If you are aggressively intercepted in any way, your instructions are to defend the shipment to the last man. Understood, Commander?"

Bringing his hand to his forehead in a full salute, Parmenopolos declared, "To our deaths we will defend this shipment, sir."

40.2

Major General Perdiccas Manolis stood before Tyrimmas Archelaus as a man stands before a god.

"I deployed the Special Forces to guard the counterfeit fruit," said Archelaus, with cold, unemotional strength. "And you will remain here, with ten soldiers of the Honor Guard Battalion."

"Yes, sir," responded the general.

"You've been given your orders by the Minister of Defense?"

"Yes, sir."

"Are you comfortable with them?"

The strange question appeared to catch the general by surprise.

"I am a professional soldier, sir. I will execute my duty."

Archelaus moved closer to the commanding soldier, boldly within inches of him. "Do you know who I am?"

The general paused, contemplating the man with the care of a disciplined soldier. His forehead creased over as he strained to ascertain the man's identity. "I think I…" Another wave of silence flooded the repository.

Seemingly angry with himself, the soldier deliberately stated, "No, sir. You're familiar to me, but I can't pinpoint why."

Archelaus took a step back. "Look closer," he commanded.

Archelaus's appearance changed right before the general's eyes.

"It can't be," the general stammered, shaking his head. "You...can't be my..."

"I can be all things, to all," declared Archelaus, his face returning to its original form. "What issue do you have with the orders? Speak your mind."

Struggling with the vision he'd just witnessed, the general replied, "We sent the bulk of the Volci troops to Berovo. Only the ten soldiers here will accompany us. With all respect, sir, they're not enough."

Once again, Archelaus moved closer to the soldier. "You say that to me, knowing who I am?"

The general lowered his head. Falling to his knees before Archelaus, reduced to the fullness of his human frailty, he announced, "You are the god of my people—the god of the Macedonians. You are Zeus-Ammon, in the flesh. Nothing, or no one, can stop you."

Chapter 41 Sword of the Spirit

And he came thither unto a cave, and lodged there; and, behold, the word of the LORD came to him, and he said unto him, What doest thou here, Elijah?

—1ˢᵗ Kings 19: 9 KJV

His spirit perceived the question as he approached the location of the first bottomless pit. As he walked through the ruins of ancient Babylon, he discerned the spiritual remnants of a great power.

Out of the ruins came a small voice. *What are you doing here?*

"I must find her. I cannot lose her." His whisper shook the rubble under his feet; his pain stirred the palms in the distance.

The cave's coldness cut into his bones. In his mind, the vision of Ariella came to him and her smile warmed him. He dreamed of her long hair and the smoothness of her skin.

"When you swear an oath to God," he recalled deKharouf instructing him, "the promise doesn't end on this earth. Perfection will judge you on your faithfulness."

"Tomorrow," he whispered to the rock and stone. "Tomorrow I will return to Siwa and cultivate the fruit. Tonight, I wish to dream of Ariella and our happiness."

Within the hardened stone an angel appeared and looked down upon the brokenhearted warrior with amazement and sadness.

41.2

The sword protruding out of Uziel's mouth was a sharpened instrument able to cut apart the physical and the spiritual. He drew the blade and plunged its point into the flesh, beyond into the spirit.

The piercing scream of the devil carried across the space of the valley.

"Why do you torture us, Son of Man?" the devil—a disembodied entity, incapable of experiencing the full scope of existence—pleaded. "We told you we do not know where she is!"

Uziel cruelly twisted the sword violently, the blade ripping open the ethereal.

Once more, the devil screamed out into the night.

As his blade impaled the devil, he drew his mouth closer to the spirit. "I've had my fill of your lies!"

Swinging his sword around, the blade cut the devil open, leaving the remains of the evil spirit in the air and the dirt.

The quietness of the Valley of Devils caused him to judge his destruction complete.

There existed gates beyond the main gateway, guarded by the evil spirits of the city. Beyond the gates, caves led into the earth, curving and twisting like a snake.

Uziel came upon the first stronghold of the underground.

An evil spirit, possessing the spiritual form and appearance of a frog, blocked the entrance. "What do you want here, Son of Man?"

"I care not about the affairs of Assur," Uziel quickly answered. "I seek the path of the hosioi."

The frog spirit pushed against the gate viciously. "Our allegiance is not to Pytho. Leave here!"

"In the days of the perdition, your mystery will entice the beast, and he will bring you under his subjection."

"Never! Go away slave of Elah, I will never relinquish this gate to you!"

Sword drawn, hardly making a sound, Uziel's blade ripped through the gate and sliced off the head of the devil.

Instantly, Uziel perceived the chief angel of the underground moving through the caverns in answer to his violence.

A great light appeared around him.

Outside the realm of time, Uziel translated back to the empty valley.

There appeared the Seraphim of the Lord. "I am the angel of the underground. Tread softly, Son of Man," commanded the seraphim. "We cannot allow you to enter through this gateway. This city is the habitation of devils and unclean spirits. Leave now."

Uziel stood in defiance.

The mighty angel reached down and held him in the spirit.

Uziel remained frozen in time and space.

The mighty angel lifted him into the realm of the bottomless pit. "If I hold you here, you will never see her again. She'll be left alone."

Placing Uziel back on the valley's cool ground, the angel stood over him and commanded, "Leave."

Seeing he couldn't defeat the mighty angel, Uziel translated out of the Valley of Devils.

Chapter 42 Task Force Superman

There hath not come a razor upon mine head; for I have been a Nazarite unto God from my mother's womb: if I be shaven, then my strength will go from me, and I shall become weak, and be like any other man.

—Judges 16: 17 KJV

The DARPA Project Report provided the SMU hunter-killers much information. The subsequent order of events led to Nabil, Merlin, and the rest of the whiz kids coming face-to-face with the emotionless hunter-killers who would orchestrate the operations of Task Force Superman.

Underneath an elementary school, in a West Virginia suburb, outside of Charleston, the slayers and the nerds discussed the details of Operation Kryptonite.

"We've gone over your analytics of propositions," stated Daniels, puffing on his Montecristo No. 2 torpedo. "We need you to tell us something."

When Nabil didn't respond to Daniels's statement, Corliss gave him a sharp look.

Merlin carefully studied the killers, but said nothing.

The other members of the DARPA team also remained quiet.

"How do we kill this super soldier?" asked Daniels.

"The mission shouldn't be to kill the specimen," corrected Nabil.

"I'm a hunter. I'm a killer." The declaration came from Gary "Predator" Cullum.

Daniels shook his head and looked down briefly. "We know the mission," he replied coolly. "We're a hunter-killer team. We've drawn up *kill methods* into the CONOPs. This is a badass motherfucker. We can't afford a single mistake."

Strange calm emerged across Nabil's features. With his spiritual powers of discernment, he realized the killers before him were composed on the outside but highly anxious on the inside. "You can't kill him," declared Nabil.

One of the hunter-killers, sitting directly behind Johnson, calmly declared, "Everyone, anything, can be killed."

In anger, Daniels yanked the torpedo away and flashed a menacing glare. "If we're going to draw up clear CONOPs, we need all the information you possess."

"The origin of their power comes from their hair," said Nabil.

Daniels set his torpedo on the table. "Hair? What the fuck are you saying?"

Nabil adjusted his glasses before answering. "He's a Nazarite. You know? Like Samson in the Bible."

"If I hadn't seen the Superman Library myself, I'd say you were full of shit." Daniels picked up the Montecristo No. 2. After taking a few puffs, he leveled his gaze. "As I recall my Bible studies, Samson had a weakness for wild women."

Cullum snickered. A few other hunter-killers followed suit.

"Let's start there. I've been looking over your DARPA Project Report." Daniels looked down and went over his notes. "What's a Pythia?"

Nodding his head, respect flashed across Nabil's face. "She's a prophetess. A diviner," he answered.

Out of the room's spaciousness, Johnson said, "A Pythia existed a long time ago."

"I believe the Oracle still exists today."

Cullum looked at Nabil with the same expression a scientist would give a bizarre specimen.

Daniels resumed his questioning. "Can she do the things we've witnessed in the library summaries?"

"No, but the five hosioi who guard her can do some extraordinary things.

The prophētai are fewer in number, but they're even more powerful."

"Can they be killed?"

The directness of Daniels's question further impressed Nabil. "Yes," he answered directly.

"Using conventional weaponry?"

Again, Nabil kept his answer short. "It'll take a lot, but it can be done."

Inquisitiveness led to Daniels's next question. "What's the best way to kill it?"

"The best way to kill it is with spiritual weaponry."

Daniels became pensive. Out of a reservoir of military experience, he asked, uneasily, "The Pythia…can she help us?"

"You mean help you kill one of them?"

"Yeah. Something like that."

"She can, but she won't. The hosioi and the prophētai are her protectors. She'll never go against them."

Chapter 43 Spiritual Love Story

But the fruit of the Spirit is love, joy, peace, longsuffering, gentleness, goodness, faith, meekness, temperance: against such there is no law.

—Galatians 5: 23, 23 KJV

She yearned for love's soulful kiss. The hunger in her loins amounted to more than just a yearning; she desired Uziel to produce in her the most precious part of her womanhood.

Out in the wilderness, as she followed the Pythia's caravan, instead of romance, an oath kept her warm. Instead of a touch, the commandments of God comforted her. Instead of companionship, her period of separation kept her company. She needed none of the comforts humanity clung to, her heart and soul consecrated to a higher calling.

"Darling?"

She dreamt of her marriage to Uziel.

"Yes, my beloved."

"How do I look in this dress?" Ariella turned her body so he could view her from different angles.

"Like heaven," Uziel answered.

"No, really."

Uziel got up and strode over to where she stood before a mirror. Without saying anything, he took her in his arms and kissed her as if searching for treasure inside of her.

The kiss burned long and passionate. When he released her, he said in a husky voice, "That's how good you look."

She trembled and gazed up into his eyes.

He stroked her hair.

She pulled away, slightly. "Do you think God forgot about us?"

Uziel went still. "He doesn't forget anything."

Her eyes became the steel of women. "Then what is he waiting for?"

"Our oath," he reminded her.

She exhaled forcefully, clinging to him with all of her strength. "I'm a woman now. I'm twenty-two. My body's on fire."

Nearly dead with passion, Uziel said, "We're his clay. We gave our vows."

"No!" Her voice cut into his spirit. "We're not just shadows in time. You're my love. My entire body cries for you every second of the day. Can't you feel my needs?"

43.2

At *Melá Mountain, near Sumela Monastery,* Uziel and Ariella lived a spiritual love story.

They created a secret dwelling within a cave cut into the steep cliff. The simple abode, buried in the thick forest, close to a summit watercourse, inhaled the pleasantness of the unpolluted mountain air of summer and the cool winds of the fall. The *Pontic Mountain range, in the Maçka district of Trabzon Province,* presented the backdrop of their profound friendship and conflicted yearning. Every morning the scent of her freshness stirred Uziel's spirit like a heavy wind. Every night, the fragrance of her body raised his affection to a peak.

Holding his head in the softness of her hands, Ariella loved lying beside Uziel in the warmth of the rising sun until it covered them like a blanket in the Turkish daybreak.

"Oh Uziel, I love you so much! I'm afraid my heart will burst!" The passion of her conviction, and the energy emanating from the center of her body, saturated her youth and freshness.

Their emotions flowed between them as their bodies merged and became one flesh. In great intimacy, they joined in their spirits.

Uziel's immense power and transcendent rage became peaceful in the freshness of the morning air.

Playfully, Ariella ran her hands through his long flowing hair. "My darling, only the Almighty can make me more complete."

They first came to their secret Melá Mountain dwelling when they were in their twenties. Uziel learned about the extraordinary place from High Priest deKharouf.

Having just completed morning devotions, the men were preparing for one of the cross-country training treks they regularly embarked upon through the Turkish countryside.

"I know it can be difficult waiting on the Almighty, suffering through the affliction of your nazar."

Dropping his vision, deKharouf walked over to the stone bench along the side of the temple courtyard and sat down.

Uziel followed the priest and sat down next to him.

"Ariella? How is she?"

The question caused him to hesitate.

"If you don't want to tell me, I understand."

"She's confused."

After a few seconds, deKharouf said, "It's the way of women to pull away from Nazarite concepts."

Uziel searched the high priest's face. "What did you and Mom do?"

Unsure how to answer, deKharouf lifted his eyes to the overcast heavens hanging over the mountains in the distance. "When we realized our fate, we hoped to join together in another way. We separated ourselves to a spiritual place and joined in our spirits."

Soon after, in the hope of a future matrimony, Ariella and Uziel translated to the extraordinary sanctuary. In time, their souls fused into one spirit.

Every night, Uziel promised Ariella.

Every sunrise, he vowed to her.

As the years went by and she approached her thirtieth birthday, conversations about their future became tainted. Late one night, below the heavenly stars, Ariella broke down. "Master deKharouf says this nazar will be different. He says we'll see and hear what no other Nazarite has ever seen or heard."

Far below, Uziel sensed the flight of the white-winged Tern angling its flight toward the coast. Through the tangles of her hair, he gently kissed away her tears.

"Please say something, my love," pleaded Ariella.

Uziel shook his head. "Master deKharouf can't see outside of his own conclusion. This will never end until it's accomplished."

"Or we're all dead," Ariella finished.

43.3

Ten more years past and their nazars went unfulfilled. These were long years of heartache for Uziel and Ariella—painful years of asceticism.

Three days prior to her fortieth birthday, while they slept below the starry Turkish sky, the angel of the Lord appeared to them in a dream.

The voice of the angel came like the rushing wind and the brightness of his countenance lit up the mountain. "Be of good cheer; the Almighty has overcome the world."

While the angel's proclamation inspired Ariella, a lingering melancholy set in.

"What's the matter?" Uziel questioned.

In obvious pain, Ariella lifted her head to heaven. Amidst the beauty of the Pontic Mountains, underneath the starlight umbrella, she considered her life inconsequential, resigning herself to her fate.

Chapter 44 Love in Our Souls

"Ours is a lifetime love," Othniel promised Rhea.

Holding each other close, they looked out into the raging sea.

"Do you remember Melá Mountain?"

"Yes, my love," she answered.

"Now Uziel and Ariella share their love on the mountain where I swore my eternal love to you."

Rhea clung to Othniel. She sighed, recalling the memories. "We loved in our souls there," she whispered. "For one hundred and forty-five years, I've loved you. I've never asked for more than you could give me." A distant look crossed over her features. In answer to her pain, the sea wailed in its deepness. "You can't save the whole world, Othniel," she said, softly.

Releasing her, deKharouf turned and walked to the edge of the Mediterranean, looking out into its savage depths. "It's not the world I hope to save," he said.

Rhea moved to his side.

He didn't turn. "It's those who come after us. I intend to stop all of this."

Rhea listened fearfully when he spoke of his intentions.

He's leaving this time.

"Othniel, you mustn't do this. We can't stop what he's prophesied."

Turning, deKharouf touched her face tenderly. In pain, he said, "I've been a servant to him my whole life. I'll always be his slave."

"I'll come to Siwa with you, then."

"No," deKharouf replied. "Stay here."

"I can't bear to lose you," Rhea called out through the crashing waves. "I'll fight by your side."

Chapter 45 Will the Almighty Be a Liar?

Let God be true, but every man a liar.

—Romans 3: 4 KJV

Sevilo De'Esanatasos came to stand in the courtroom of the Almighty.

In the heavenly court, by the far sides of the northern lights of the universe, De'Esanatasos and the Almighty took up the matter of the Law.

"I come from going to and fro in the earth, and from walking up and down in it," said De'Esanatasos. As he spoke, he removed his earthly image and took the form of a goatman, possessing the head of a goat and the body of a man. "There's rebellion through your ranks Elah."

The Eternal Fire hardly moved.

"You declared prophecies from old. Your prophets proclaimed them. No one can prevent them. Nothing can stop them. Will the Almighty be a liar?"

The Fire of Elah remained unmoving.

The cries from De'Esanatasos fashioned into a desperate rage. "They're your prophecies Elah! Your word cannot return to you void! The image of the king of Macedon must stand in the temple!"

Chapter 46 Urim and Thummim

And he put the breastplate upon him: also he put in the breastplate the Urim and the Thummim.

—Leviticus 8: 8 KJV

Deep within the rock and guts of Mount Yeroham existed the sacred temple, wherein the high priests walked up and down amidst the Stones of Eternal Fire.

No physical gateway allowed entry into the temple. Only through spiritual translation could the temple's sacred chambers be reached.

High Priest deKharouf and the six high priests—the Seven—assembled three times a year to question the *Innocent Lights of Perfection.*

The high priests, known to only a few, were the masters of the Law and the guardians of the Urim and Thummim.

Wearing the Breastplate of Judgment, deKharouf knelt before the Stones of Fire. To each side of him, the high priests also knelt before the Fire.

"Place the Tablet of Virtue and Fault upon the Altar of Fire," commanded deKharouf.

Carefully, the high priests lifted a seven-sided tablet composed of *red diamond, black opal,* and *musgravite.* Placing the tablet on the four columns around the fiery altar, they stepped back as the Fire became larger. Besides the genuine rare gems composing its surface, from left to right: an emerald, a white diamond, a ruby, and a sapphire adorned the tablet.

"What is the first enquiry before the Lord?" asked deKharouf.

From the first question, until the last, the priests consulted the Urim and Thummim. Finally, there remained one final enquiry.

"Come forth, one and all, to hear the counsel of the Almighty!"

A familiar face appeared before the hot Fire: a former priest who betrayed his oath. Kneeling before the Fire, the priest humbly called out a lowly petition. "I beg the Assembly of the Wise to allow me to ask twice of the Eternal Fire."

The Fire lifted and raged around the tablet, causing the stone bench and the precious stones to burn radiantly.

"Discover the Revelation and the Truth from the Stones of Fire," called out deKharouf to the priests gathered round the Table of Judgment.

Savagely, violently, the Fire burned hotter. The great heat caused the precious stones upon the surface of the Tablet of Virtue and Fault to burn brighter than before.

"Elijah Basra, if the emerald and white diamond put forth the light of the Fire, then the reply is no. If the ruby and the sapphire put forth the Fire's light, then the answer is yes. Do you understand?"

Elijah answered weakly, "Yes."

Through the stone surface, the hotness of the Fire scorched the red diamond, black opal, and musgravite ornamenting the Tablet.

Waxing hot on the right side of the tablet, a gentle light gushed out of the cuts of the ruby and the sapphire. Continuing to grow, a powerful stream of light issued out of both precious stones, radiating throughout the temple.

"Behold," called out deKharouf, "the judgment of the Almighty declares innocence. Elijah Basra, the Lord God finds your heart unimpeachable. You may ask your two enquiries."

Remaining on his knees, the former priest spoke in a discreet manner. "Mighty God is my atonement pleasing to you?"

Again, the Fire waxed hot on the right side of the tablet. Light flashed out from the ruby and the sapphire.

"Elijah Basra," announced deKharouf, "your sins are found out."

The former priest remained prostrate on the ground.

"The Fire awaits your last question," announced deKharouf.

Elijah slowly raised his head and looked directly into the eyes of deKharouf. "Almighty God, are you pleased by my son's nazar?"

High Priest deKharouf considered the former priest in anger.

The Fire exploded in and around the left side of the tablet.

Immediately, the emerald and the white diamond released their brightness, pulsating and splashing against the hard rock of the mountain temple.

Keeping his attention on the unpretentious priest, deKharouf declared, "The Almighty is not pleased!"

Elijah pleaded into the Fire. "Lord God, take pleasure in my banishment and lowly post before the Assembly of the Wise. But, my God, I beg you, do not judge my son in anger. It's not his desire to provoke you."

"Enough!" shouted deKharouf, his rage transparent in his features. "The Almighty has spoken! All men be silent!"

The outcast priest lowered his head in silence before the Fire.

"This ends the sacrament of Revelation and Truth," declared deKharouf.

After the high priests lifted the Tablet of Virtue and Fault off of the Altar of Fire, and carried away the Urim and Thummim, Elijah rose to his feet. "I seek your counsel, High Priest."

"You received counsel," replied deKharouf, firmly.

"From the Holy Fire, yes," countered the former priest. "Now, I seek your counsel."

46.2

Apart from the Hall of Ceremony, in a modest chamber, the men met.

"You can't do this." Elijah Basra stood defiantly against the high priest.

"What are you talking about?" asked deKharouf, in righteous anger.

"This nazar you've appointed my son to perform—jettison him from it."

"It's none of your concern," stated deKharouf, coldly. "You're no longer part of the Assembly of the Wise."

The blow struck deKharouf on the side of the forehead. Although not meant to be a kill blow, the force of the assault drove the high priest back against the wall of stone.

Allowing his back to absorb the hard impact along its entire surface, deKharouf spun to the side and viciously drove his elbow into the former priest's ribs.

His air supply cut off, Basra managed to lock deKharouf's arm and pin it next to his body. Savagely, he gripped the high priest's throat and slammed him against the wall.

Lowering his body and twisting away, deKharouf broke free.

"I won't allow you to use my son this way!" Basra shouted. "Don't you see, Othniel, you can't win? You're playing a dangerous game and putting my son between God and Satan!"

"Who are you to make demands? The Almighty judged and expelled you. You have no say in the temple's business."

"I'm here to stop you from destroying my son's life!"

"He's my son too!" exclaimed deKharouf, trembling with emotion.

Full of rage, Basra unleashed a savage kick to the abdomen, once more sending deKharouf slamming against the wall.

The high priest rolled off to the side, his body spinning away from the attacker, allowing him to reposition. Launching a counterattack, the blow caught Basra on the side of his head, sending him reeling to the ground.

Blackness overwhelmed Basra. Quickly recovering, he kicked the foot of the high priest, knocking him off balance.

Both men grappled on the ground. First one, and then the other gained the advantage. Held in each other's death clinch, the men lay on the ground, their faces inches apart.

"I'm an outcast because I succumbed to the needs of my flesh. But you, deKharouf, did far worse," Basra accused the high priest, through clenched teeth. "You're a man! Nothing more! Yet you dare to place your position above God!"

Continuing in their titanic struggle, both men's bodies smashed against the wall of rock, neither able to gain an advantage.

"And now you wish my son to join you in this insane mission?" The outcast priest spoke of horrific pain and dreadful suffering. "I entered the vapor…and look what it cost me! My son has a chance to live a better life. I won't let you take it from him!"

Once more, the men crashed into the wall, the vicious impact loosening the rocks. Unable to gain an advantage, the men lay exhausted from their titanic struggle, neither willing to release the other from their death hold. No longer having the strength to continue the fight, the men remained on the floor, exhausted.

A few seconds later, the other high priests learned of the struggle. Entering the chamber, they pulled the men away from each other.

"Remove Basra," ordered deKharouf, keeping his attention focused on the outcast priest.

"Giving into the appetites of the flesh is not permitted in the house of the Almighty," imparted the priests, dragging deKharouf away. "Resist the impulses of earth and death."

"Not my son, deKharouf!" roared Basra, struggling against the priests. "Not my son!" He stopped resisting the priests, allowing them to pull him out of the chamber. "This is not over! Do you hear me, deKharouf? This will never be over!"

Chapter 47 Spiritual Translation

By faith Enoch was translated that he should not see death; and was not found, because God had translated him: for before his translation he had this testimony, that he pleased God.

—Hebrews 11: 5 KJV

"Siwa is a place where even the birds entertain secrets," an old man once told Uziel.

An oasis outside the worldly dimension, absent of written history, only the spoken word brought knowledge of Siwa's history from ancient times.

"It's the way of the oasis," the old man explained. "The key to conquering Siwa—if one is so inclined to dare to conquer land belonging to the god—is through the spiritual paths."

47.2

"Transformation is not change, as the dictionary says," High Priest deKharouf repeatedly taught him. "It is the revelation of the spirit, over the flesh. Always remember, it is the right of the spirit to dominate the flesh."

Spiritual translation required the capture of eternity. In the custody of infinity, the Nazarite passed through the portal of limitlessness.

Ownership of ground—a legal declaration to gain and capture ground—

threatened the security of a translation. If a Nazarite translated into captured ground, the spiritual authority who possessed the ground—if strong enough—could capture the translator and prevent escape. In some instances, even cause the translator's destruction.

47.3

In his mind, Uziel returned to the first day High Priest deKharouf instructed him about the most powerful manner of travel.

"Look around you," commanded deKharouf. "What do you see?"

Twelve-year-old Uziel looked out into the Turkish countryside. "I see trees and hills…the rooster and his chickens…and corn stalks." Uziel appeared confused.

"Look closer."

Uziel looked again. "Master, that's all I see."

"Science tells us most of the universe is invisible. Science is finally catching up to the reality of our existence." In a voice of warning, deKharouf said, "You cannot make war unless you see the enemy you are fighting."

"But Master, how can I see what cannot be seen?"

Respecting the young boy's question, Master deKharouf spoke gently to him. "Grow new eyes. Learn to see the spiritual things, as you can see the physical things."

"Teach me, Master," the boy requested, in a voice much older than his years. "To see the unseen."

Master deKharouf pulled a cloth from his pocket and blindfolded the boy. "What do you see now?"

No longer distracted by the earthly things, the boy strained to see the spiritual world.

The blindfold prevented him from seeing anything.

More confused than before, Uziel blurted out, "Master, I can't see anything."

The high priest removed the blindfold. "Never forget what you learned here today."

"But Master," cried out Uziel, "what did I learn?"

In frustration, Master deKharouf replied, "When you see nothing, it is then the Holy Spirit can reveal to you what he desires you to see. But beware: an angelic prince dominates each earthly territory. If the controlling angel of an earthly area is not bound, and the spiritual forces under his command are not controlled, or eliminated, the particular territory you intend to translate to, is not free.

If the enemy forces controlling the land detect you, the chances of your survival will not be good. Translation is not a matter of speed and time," deKharouf explained. "It's a matter of sovereignty and spiritual legality! When you translate—time is no more."

47.4

Bound to a heavy pole, in the middle of a cornfield, a young Uziel strained against the thick rope.

He remembered the day clearly.

"Concentrate!" High Priest deKharouf commanded. "If you do not stay focused in translation you will not be precise in your revelation, and you won't render to the exact place of your spiritual and physical completion. You must attain singularity. Flesh cannot withstand the spiritual forces arrayed against you. Your body will be destroyed."

Uziel didn't give voice to his fear, but he felt it. In the heat of the summer day, he struggled against the heavy rope binding him.

"As you think it, so it will be," stated deKharouf.

Uziel emptied his flesh of everything but the path he envisioned in his spirit.

"Discern the location you will be translating to," said deKharouf, calmly.

With all of his might, Uziel concentrated. Traversing across the cornfield, his spiritual vision saw an adjacent wheat field, three miles away. In the field stood a similar post impaled to the ground.

Letting go of all physical connection, Uziel's body melted into the measurement of forever. Time, space, and the planetary elements burnt beyond the threshold of earthly fire.

All of earth departed.

Infinity endured.

While his body remained confined to the post in the cornfield, his spirit stood by the post in the wheat field, three miles away, concurrently.

Later, over a dinner composed of yogurt salad, fish in olive oil, and stuffed and wrapped vegetables, Uziel questioned deKharouf about the details of the incident.

"How can I be in two places at once?"

A soft breeze blew in off the Dardanelles. The young man and his teacher ate together on the terrace of the modest house, conversing about the mysteries of spiritual warfare.

"You ask because of your sense of omnipresence?"

"Yeah," Uziel replied softly.

The high priest put down his glass of water. His demeanor took on a serious aspect. "Translation is a mode of *dimension travel*. Recall your teachings about the mystery of dimensions?"

"The distortion of *proportions, magnitudes, and measurements?*" replied Uziel.

"Yes," confirmed deKharouf. "The Nazarite must be the master of the earthly environment, and the laws of dimension. To see and hear in the spiritual, we comprehend the true earthly creation. Omnipresence is a spiritual revelation. In the Garden of Eden, humanity controlled the keys to translation. Because of sin, many have lost this gift."

"So, in translation, I am in two places at once? In translation, I'm not moving?"

The master took another drink of water. "To translate is to occupy the entire universe, not just earth." A special radiance arose from deKharouf's visage. "The power of translation is the power to be like the Almighty." Raising a warning finger, deKharouf said, "Be careful when exercising such power."

Giving total attention to deKharouf's words, Uziel asked, "Master, can the enemy translate?"

"No," deKharouf answered, "but beware: the enemy princes who stand against us are the princes of the power of the air. They travel and go to and fro in the earth, and walk up and down in it. If you translate anywhere across the places they control, you could be acquired and controlled by the vapor."

"Master, my sword, my spiritual sword. How do I wield it?"

A soft breeze passed through the window. "Do not rush your preparation," deKharouf answered. "The time of the sword will come."

"Master, I just want to—"

Raising a hand, deKharouf said, "You covet the things of the Lord."

"I answer the Spirit's call in the night. When I hear the voice, you told me to answer."

Pleased by the boy's spiritual appetite, deKharouf smiled in his heart. "The sword of the Spirit is the completeness of the Word of God."

Uziel stopped eating. "The Word *was* God. The Word *is* God."

"Yes," deKharouf confirmed, paying homage to the boy's sharpness of mind. "Now you appreciate the patience required to brandish such an awesome sword of power."

Uziel ate ravenously, content in his newly acquired knowledge. The Levant breezes ran through his long, wavy hair. Suddenly he stopped, eyes bright and fresh, and said to deKharouf, "Concerning the work of my hands, command ye me."

Marveling at the pureness and comprehension of the young warrior in the making, deKharouf nodded, "Yes, it is good your spiritual sight is getting clearer. Align your words to the Almighty's. You exercise your spiritual sword in faith. Like the Almighty, your words will not return to you void. Everything you say will be. This is the Sword of the Spirit."

47.5

Propelled by their ever-developing spiritual powers, the love between Uziel and Ariella took on new dimensions.

In the fall of 1940, his Nazarite vow took him away. While the world burned in the flames of war, he vowed to fight for the things of God.

Uziel turned twenty, Ariella sixteen.

"Translate with me," Uziel gently coaxed, as he fondled her cheek.

Ariella arched her back, her long hair swaying behind her. "I'm not good enough yet."

"Just hold my hand. I'll take you," he assured her. "I'll protect you. I won't let anything hurt you."

As the Turkish sun sank behind a forest in the distance, he pulled her toward him.

Equally, she pulled away. Breaking free from his arms, she walked to one side, lost in her thoughts.

"What's the matter?"

"It's wrong to use God's power this way."

"Baby," Uziel whispered into her ear. "God gave us gifts for us to use. They're our gifts."

She held him tight to her breasts.

"Ariella?"

"Yes."

"I love you. I won't see you until this war ends and my vow is complete. Please translate with me."

She held him tightly, feeling his heart race. "Yes," she said into his chest. "Yes, Uziel, I'll translate with you."

Chapter 48 Archon

Not long after Macedonia's global recognition as a sovereign nation, Tyrimmas Archelaus recreated the Amphictyonic Council. His work went without much press or fanfare.

Its position in the Greek and Macedonian Governments listed as low level and consultatory, many considered Archelaus' efforts to be more in honor of Grecian history than a political scheme. Few government officials perceived the enormous influence the religious council exerted upon the government.

Five *amphictyons* were appointed to the council. Because of his exertions in restoring the council, the amphictyons appointed Archelaus *archon* over the assembly. Behind the scenes, the influence of the council dominated the activities taking place at Delphi. In a short period, the council came to gain political control over preeminent central divisions of the Macedonian and Greek Governments.

"Amphictyons who oversee the well-being of the Temple of Apollo," Archelaus declared in the quiet parliamentary meeting room. "I bring news of historical and political meaning. The bones of our greatest king—Alexander the Great—have been recovered from the royal tombs at *Vergina*."

After a sharp intake of breath, one of the amphictyons asked, "Are we certain of the identification?"

Archelaus reflected on the question deliberately. "Yes," he answered, firmly. Getting up from the table, he walked to the front of the room as the lights dimmed. A large conference screen dropped down from an encasement in the ceiling and photos of the diggings began displaying on the screen. Pictures of the artifacts recovered from the dig cycled through, one after another.

"The markings on the golden larnax are unmistakable. The human remains are being tested."

"Where are the archaeological items being protected?"

"At an unregistered military site under Volci armed guard."

"Less government involvement is best."

"I agree," confirmed Archelaus, resuming his seat. "Under military aegis, we can preserve the artifacts, and control the media impact."

One of the amphictyons said, "The shielded method of the Pythia's journey to the oasis should ensure the bones arrive intact. The scientific modifications made to *Ammon's Temple* have been classified as repair and preservation."

Archelaus gestured in a broad manner. "The three major elements to the actualization of the image—the bones, the chosen Pythia, and the elixir—are fulfilled."

"What is the final timeline?"

"Egypt is instructed to allow entry into its borders all of the elements commanded by this council before the next solstice. The Sacred War will follow soon after. The Nazarites will attack *Aghurmi Hill* in an attempt to stop the prophecy of the king."

"Speak Archon Archelaus," the council said, in unison.

"The winepress is readied," declared Archon Archelaus. "It is the commencement to pour the wine."

Chapter 49 Siwa

To ensure his movements into Siwa weren't detected, he translated into the Qattara Depression, West Gazalat. From there, he used conventional modes of transportation.

Adrère Amellal Resort stood nearly three kilometers away from *The Temple of the Oracle.*

The porter set the luggage by the bed, in the candlelit room, and disappeared into the eerie silver shadows of the night.

Uziel surveyed his surroundings.

Nestled amongst a thick cluster of palm trees, the hotel took advantage of the seclusion the aridness of the area produced. Constructed of salt-rich mud, in the traditional Siwan style, the resort sat next to a white limestone mountain. Absent of electricity, all lighting, cooking, and physical comfort relied on natural sources—the earthen buildings maintaining the warmth of the sun in the winter and providing coolness in the summer heat. The rooms, illuminated by beeswax candles, complemented the wholeness of the place. Absent of phones, or even a reception desk, Adrère Amellal Resort enticed the visitor who desired isolation and solitude, above all else.

Looking down from the window of his third level room, Uziel reviewed the linear fountains dignifying the open court. The hotel, plush and high priced, notwithstanding its lack of modern amenities, offered a perfect location to prepare.

"How long will you be staying, sir?" asked the staff member, setting down the olive jam next to a breakfast of bread, beans, and eggs. The man flashed Uziel a smile, giving hint of more than pleasantries.

"It's been outlawed, but Siwa still has a homosexual population. Don't outright refuse the homosexuals if they make advances," he heard deKharouf's detailed instructions in his mind. "Connect with the *zaggala,* no matter if the homosexuals are the link to them."

Uziel made it a point to flash an equally welcoming smile to the man. "Open calendar," he answered.

Making certain to wear a wedding ring when he came to Siwa, it presented an excuse to leave unexpectedly, or cancel a planned sexual rendezvous.

"Will you be having dinner somewhere in the city?" the man continued. "I can offer some suggestions."

"Sounds great," replied Uziel, "but I'm afraid business will take me late into the night. Can you ask the chef to prepare a plate for me?"

49.2

The night spread across the balminess. The taxi offered little comfort. Absent of air conditioning, the old vehicle cultivated the sweltering thickness.

"Where go you?" the taxi driver asked, in broken English.

Uziel replied, "Aghurmi."

Ten minutes later, they reached the town center of Siwa.

"I've changed my mind. Drop me off," Uziel called out.

Next, travelling in a Siwa Taxi—a carriage pulled by a donkey—Uziel instructed the driver to the Aghurmi Hill where existed the ruins of the Temple of the Oracle. "Pull over," he commanded.

The taxi pulled over to one side of the dirt road.

Requesting the taxi driver to wait, Uziel used spiritual sight to reconnoiter the surrounding area. Detecting a host of angelic forces aligned in and around Siwa Hill, supported by legions of devils, he recalled deKharouf's instructions. "The spiritual principalities you're facing have powers of discernment equal— perhaps even greater—than yours," the high priest warned. "You mustn't venture too far into Aghurmi Hill, until the actual assault."

In the past, families commonly lived in the temple. In recent times, certain underground groups started to discourage the practice.

"Take me back," commanded Uziel.

Upon returning to the market square, Uziel trekked back in the night. Positioning east of the hill, he resumed his spiritual search prudently and delicately.

Not until the first streaks of dawn crept up on the hill's edges did Uziel conclude his reconnaissance. Although he failed to locate an angelic source, he discerned much activity of disembodied entities guarding the entrances to the hill.

Arriving back at the hotel before the sunrise, Uziel threw out the food left outside his door. He never ate food from an unknown source. A diet of locust, honey, seeds, fresh caught fish, and manna helped him control his physical impulses.

After checking his room to make sure all points of entry were secure, he lowered the shades and fell fast asleep.

Chapter 50 Something's Changed

Merlin followed Nabil down the hallway to the cafeteria.

Sitting down at a corner table, Nabil noticed Merlin.

"Care for company?" asked Merlin.

Nabil gave a slight nod of his head.

A nearby window let in the shadows of the dreary day, raindrops tapping lightly on the glass.

"You didn't say much in there, Prophet," said Merlin, taking a bite of his ham and cheese sandwich.

"I didn't see a need to," Nabil replied.

"You mean, because of the ghosts?"

Nabil ate some of his meatloaf and mashed potatoes before answering. "Yeah."

Merlin squinted and took a gulp of his buttermilk. "Nah," he accused. "You didn't say anything because you've already drawn your conclusions."

Nabil chewed his food slowly, neither acknowledging nor denying what the man said.

"You didn't buy what Wilson and Praetor said. Why?"

Putting down his fork, Nabil took a drink of orange juice. "I don't believe the images we saw in there originated from us."

"You mean the United States?"

"I don't believe the CIA sourced those images."

"How can you be sure?"

"Because there's no way fifty years ago, or even today, CIA operatives could get near a Nazarite, much less snap a picture of one."

"You think this project isn't what it appears to be?"

"You, me, we're not military. DARPA's ordered under US Military organization. We're controlled civilians."

Merlin finished eating. Throwing his napkin on top of his tray, he asked, "So what do you say is happening?"

"Someone fed the DIA the reports."

"Who?" Merlin's strained voice sounded tired.

"The hosioi, perhaps."

Merlin quickly pounced on his answer. "But, according to you, the Nazarites and the hosioi are destined to fight a war, in fulfillment of prophecy."

Nabil looked up in surprise. He thought Merlin hadn't paid attention. "Not against each other."

"They're on the same side?"

"Not on the same side," answered Nabil. "Regarding the prophecies of the beast, the Nazarite's are bound by their vows to make sure the beast prophecies come to fulfillment. This makes the recent events puzzling."

"In what way?"

"The satellite images don't make sense. Macedon, Egypt, Syria, and Turkey all play a key role in Bible prophecy." Nabil brought his hand to his chin in deep thought. "The SCI data indicates strange activity taking place in the strategic areas of the trail of Alexander."

"Which means the reported activity corroborates your words."

Nabil stared out at the rain.

"What's the problem?"

"The increased activity in those areas could only mean one thing."

"What?"

Nabil shook his head. "I've been carefully studying the activity and believe I've created a strategic map showing the movements of the Nazarites. And the hosioi." Shifting in his chair, he said, "The strategic map doesn't fit Biblical prophecy."

Carefully, Merlin said, "Give me conjecture."

In Nabil's mind, only one conclusion made sense. His words detonated like a bomb. "The activity seems to suggest the Nazarites are trying to prevent the passage of the Pythia."

The brightness of a lightning bolt flashed into the cafeteria.

The storm outside worsened.

Chapter 51 Elixir of Immortality

Akhenaten Ptahhotep met the zaggala on the south quarter of the date grove, enclosed by a modest ridge, to begin cultivation of the next season's Aghurmi Amasis dates.

Preparation of the trees commenced at the bark. Delicate removal of segments of the cortex of pyramid trees in specific intervals, advanced to the collection of the seeds, and further analysis and study. Even agrology played a vital role through the generations.

"Observe not only the genders within the grove," Uncle Phoe repeatedly counseled him, in his boyhood training. "Discover the trees creating oncogenesis transformation. Perform a precise biopsy. Take the immortal cells and introduce the gene accelerant."

The immortal cells were a generation of tumors present in the selected trees. Some of the trees possessed generations of tumors. In his adolescent ignorance, Akhenaten recalled asking his uncle questions about the method they used to develop the elixir.

"Why do we work with tumor cells?"

In his longsuffering way, Phoe spent the better part of two decades teaching him the singular answer to his question. Even now, in his adulthood, Akhenaten did not comprehend the entire complexity of the progression.

"I've spent my life learning about the immortal elixir compound and barely scratched the surface of its immense complexities," Phoe often told him. "It is wise to focus mostly on the growth seasons, not the cells."

Early afternoon hotness swarmed over the grove where the zaggala and Akhenaten set about their work.

Akhenaten reminded the zaggala of Camden Miller's commands. "Since the dateless past, your tribe developed two groves of the Aghurmi Amasis Date," Miller confirmed. "You will now support only one grove. The other will no longer be cultivated in the holy ways. Do you understand?"

"Of course, Master," Akhenaten answered. "But won't this leave us short on our supply to your servants, the hosioi?"

Miller, slightly irritated by the question, uncrossed his left leg and crossed his right leg, before he replied. "Don't be concerned. It's not a trial. We're in the final stages of the elixir's perfection. One grove will be sufficient."

"You wish to deceive the stranger from Karpos Peristera Incorporated?"

Miller shook his head. "He won't be deceived, simply delayed. He'll discover, soon enough, you're not being straightforward." Miller's features dimmed in thought. "He'll need to take action to unearth the true grove. I'll be waiting for him when he does."

Akhenaten bowed his head. "We will heed your counsel, Master."

"Work the southern barrio of the grove. Leave the northern barrio for the stranger from Karpos Peristera Incorporated," instructed Miller, his voice containing a sinister quality not lost on Akhenaten.

Chapter 52 Detected

After Uziel approached the Ptahhotep Aghurmi Tribe about purchasing the Aghurmi Amasis cultivations, he tapered his movements throughout the Siwa Oasis.

"The enemy is the prince of the power of the air," he heard deKharouf's voice in his head. "The enemy holds many rights and laws on the ground, and the air, around Siwa. It limits our concentration of spiritual force there. Once you expose yourself to the Aghurmi Tribe, exercise secrecy."

Weeks later, during a late-night venture through the palm grove of the northern barrio, Samuel Nemaeus confirmed the falseness of the palms and harvest he'd purchased.

As the Nazarite high priests expected, the Ptahhotep Tribe protected the barrio containing the perfect trees.

This date fruit is not from the perfect trees, concluded Nemaeus, recognizing the false yield. The moonlight passed over him as he searched the adjacent southern grove. In a dangerous move, he continued to move further south, inspecting the palms.

Out of thin air, the attack exploded over the cultivated ground. Pivoting to his right, he parried the blow from the zaggala sword.

Discarding the image of the businessman, Nemaeus, Uziel assumed his spiritual likeness. Pivoting out of his defensive stance, he thrust his sword into the torso of the zaggala. Twisting the whetted instrument savagely, Uziel pulled back his blade, the sharpness jetting the lifeblood out of the sentinel.

Before the lifeless body of the zaggala hit the ground, the remaining three sentries converged upon Uziel.

Taking a step back, Uziel slew the zaggala to his right, slashing off his arm.

The two remaining zaggala gave ground, first slowly, then with urgency.

Too soon. They relinquished the barrio too quickly.

Before Uziel could retreat into the shadows, the prophētai discerned his spirit.

There's six of them. It's a setup to confirm my identity.

Now it was Uziel who gave ground speedily and sought out the clearest path of escape.

Having learned my identity, the enemy will reposition, he scolded himself. *Their movements will disrupt the trail of the perdition and place Ariella in greater danger.*

As he came to the edge of the southern barrio, he took less caution and speedily made his way out of the grove.

Chapter 53 I Am Promised

Far away, in the sands of the *Jordan desert*, the Pythia and her guardians came to the southern edge of the *Dead Sea*. More than 400 meters below sea level—the lowest place on the earth's surface—the cavalcade stood on the water's brink.

Following the slow-moving caravan, Ariella trailed from a safe distance.

In Jordan, it became harder to remain concealed and still keep the procession in her spiritual vision. Indeed, the closer the procession came to the boundary of the *Wadi 'Araba*, the more difficult it became to spiritually see the path the caravan travelled.

The spiritual power of the four angels out of the bottomless pit; the geographical location; her physical weakness, due to the dryness of the area—all of these factors led to her miscalculation.

As the earth's ground sank deeper, she sensed a strangeness in the air.

"Do not continue to trail the caravan if the air becomes sweet smelling," deKharouf often cautioned her, throughout her spiritual training. "The sweet smell is the scent of the Macedonian angel."

"But Master," questioned Ariella, "if I am not to trust my physical senses, then how can I know what is sweet smelling?"

"Don't allow the angel to enchant you through his earthly scent and spiritual charms," warned deKharouf.

The deeper she breached the ramparts of the enemy, the less of an escape route she provided herself.

A fatal mistake.

Two devils nearly reached her before she drove her sword through one and sliced the other with one fluid movement.

The devils screamed out in death.

Immediately after, two more devils appeared to her right.

The vapor swirled violently around her, as she moved along the spiritual fog's outer edge. Maneuvering behind the devils, her long hair falling across her shoulders, she swung the weapon violently, destroying the evil spirit closest to the vapor's edge.

"The vapor is their ground," she remembered deKharouf's warnings. "Let them keep it."

Realizing the danger, she dropped closer to the ground, attempting to retreat.

In a frenzy, the violence came out of the vapor, smashing into her shoulder and sending her crashing into a rock edge. She clawed the dirt and pushed up from the earth just as the second attack reached her.

Twisting to her left, she swung the sword across her body viciously, the sharpness cutting the evil spirit to the pith.

Emitting a horrific squeal, the devil fell off to the side.

Struggling to recover her footing, another devil fell upon her, striking her on the side of the throat, barely missing the killing blow.

Ariella rolled away. Bringing up her sword, she drove the deadly point into the devil's ethereal substance. Rapidly rising to her feet, she stood over the hellish thing and plunged her sword into its center, destroying its evil.

A strong wind blew out from the twisting miasma, the gust blowing back her long hair. Underneath the moonlight, standing in battle posture, hair blowing in the wind, her femininity displayed a ferocious spectacle, revealing a womanly deadliness.

From where she stood, she saw the Pythia, her pentakis aligned hosioi, and the vicious *hex-prophētai*.

Forthwith, the vapor took control of her flesh and held her in its spiritual power.

53.2

All around, the spiritual warriors of the four angels stood.

"Bring the Sibyl out!" commanded the chief prophētai.

Two hosioi brought out the Delphic Sibyl, a mystic of renowned powers.

"Bring out the Pythia!" the vicar prophētai called out again.

The defending warriors of the Delphic Oracle brought the Pythia and the Delphic Sibyl before the priest.

Dressed in the blue embroidered *tarfottet*—their faces completely covered—the women walked in measured cadence.

From out of a small earthly cavity, a thick vapor collected around the party of warriors and the women, engulfing them within its smoke and fire.

Raising his arms, the chief prophētai called out, "Let the breath of the prince of the power of the air join with the breath of *Zeus-Ammon—the great-horned god*—and fill the bodies of the vessels."

The vapor entered the Sybil and the Pythia, subjugating their spirits and conquering their flesh. Their bodies became straight and rigid.

The priest's voice filled the air. "The mighty god commands the bodies of these ewers to be purified. Let them be purified in the bath of..."

The priest stopped, his spirit sensing something.

53.3

Under the angel's spell, Ariella lost control of her physical yearnings, captivated by the angel's magnetism. The air surrounding Wadi Araba threatened to smother her.

You're so beautiful, Ariella declared in her heart, staring into the countenance of the *morning star* angel.

Next to the angel, as if cut from a rock, the Grecian angel appeared. Giving way to wavy hair blazing like the brightness of the sun, the angel's masculine, powerful chest carved down into a splendid trunk and sculpted legs.

Reaching down, the angel ran his fingers through her hair.

Ariella's knees went weak.

The next thing she knew, she stood before the vicar prophētai, next to the

Sibyl and the Pythia.

"Let us offer libations and nutriment to Zeus-Ammon," announced the head prophētai.

The women walked into the salty wetness, cleansing their bodies.

In formal ceremony, the priest called out above the stillness of the air. "This is the flesh and blood to complete the elixir. These are the containers of Zeus-Ammon."

Intoxicated by the mighty angel's vitality, Ariella's mind comprehended the meaning of the priest. Somewhere in the far reaches of her mind, she realized the angels of the perdition and the unclean spirits would zealously guard her to ensure the caravan reached Siwa. There, she, the Pythia, and the Sybil would become the possession of the temple angels and carry the offspring of their desires.

Confronted by the inevitability of defilement, the vision crushed her spirit. *I am promised to my love. I cannot belong to another.*

53.4

Dense spiritual foulness permeated the vapor along the ancient trail of the perdition, contrasting the span of arid infertility leading to the wetness of the oasis. Not until they reached the edge of the Levant did Ariella come out of her trancelike state and recognize the vileness of the impure vapor.

On one side of *Jebel al-Madhbah,* in the heart of the hurried overhangs of the *mountain of the altar,* the caravan stopped.

Ariella gestured to the attending Pythia. "I cannot..."

"Shush," the Pythia shook her head, motioning to the ominous figure of a hosioi standing guard nearby.

Ariella went silent until the hosioi resumed his patrol.

Holding out a flask containing the waters of *Kassotis* and a tuft of laurel leaves, the woman commanded Ariella to drink.

Reluctantly, Ariella drank from the unique flask. The cool water, to some degree, recovered her senses and she determined the youthful Pythia to be younger than she'd first thought, no more than fifteen or sixteen.

"I'm promised to another," she tried to explain to the young woman. "I cannot be given to the god."

"We've awaited your arrival for centuries. The prophecies declared your coming."

"It can't be," Ariella protested, drinking more of the intoxicating water.

"The god is all knowing. He chose you from the sands of women. You are promised to him."

"Please, help me. I am vowed to another."

"The god led us through the promised route, here to *Wadi Musa*, to revere and prophecy. The god wishes you to meditate into the leaves."

Grasping the laurel leaves, Ariella feared the worst. Tears fell from her eyes. Despondently, she looked around the barren peninsula and wondered how she could escape.

It doesn't matter anymore, she concluded. *I'm no longer a Nazarite—I am defiled. I've been touched by the vapor.*

A revulsion entered Ariella's heart. Because of the aversion, dark emptiness descended upon her soul and further devoured her sensibilities. In her hate, a cold vengeance swelled.

Forgive me Lord. Before, my heart only had room to love you and Uziel. Now, I devote my life to destroying those responsible for bringing this horrible tragedy upon my nazar.

Renewed by the immensity of her hatred, she recovered from the lowest elements of her despair. Hope lifted her out of her anguish, and she discerned a change in the swirling vapor.

She knew the change.

"The journey from the Jordan desert to the Siwa Oasis is a sacred odyssey. I've travelled the path many times," explained the young Pythia to Ariella, on another of their stops. "On this ancient caravan route, used by Alexander the Great on his travel to Siwa, our sacred pilgrimage defies the physical dimensions of the planet."

Across the spiritual realm, from height to depth, the unclean forces of the four angels subjugated the trail of the perdition, leaving a revolting granularity upon the desert sands.

"The god who dwells at rocky Pytho, the god of the Hellespont, the god of Assyria, and the god of the Pharaohs claim the sands of the oasis," said the young Pythia to Ariella. "We are their supplicants."

Drawing nearer to the oasis, the desert sands coagulated, allowing the caravan ease of travel. The miraculous event revealed the god's conquest of the physical laws of the planet.

To safeguard the well-being of the caravan, rains fell, and ravens and other strange birds appeared in the blinding desert to lead them to their destination.

In the horizon stood the date palm trees of Siwa.

Unopposed, the angelic forces led the caravan's slow mundane advance until it reached the border of the oasis. Soon after, the caravan unhurriedly ascended up Aghurmi Hill, eventually swallowed up by the sinister, otherworldly vapor ominously pervading every inch of the ancient site.

As the killing vapor of death surrounded her, Ariella suffered heavy gloom.

Chapter 54 Perfect Trees

Months later, they concluded their first inspection of the southern quarter of the grove. The hosioi, dressed in their Doric chitons, confronted Akhenaten and the zaggala.

In awe, Akhenaten perceived the mysterious strangers to be slayers beyond human comprehension. Fear gripped him.

One of the five hosioi motioned to the zaggala.

Immediately, the zaggala made their way to where the hosioi stood inspecting a select cluster of date palms.

Akhenaten started to move toward them but the hosioi motioned him to stop. He waited until the hosioi finished speaking before he resumed his duties in the grove.

The next day, the prophētai arrived to inspect the same clump of trees. Unlike the hosioi, who were short in their verbal communication, the prophētai spoke, but only through prophecy and divination. When they provided the zaggala the foretelling, Akhenaten listened.

"This palm pollen will produce the highest concentration of elixir," the prophētai prophesied.

Skeptical of such predictions, even though his uncle honored the near perfection of the prophētai in their prophecies, Akhenaten nodded his head in respect. More scientifically minded than his uncle and less inclined to believe in art forms or religious customs to determine the proliferation of the dioecious trees, he remained unconvinced.

"Don't be quick to dismiss their predictions," his uncle cautioned him. "Date palms are one of the most difficult trees to predict sexual identity. It offers us great advantage to know the sex of a tree."

"These date palms," the prophētai continued to prophesy, "are the complete and perfect trees."

The complete and perfect date palm tree possessed both male (*androecium*) and female (*gynoecium*) reproductive systems.

The prophētai wore the hooded gowns of antiquity, a representation of pious devotion long forgotten by the modern world. In all the years he'd labored in the groves, the prophētai never directly communicated with him, as if his attendance in their business was a temporary bother they willingly endured until they completed their holy task.

Akhenaten nearly fell backward in astonishment when the six prophētai turned to face him, their darkened gaze menacing under the long hoods.

"These are the perfect trees of all generations," the head prophētai said to him. "From the fruit of these palm dates we will create the elixir of immortality."

Akhenaten stood transfixed, stunned by the declaration.

Brandishing their sharp weapons, the zaggala took up a perimeter around the southern barrio, unresponsive to anyone except the prophētai. Their defensive posture indicated the seriousness of their commitment to the commands the prophētai gave them.

No longer regarding him, the prophētai commanded the zaggala. "Do not allow this southern quarter to be molested by anyone, neither of flesh or spirit."

Chapter 55 Conqueror of Tyre

Son of man, take up a lamentation upon the king of Tyrus, and say unto him, Thus saith the Lord GOD; Thou sealest up the sum, full of wisdom, and perfect in beauty.

—Ezekiel 28: 12 KJV

The second critical battle Uziel fought in his attempt to gain control of the trail of the son of perdition was at the ancient Phoenician Harbor of Tyre, Lebanon.

Since the time of the ancients, the visible pathways controlled by Tyre's strategic placement were critical to anyone wishing to control the earth and dominate humanity. Alexander the Great refused to progress his Persian Campaign, until he gained power over it.

However, its spiritual importance took on far more relevance than its physical prominence.

"I seek to pass," Uziel said to the two devils governing Tyre's physical pathways of water and earth.

"Enter elsewhere, Man of Elah. Our spiritual king's authority rules this gateway."

Uziel drew his sword and ripped them open.

The other devils, wanting no part of his viciousness, departed the area.

Uziel searched the residues of the ancient city. Innumerous devils littered

Tyre's spiritual air. Three days later, he found the rudimentary portal where spirit and flesh passed from one realm to the other, and back.

Did the hosioi and the prophētai bring the Pythia through this gateway?

Moving though the portico, he entered an interior chamber, sealed by a heavy gate. Upon passing through the chamber, five devils attacked out of the thick spiritual smoke, driving him back into the chamber. Pivoting to his left, he swung his sword through their incorporeal substances, destroying all five with inconceivable ferocity.

Making his way through the entrance, Uziel found himself residing between spiritual and physical ingresses. On the other side of the heavy gateway, comprising one way in and one way out, a stairway led to the celestial towers.

Uziel's spiritual vision detected two guardian cherubs on each side of the celestial gateway, monitoring his fierce attack. They came at him from perpendicular lines of attack. Lowering himself, he drove his sword into the elements of the cherubim, holding them in place.

Pushing through them, Uziel ascended the stairway into the spiritual levels. On the other side, the stairway led back to earth.

When Uziel emerged from the celestial gateway, he secured spiritual and physical authority over Tyre and the region it controlled.

"Your lifelong nazar is to take captivity captive, to save the weak, to uplift the lowly," deKharouf told him as a boy.

All of his life, in the likeness of a spiritual warrior, he fought the fight of a hero, and battled as a protector. In his virtuous labor to raise the dead and destroy the wicked, he drew spiritual sword to destroy the destroyers of humanity, and kill the killers of the living.

Yet, the conquest of Issus, and then Tyre, were not the undertakings of a hero, or of a protector.

Conquest was the business of the conqueror.

Chapter 56 The Son of Perdition

Let no man deceive you by any means: for that day shall not come, except there come a falling away first, and that man of sin be revealed, the son of perdition; Who opposeth and exalteth himself above all that is called God, or that is worshipped; so that he as God sitteth in the temple of God, shewing himself that he is God.

—2 Thessalonians 2: 3, 4 KJV

Once again, Merlin trailed Nabil. This time to a small café on the outskirts of town. They ate a dinner consisting of roast beef with delightful mini Yorkshire puddings, and a complement of stewed vegetables.

After eating, they walked across the street to a secluded park. In the twilight shadows, a soft mist lingered in the air. A small group of children, defiant against the wetness and impending darkness, played in the park, their laughter offering some relief to both men.

Merlin leaned back on the park bench, relishing the coolness of the soft breeze.

"The Son of Perdition prophecy is long and complicated," said Nabil. "And it's about to be replicated."

Nabil waited to see if Merlin reacted to his revelation. He didn't, remaining deep in thought, his eyes closed.

Another soft breeze passed over the men, prompting Nabil to resume his enlightenment.

"His mother will be a chosen woman of a select class."

"A human female?" Merlin's eyes remained closed.

"Yes, she'll be human. But the father—the fathers…"

Merlin's insides churned in agitation, yet he remained motionless.

"The fathers of the son of perdition are the same angelic fathers who sired the greatest warrior in the history of warfare—Alexander the Great of Macedon."

The revelation struck Merlin like a lightning bolt. Opening his eyes, he sat up on the bench. "Alexander the Great?" Merlin asked, incredulously. "Macedon? The modern state of Macedon is not a genetic descendant of ancient Macedon. They're not even the same geographically."

"You're correct," responded Nabil, respecting the quality of Merlin's mind. "However, their geographical location existed as part of the Macedonian Empire in antiquity, which is all that matters."

Merlin, enthralled by Nabil's disclosure, sat expressionless. Not even the children's laughter mollified the dread creeping into his intestines.

"The spiritual laws that once governed our existence all changed when *Eashoa Msheekha* died on the cross and arose from the dead."

"You use the ancient Aramaic to say Jesus the Messiah?"

"Jesus is called a counselor in the Bible—a lawyer. It's best, when dealing with legal matters, to be as precise as possible. So yes, I denote to Jesus the Messiah in the ancient Aramaic."

"What laws are you specifically referring to?"

"There are many. For the purpose of clarity, I emphasize the laws of biology."

"What about them?"

"In the days before Eashoa's death, and his subsequent rise from the dead, angels legally traversed the spiritual plane and physically mated with human females. After Jesus conquered the spiritual and the physical, and took captivity captive, angels were precluded from copulating with earthly women, as well as prevented from carrying out many other physical actions on earth."

"How can angels mate with human women when they're spiritual beings and earthly women are physical?"

"Angels are able to take physical form. In the ancient past, they did so much easier."

A burst of laughter sprang forth from the small group of children playing in the park.

When the sounds of the children subsided, Nabil resumed. "Alexander the Great was the progeny of an angelic union with a human woman. The four angels out of the bottomless pit fused their angelic seed and mated with Olympias, the mother of Alexander the Great. What makes this critical are the subsequent promises the angels made to Alexander. Promises relating to his conquests on earth, and conquests involving future campaigns he would undertake in his next life on earth."

Chapter 57 Oasis

Siwa—a warrior city—appears to sprout out of the desert.

The city remains in the ancient past. Time stands still there.

In *Amazigh,* Siwa means *"Bird of prey which protects the god Amun."*

Having the semblance of a bird of prey, the vast desert surrounding the city gives the impression of huge wings connected to the body of a bird.

Beyond the market square, in the gardens and private groves, the genuine character of the oasis takes form. Away from the marketers and the sellers dwell the real people who give Siwa its reputation for hospitality and unequaled peace.

In the gardens and coppices of the oasis, life is relaxing and timeless. The world can pause until the pot of tea is finished. Nothing is more important than finishing an enjoyable meal.

Siwa has seen it all, done it all—the world can wait.

There is no history in the ancient dregs and orchards—no books exist of the city's rich past.

While the heart of the city adopts strains of modernization, further away from the market square, all remains frozen in time. Beyond the abundant palm copses, enclosed gardens, and olive groves, above the numerous freshwater springs and salt lakes, sits the impressive remains of the ancient fortress town of *Shali.*

Moving through the ancient place, Uziel sensed the thickness of the devils and unclean spirits. Looking to find the best point to enter the vapor, he walked slowly through the ancient streets, taking in everything, seeing the oasis through his spiritual vision. Confident he hadn't been detected, he entered a café.

To the outside world's perception, he was a smuggler perhaps, back from a dangerous mission to the border. Unwashed clothes and unkempt body rarely led to questions.

There are many secrets in the oasis.

Drinking his tea near the heart of Siwa, he held his attention on two men emerging from the *Hotel Kelany*. Dressed appropriately, long, white Egyptian galabeya, over white pants, the men were not too boisterous, nor overly sedate, in their conversation.

The fact they fit in perfectly to the oasis raised Uziel's suspicion.

Spirits possess the men, he concluded.

The people of Siwa believed in ghosts and evil spirits. Many Siwans possessed amulets to protect them from the evil spiritual forces they feared existed in the ancient city.

Concentrating on the two men, Uziel attempted to determine the identity of the evil spirits who possessed their bodies. A dangerous undertaking as it exposed his own spirit to detection.

Following the men with his spiritual eyes, Uziel discerned the images of the evil spirits.

One of the evil spirits appeared in the shape of a falcon, its audacious colors bright like the sun. The shape of the other evil spirit was a ram, its horns pushing out of its head like strident lances seeking to impale.

They're waiting, Uziel determined. *They're sentries.*

"Spiritual warfare is a titanic struggle," he heard the voice of deKharouf, in his head. One of many learning sessions, that littered the story of his life. The particular learning session he called to mind took place when he was fourteen.

"Spiritual struggle is so concentrated even the easy act of basic communication is magnified and is nearly impossible during spiritual war. To communicate from one point to the next takes great ingenuity and thought."

To further emphasize his meaning, deKharouf drew a line on the blackboard. "Consider physical warfare. Anything you try to do on the physical battlefield, your enemy will try to prevent you from accomplishing. If you try to communicate with fellow units, the enemy will be concentrated on stopping you by jamming your signal or other means."

Drawing an *x* through the line on the blackboard, he continued. "It's the same way in spiritual warfare. Only the power and focus of the attack is much more intense. From movement, to communication, to the whole spectrum of logistics, every single inch of the spiritual battlefield is contested."

From deKharouf's many teachings on spiritual warfare, Uziel's proficiency in spiritual combat increased on many levels.

The sentries are here to prevent me from moving around too freely, and to restrict my ability to communicate or signal.

I'll trail them, and find their point of entry in the vapor.

Starting in his soul, a powerful sensation overtook Uziel's body, creating a wave of jubilation at the center of his core. Every emotion raged inside of him, every weakness pulsed in his nerve endings and glands.

"When you arrive at Siwa, you will be as we are," explained High Priest Munius Spatha and High Priest Kilij Marslan. "Like Eashoa Msheekha was when he drank the cup of damnation, and Samson was when he went down to *Timnath* to find a wife from the daughters of the Philistines—you'll be outside the lawful spiritual safety of the Almighty. Because you'll be more subject to the principalities and powers of the planetary air, your angelic support, and your ability to communicate with the Kingdom of Heaven, will be severely limited."

"To risk concentrated spiritual involvement will draw more enemy response, my child," pointed out High Priestess Ruth Mara.

Uziel adored High Priestess Mara, and clung to her almost as much as he did High Priestess Korban.

"As you know, Siwa is the territory of the angels of perdition, namely the angel Zeus-Ammon," interjected High Priest Enoch Chiavona. "Because of ancient laws in the dateless past, and certain prophecies, Heaven's Kingdom is strictly limited in its influence there."

Across the dirt street, sitting at one of the outside tables of a busy restaurant, the image of a young man caught his attention. Swallowed up by the throngs of people passing by here and there in the midafternoon sun, the young man's calmness diverged from the noise.

Quickly retracting his spirit, Uziel decided on a safer course of action, relying on his physical senses to make a closer study of the young man.

Stunning to look upon, the young man's comeliness enthralled Basra.

I must examine the man's composition with my spiritual sight.

Human organs, flesh, secretions—these meant little in spiritual space. Going much deeper, Uziel discerned to the spiritual matter of the young man's soul. Methodically, he probed the man's spiritual composition, cautiously searching the barrier between the man's spirit and body.

That's not right.

First wonder, then confusion, layered Uziel's curiosity.

There's no soul, Uziel concluded. *If there's no soul, then…*

Shock came over Uziel. A cold chill passed through him. He sensed the deepness of the spiritual layers and saw the images imprinted upon the man's spirit.

I'm looking at an angel.

Across the back of his neck, the hairs stood up on end, as he realized the identity of the angel.

In splendor and exquisiteness, the angel's spiritual image reflected the brightness of diamond, onyx, jasper, emerald, sapphire, and other precious stones.

As the angel radiated in the hot sun, Uziel discovered ancient wisdom and perfection in every movement the angel made.

The covering cherub, Uziel thought in astonishment.

"Be careful," deKharouf repeatedly cautioned him, throughout his education. "The angel known as the morning star is beautiful and comes as an angel of light. Be not deceived."

When deKharouf first spoke to him about the covering cherub, Uziel's curiosity got the better of him.

"How will I detect him when I encounter him?"

Deliberately, deKharouf lifted a hand in front of young Uziel. "Never seek to encounter the Morning Star. However, he'll certainly seek to acquire you. If you search out his spirit, you'll ascertain a vastness only eternity and divinity can comprehend. Within infinity's heavenly veil, Lucifer's sin is interned."

Lucifer, marveled Uziel. *Just outside the Aghurmi perimeter.*

It took all of his skill, but Uziel covered his physical movement and departed the café. *If the prince of the power of the air detects me, I'm sure I won't survive his attack.*

Cautiously, Uziel avoided the mighty angel, delicately fading away from the market square. Repositioned in a private garden, he located the two evil spirits from the Hotel Kelany. Remaining hidden amongst a line of olive trees, he trailed the evils spirits as they followed the ancient path leading to Aghurmi Hill.

Waiting near a clump of *halfa grass,* Uziel observed a third spirit take the place of one of the two spirits at the edge of the perimeter.

The evil spirit who departed is going to report. Here's my chance.

Being extremely meticulous, Uziel maneuvered behind the two spirits. Unleashing exact ferocity, he demolished the body of the spirit closest to him, hardly making a sound. Turning on the other spirit, as it spun to escape his attack, he crushed its essence.

Tens of thousands of spirits erupted in ethereal torment across the hill, reacting to the break of spiritual contact.

Attaining the next height, Uziel's destroying angels advanced toward the dark shapes of the Aghurmi Hill dwellings. As the angels reached the ancient abodes, a legion of evil spirits formed a protective shell around the dwellings, even the open space leading up to them.

A spiritual battle—short and fierce—broke out. Within seconds, Uziel's angels destroyed all but a small group of spirits who sought to escape the spiritual carnage.

Having no place to exist in the physical world, the remaining spirits could not escape their spiritual destruction. Uziel's angels destroyed them completely.

Within seconds, Uziel breached the perimeter. Straightaway, he entered the vapor and rejoined with his angelic host.

Chapter 58 Hunter-Killers

In the valley of the devils, near the place of birth of Babylon, Lieutenant Daniels and Sergeant Johnson led their SMU hunter-killers on a search and destroy mission to find a hunter-killer of astonishing deadliness.

Daniels and Johnson assembled the team under new strictures, incorporating a CONOPS relying on technology. The SOCOM team—equipped with both TALOS and Atlas technology support—possessed a decisive advantage in the field.

The TALOS advanced equipment, namely the Kinetic Operations Suit, would be restricted against the super soldier they were hunting. The Atlas robotic support, on the other hand, provided great assistance, even if only in the areas of carry and payload.

One task force directive confined the "black" activity.

"You can't jump lines," Colonel Lasker warned. "No one can discover GF99's existence."

Jumping lines referred to the national borders of countries, where the probability of detection increased, appreciably.

The assembled hunter-killer team numbered fifteen killers, five killers to a squad. While the squads served as moving parts to the whole, Daniels gathered and reassembled them into one cohesive killing force.

"There'll be own individual C2," Daniels briefed his hunter-killers. "The *INTSUM* (Intel Summary) puts the *HVT* (High Value Target) in the vicinity of the eastern bank of the *Euphrates River*."

"Why?" asked Cullum.

"It's uncertain why the HVT comes and goes from this particular site, but each time he does, he concentrates his activities within the ancient ruins near *Al Hillah*."

Group Ham, which stood for *Hammurabi*, took a position south of the ancient palace of *King Nebuchadnezzar*. *Group Ish*, which stood for *Bab Ishtar Babylon*, took a position north of the ancient palace.

Lastly, *Group Neb*, which stood for Nebuchadnezzar, took position directly within the ruins, assuming the role of mobile field command, and the network field link.

In an attempt to avoid any interference from outside forces, Grey Fox used elaborate archaeological covers to mask the groups. The United States Secretary of State sent high-level messages to the Babylon Museum informing them that a preliminary survey group would be sent to initiate repairs on the ancient Babylon Temples.

"We're the preliminary survey group?" asked Daniels.

"The area will be clear, indeterminately," Colonel Lasker replied. "The Iraqis will be thrilled to see us taking some responsibility for the damage they accuse us of inflicting on their temples. This'll provide us a safe window to operate in."

Daniels placed himself within Group Neb, coordinating all task force operations. Johnson commanded Group Ish.

Because the INTSUM showed the target's excursions nearly always began in the north, the CONOPS placed Group Ish directly in the path of first contact.

Cullum assumed Group Ham's lead.

"You'll be a free-moving reserve," explained Daniels. "Remain in position until first contact, or you'll become a liability. We need to pinpoint the counterattack, and this can't happen if you're free-moving before the defense."

Because of his hair-trigger personality, Daniels considered Cullum the weakest link. However, in the role of counterattack, his personality and mental profile fit the function perfectly.

"UAV support will be necessary," Daniels commented to Lasker, during the logistical preparations.

Lasker leaned back in his office chair, eating his candy treats. "This'll be accomplished through the most recent shipments to the Iraqi Government. We'll allocate two UAVs to patrol the AO. Acceptable?"

After sealing off the AO, the three groups linked up in the ruins of the palace. In quiet introspection, the killers made final preparations.

Anxiety covered the air like a blanket. The hunter-killer groups appeared solemn as they looked after their weapons and gear. Then, adjusting their *shemaghs* and AN/PVS-21 night vision goggles, they readied themselves for the hunt.

At 2300 hours, Group Ham moved out.

From out of the blackness, Cullum gave a sharp command to one of his killers, "Man the Ma Deuce."

"I got the *fitty*," the man said, gripping the .50 caliber and tagging along behind the other four killers heading into the dark countryside.

"Pick it up, meat eaters," Cullum softly called out. "Let's go play in the sandbox."

Without another word, Cullum pushed Group Ham to its POO hunting position.

Even though they were hunting a killer who didn't require conventional firepower, the habits of hunter-killer combat prevailed throughout the groups. *Point of origin* (POO) was a critical method of detection in their hunting and Daniels dared not discard the hunting technique.

At 0100 hours, Johnson's Group Ish left the improvised C2. Before leading his killers out, he drew up to Daniels in the dark palace ruins. "Let's get this Charlie Foxtrot on the road," he whispered.

The men shook hands in the night.

Breaking away, Johnson gripped his M4 and led Group Ish to the prescribed northern site drawn up in the CONOPS.

58.2

The night turned black. Clouds covered the near fullness of the moon.

The fifteen task force members were accustomed to the agony of the hunt. The intensity of the wait; the coldness of the elements and the sweat from the heat; the constant stress and anticipation—these things bothered the quality of the hunt and the hunter needed to overcome them.

It is one thing to remain focused. It is another to remain motionless and focused for days, and then, in a split second, explode with irresistible power and energy.

We're like spiders, thought Daniels, in the cold March night.

As a boy in school, he'd learned the brown recluse spider could survive up to ten months without food or water, and up to 6 months without air. Fascinated by spiders, Daniels often studied them, especially the hunting variety, to develop better methods of hunting and killing.

We'll need every trick to survive this hunt," Daniels thought to himself in the night.

Even though Daniels was an efficient and ruthless hunter-killer, the image of the dreadful killer they were hunting gave him a moment of pause. Looking out across the moon-dust covered landscape, he became intensely aware of his mortality.

To survive, many times a Special Forces killer discarded parts of his humanity. The perception existed that men like him were different and did not feel fear like others.

Fear is my friend.

The old saying gave him little comfort.

I'm afraid of you.

"Sir?" One of the killers of Group Neb stopped his preparations to study him.

Daniels realized that he'd whispered the words, *"I'm afraid of you,"* not thought them. "Just thinking out loud," he replied.

With each order he issued to the central group in the palace, the dread— far different than any he'd experienced before—lingered and grew in his mind.

58.3

The first few nights were quiet, the moonlight becoming brighter each night as the cloud cover dissipated.

The *RQ-180 Shadow*, accompanied by its predecessor, the *RQ-170 Sentinel*, covered the area from the skies. Soaring fifty thousand feet overhead, the UAV's *electro-optic camera* sent the collected real-time imagery to the *GCS* (Ground Control Station) operators below. From there, GCS transmitted the data to the hunter-killer teams on the hunt.

By the fourth night, subtle movements occurred. On the ninth night of the hunt, the super soldier unexpectedly entered the AO from the south. Astonishingly, the UAV tandem did not detect the episode.

"I got smoke, possible fire."

Cullum's murmur splashed cold in Daniels's headset.

"Hammurabi, lay down," Daniels immediately commanded. "Ishtar left flank, you're hot."

Hoping to create a holding line, Daniels moved his team from the west with the intent of folding the super soldier into the two other teams.

The delicate moving operation needed to be perfect to work.

"Marduk," whispered Daniels into his headset, "we're live."

Marduk was the codename of the GCS coordinating the activities of the RQ-180 and the RQ-170 drones flying overhead.

"Copy Neb. We're getting skip, nothing definite."

Skip? What the fuck? "From Group Ham gate?" Daniels asked.

"No. It started from the Ish access. Then it disappeared. Now it materialized at the Ham gateway."

"Is it still there?"

No answer.

"Marduk, respond!"

Finally, the GCS replied. "I can't tell."

Stop this shit, goddammit! Daniels screamed in his mind. "Marduk, I need to see what you see."

Another plea.

Seconds seemed like hours.

Then, in the Iraqi darkness, Daniels heard the strange transmission in his headset.

"There it goes! My God! Neb!—It's outside of your right flank!"

Daniels raised his fist.

Seeing his signal through their night vision goggles, his team halted.

His head on a swivel, Daniels turned to his right and scanned across the star dusted desert landscape. *If the fucker's outside of our right flank, then we need to withdraw,* Daniels reasoned to himself.

"Do you copy, Neb?"

The GCS operative sounded excited in Daniels's ear.

"Yeah, I copy," responded Daniels, hesitating. To call a withdrawal would leave the other two points of the killing triangle open and vulnerable.

"Back up, Rog," said Johnson, in his ear. "We'll be okay."

Reluctantly, Daniels gave the pullback signal and Group Neb started to withdraw, leaving a wide gap between his right flank group and Group Ham in the center.

58.4

In quick response, Group Ish pushed straight across and to the left front of Group Ham, spinning the combat zone left to right to compensate for the absence of a right flank.

It was the correct maneuver, had the double flank movement not been anticipated.

"What the hell's that fog?" Johnson asked into his headset.

It's dry, how can there be fog out here?

What he saw next was unbelievable to Johnson. As the fog slithered across the desert sand in uneven layers, there emerged the fiendish form of what he imagined a devil to be. Horns and hoofs clothed in a long robe.

His training allowed him to overcome his shock. Aiming his M4, he fired into the fog.

58.5

Taking advantage of Group Ham's exposed right side, the fiend in the desert night cut though the group's diamond formation, killing the first man instantly.

"Rip him up with the 50!" commanded Cullum, whirling to his right. In one fluid motion, Cullum unleashed the fury of his SCAR-H, lighting up the darkness in savage retribution. The 7.62×51mm rounds flew wildly upward and to the side, terribly missing their mark.

Toward the rear of the formation, the near silence exploded with the ugly sound of body armor impact, as the first man killed met his fate with astounding suddenness.

The residue of the lifeless soldier saturated the dry air in a copious mist.

An instant later, the darkness returned to quiet.

The movement of the attack countered Group Ish's left wing measure. The whirlwind prevented Group Ish from being able to engage the assailant, due to crossfire.

With incredible speed, the attacker continued to spin around Group Ham's position, killing the next two men before Cullum could adequately turn and respond to the assault.

Upon losing his third man, the thought occurred to Cullum that if his entire group was about to die then they had nothing to lose by unleashing the ferocity of their weaponry.

With the shadow of death bearing down on his position, Cullum caught a momentary glimpse of the attacker. Taking direct aim at the imp-like specter, he fired wildly.

Pulling the tape on the M67 grenade, he tossed it into the strange fog. Throwing himself to the side, he released unbridled ferocity from his SCAR weapon, just as the blast of the grenade roared throughout the southern section of the ruins.

Seconds later, he heard the sound of impact upon body armor and realized he'd lost his fourth man.

I'm all that's left of my group! The motherfucker killed my men!

The strange fog and mist overtook him.

Leaping to his feet, he searched frantically for the attacker.

58.6

"The fog's overrun Group Ham," announced Johnson. "I need more field data!"

"Marduk, did you copy?" raged Daniels into his headset. The lack of clarity coming from CSG fed his fury. "Marduk!"

"Group Ish, stand by for determination of its source!" exclaimed the CSG operator.

Ignoring the request, Johnson signaled his group forward. Seconds later, Group Ish plunged into the haze in a battle-ready line formation.

"Will!" Daniels cried out. "Will, wait for me! We'll go into the shit together!"

Having worked together on many black missions, across three continents—from flash military actions to covert reconnaissance gathering, familiarity formed a powerful stabilizer holding the men together. On the battlefield, they were of one mind, more importantly, of one heart.

"Too late, Roger," Johnson called out, "we're already in the shit."

"Stay put, we'll squeeze the fucker, and squash him!"

Without waiting, Daniels pushed his group south, catching the attacker in a vice between both teams.

The cool night air spread across his skin as Daniels approached the edge of the fog. As he pushed his group forward into the haze, the CSG operator tried one last time to dissuade him.

"Group Neb!" the CSG operator forcefully cried out. "Give us a chance to probe the haze!"

Daniels refused to listen, determined to seek revenge upon the ghoulish assailant who existed in the smoky vapor.

58.7

In the middle of the swirling vapor, Cullum saw the fiendish killer come closer.

A consummate killer who'd executed many killing missions in his career, Cullum always came to the battlefield overloaded with killing tools—

weapons, ammo, explosives, and all manner of sharp instruments.

I discharged everything into the motherfucker.

Absent of fear, Cullum stood frozen in unbelief, the realization of his imminent death overtaking him.

"Who the fuck are you?" he yelled out to the frightening wraith, the specter of death personified.

They proved to be his last words.

Seconds later, his remains lay upon the smooth sand, within the fog.

58.8

Group Ish inched forward in a killing crouch, weapons held close to the core. The five hunter-killers held their line formation, streams of thick fog wrapping around their armor and weapons. Coolly, Johnson and his band of killers carefully searched the murkiness for any survivors of Group Ham.

The hosioi streaked across the desert, exploding out of the shadows and striking the left edge of Group Ish's formation. With unearthly savageness, the terror in the night ripped open another hunter-killer, human entrails splashing across the cold, dark vapor.

A barrage of bullets and the eruption of grenades again shattered the night.

"Flash," Johnson said coolly into his headset mic.

In answer to his command, the hunter-killer in the middle of the formation launched the thermobaric grenade.

The heat burned intensely in the fog, as the hunter-killers from Johnson's group unloaded a salvo of vicious fire in the direction of their fallen warrior. Their fire concentration hit the fiend in the fog directly.

The hosioi, wounded and hurt, did the unthinkable and spun his rage staunchly into Johnson's group.

By penetrating the formation, because of his closeness to the innards of Group Ish, he prevented Daniels' Group Neb from issuing full reprisal, for fear of inflicting friendly fire.

Savagely, the hosioi gut the group, rapidly killing two more Group Ish warriors. The killings left a deep gash in the formation, allowing him a breakout opportunity to escape the intense ferocity of the hunter-killers.

Facing total annihilation, Johnson amazingly retained his coolness as he barked into his headset, "Fire!"

In obedience to his command, the remaining killer in Group Ish collapsed the formation into a two-man line.

Side by side, the killers crouched down, fully set to unleash their ammo in a last-ditch effort to slay the mighty slayer.

58.9

Daniels patted his HK416 A5 Model as he led Group Neb into the thick vapor. Over his headset, CSG Marduk sounded in his ear.

"Neb, we're acquiring GPS coordinates of the target." After a brief pause, "Neb," choked out the CSG operator, "Our CLs (communication links) have been interrupted." After another pause. "We lost the 170." Another gap. "We lost…the 180. Neb, we're blind!"

Daniels halted his group, fist raised.

"Get out of there, Neb!" the frantic CSG operator said. "Get out of there, Ish! We can't see!"

Ignoring CSG Marduk, Daniels said firmly into his headset, "I'm not going anywhere, Ish."

A split second later came the reply from Johnson. "I hear you, my brother."

It was a sedate rejoinder to a fanatical history of war and battle. The men had been friends, partners, and fellow warriors for over twelve years. They were prepared to live or die together in battle.

"Striker40," breathed Daniels into his headset mic.

Answering his command, the killers on the left flank of Group Neb, positioned the tripod of the Mk47 MOD 40mm grenade launcher.

Stick your head out you motherfucker, and I'll jam it up your ass. Daniels's rage boiled over. "Refused left," he commanded.

The idea behind his command was to keep the grenade launcher further back of the advancing group, the better to protect their greatest firepower until it fully locked on to the exposed target.

Come out, come out, wherever you are, you son-of-a-bitch.

In the well-crafted ruse, Daniels displayed the cunning of his vast experience in battle. He calculated to use the refused left flank maneuver to lure the enemy to attack the group's strongest set piece: the grenade launcher.

Commanding his killers to spin in a tight formation, Daniels didn't realize until too late that the killer in the vapor stopped his advance on the grenade launcher and spun to face the formation.

Ruthlessly, the killer killed two of Daniels's hunter-killers, ripping them to pieces in the wake of his storm of violence.

The speed of the assault caught Daniels off guard. "X3, X3," he said into his headset.

In coordinated movement, what remained of Daniels's squad speedily moved to the left.

In response, the fiend spun to the squad's right, keeping in tempo.

Daniels kept his sights locked on the fiend. Seconds later, the apparition moved more than one hundred, fifty meters away from Daniels's squad of hunter-killers. The added space gave Daniels the chance to fire his HK416 A5.

In unison, Daniels's remaining assault unit brought his Mk 14 to bear.

"Sitrep, alpha sierra," called out Daniels into his headset.

"Negative on that, Neb," answered CSG. "We think the P code is twisted on the L1. Before we scramble birds, we need to know what's there."

Not dismayed, Daniels spoke calmly into his headset, the lull on the battlefield causing a deafening silence. "14-1."

Directly, the Mk47 Grenade Launcher propelled a single "smart" grenade. Soon after, the noiseless night erupted in a loud explosion, the grenade going off in the general location of the terror.

Daniels kept his eyes on the enemy hunter-killer, observing the blast detonation directly beneath the fiend. In astonishment, he saw the enemy killer run right through the deadly impact. "X9! X9!" he called out.

Out of the vapor's whirlwind, the fiend converged on the left side of his hunter-killer squad.

The command to move right came too late.

The fiend ripped open the Striker operator with deadly precision, the man's viscera hanging out from his body cavity before drenching the desert sand.

Having lost three men in a matter of seconds, Daniels continued to push out his right flank in a desperate move to avoid further death.

Johnson's M4 unleashed its fury. Through the heavy smoke and vapor, Johnson's aim proved accurate, the rounds striking the target with potent violence.

It wasn't enough to prevent the imp-like figure from tearing open the last of Neb Group's hunter-killers. Thereafter, with lightning speed, the wicked figure moved on Daniels.

In desperation, Daniels fired into the hosioi, his bullets tearing the flesh of the killer.

Just in time, Johnson's M4 cut loose again, the rounds ripping open the fiend's head.

Instantly, the dreadful form of the devil landed on the cool sand, its blown open head coming to a stop next to Daniels's right foot.

In the stillness, the vapor began to dissipate. Within seconds, it completely cleared.

Weapons drawn and ready, the remaining three hunter-killers stood over the deadly entity.

Hastily, Daniels unhooked an attachment from his thin battle force backpack. Pulling out the Shadowfire communication box, he put the handset to his ear and said, "Ashur Ninurta, MRRHQ1, this is Group Nebuchadnezzar and Group Bab Ishtar Babylon. HVT is HK'd. Repeat: HVT is HK'd."

MRRHQ1 stood for Mobile Raven Rock Head Quarters 1.

"This is Rock 1. Copy Group Neb. Stay hot, we're on the way."

Chapter 59 She's in the Desert

And the woman fled into the wilderness,
where she hath a place prepared of God.

—Revelation 12: 6 KJV

On the thirty-sixth night of reconnaissance, Uziel detected powerful angelic forces converging on Siwa.

Translating back and forth from Siwa to Delphi, and throughout the trail of perdition, Uziel failed to locate Ariella, becoming more despondent.

"Siwa is the Gateway to Immortality for the angelic seed," Uziel remembered deKharouf tell him years ago. "Once you attack and destroy the Issus stronghold, the angels of the perdition will know what we desire to accomplish. The four angels will certainly alter their prophetic timeline. Perhaps even change the location of the birth."

59.2

The night encircled him.

All around the air of Siwa, the disembodied devils looked for an opening to destroy him.

His sword brandished, Uziel moved up the hill. He approached the edge of the spiritual defenses surrounding the ancient temple.

"I seek to find the trail of the four mighty angels from the pit to save Ariella, Master. I will not fight for your objectives—I fight for mine."

"You're a man influenced by your own convictions, Uziel," agreed deKharouf. "Very well. Seek out the enemy. When the enemy reacts to you, I'll respond to them."

The first devil Uziel came upon projected the hideous appearance of a maggot and reeked like decomposing flesh. When Uziel moved into position for the kill, the devil sensed him.

Crouched in his fighting stance near the bottom of the long limestone stairway, Uziel observed the devil scanning the darkness. Plunging his sword into the ethereal thing, he destroyed it.

In the starlight, the spiritual sword protruding out of Uziel's mouth glistened through the peripheries of the vapor. His every movement tight and calculated.

From the top of the stairway, the rock landing extended into a circular space, streamlining into a long hallway, which contained multiple archways. The manifold archways gave the eerie look of a tunnel appearance in the glow of the starlight.

Moving down a narrow passage leading to the temple, Uziel passed through time and returned to an earlier period when the Temple of the Oracle was first constructed. In the vision of the past, he saw the angel of the temple—Zeus-Ammon—as he first appeared, in his full glory.

The mighty angel smelled like sulfur and assumed the conflicted images of a he-goat, a falcon, and a man. Across his body, he displayed the breastplate of war, and over the horns on his head sat the laurel leaf of victory. The angel bristled with hate and fierceness.

Uziel had only witnessed the image of *Zeus-Ra* in his night dreams. Since the early days of his Nazarite preparation, deKharouf repeatedly instructed him on the dangers angels presented in spiritual warfare.

"In your reconnoitering, do not engage an angel in warfare. The destruction of an angel is not permissible without divine legal precedent. The Almighty only allows us to bind them in pits. It is an extremely dangerous undertaking—and difficult to accomplish."

I've gone far enough, Uziel deduced. *A devil close to the inner circle of the tetra-angelic command will recover much information under interrogation.*

Through another narrow archway, he entered an opening where the vapor thickened. The thickness of the vapor and smoke caused him to stop.

Within the inside breadth of the temple courtyard, Uziel observed the devil he decided to target for capture.

A destroyed devil will be of no use to me.

Keeping his attention on the surroundings of the temple square, Uziel thrust the sword and pierced the devil.

Keeping the devil impaled, he began the grueling task of escorting the sentry out of the hill of Aghurmi.

Not until the near breath of dawn did Uziel and his prisoner reach the foot of the hill. From there, he applied more speed and led the prisoner to the northern palm grove where existed a natural sunken enclosure.

Comprised of stone, ground, and root, the fissure served well as an interrogation cell.

59.3

The hosioi defiantly remained silent.

"Eternity…" whispered Uziel menacingly, standing over the captive spirit. "That's how long I'll torment you. I'll never end taking pleasure in your pain."

"Where she is, you cannot recover her."

The devil's answer rekindled Uziel's rage. "Why do they want her?"

"Her blood. She's in the desert, across Jordan," finished the devil. "She's in the midst of the four gods of the perdition."

A hopelessness descended upon Uziel.

Defeating one angel is possible. Two, nearly impossible.

All four angels?

Chapter 60 It Wasn't a Nazarite

"It went through the SMU hunter-killers like they weren't even there." Merlin pushed the report across the desk toward Nabil. The report added information to the Superman Library. "It sounds a lot like our case study."

"It's not," Nabil commented, quietly perusing the report.

"How can you be certain?"

"Because some of them survived. If they'd encountered a Nazarite, they'd all be dead."

Merlin remained skeptical.

"They encountered a hosioi," concluded Nabil.

"If we're going to draw up plans for a prototype superman soldier," pressured Merlin, "we need to move beyond the verification phase."

"Prototype?" Nabil asked.

Chapter 61 Where is She?

Now when I passed by thee, and looked upon thee, behold,
thy time was the time of love.

—Ezekiel 16: 8 KJV

Using the information acquired from the captured demonic entity, in a reckless move, not characteristic of his usual carefulness, Uziel translated to the *Rweishid Desert* in search of the Pythia's convoy.

From the distant Mountain Heights Plateau, within the sundry landscape of the Jordan Badia Region, he located the procession as it made its way south across the Jordan Valley. Following from the highlands, Uziel contemplated a cold calculation, born in the mind of a desperate paramour.

Do I go against Master deKharouf's instructions and enter the vapor, or let the caravan pass?

Quickly, he decided.

I can't lose the opportunity to gain answers about Ariella's whereabouts.

Somewhere south of the Dead Sea, the hot, dry Wadi 'Araba climate mixed with the vapor and caused strange signs in the sky. Probing the vapor, he discerned the hosioi and the Pythia, but not the prophētai. For this reason, he applied caution in his pursuit of the procession.

"Do not be surprised if the order of the march is small and minor," deKharouf often told him. "And don't underestimate it if it is. Be aware that the strongest of Hell's spiritual forces, namely the angelic force we war against, will administer its process. Edom and Moab are critical areas in the trail of the perdition. The routes in and out of the region will be heavily guarded. It is dangerous to enter the vapor, even for brief periods."

Uziel's mistake in the palm grove magnified the danger.

If it wasn't for my slipup, I wouldn't need to risk entering the vapor.

Coming down from the highlands, in the early evening, Uziel entered the valley, directly to the northeast of the vapor's trail. The moon dust swirled all around, he did the unthinkable and crossed the threshold into the smoke, unleashing his rage on the hosioi. He destroyed two before they became aware of his breach.

Hours passed.

He perceived a lone hosioi moving toward the spot of the two spiritual remains.

It's a perimeter check, determined Uziel.

Not until the sword drove through his flesh and into his spirit did the hosioi became aware of Uziel.

Swiftly, Uziel thrust out, making sure his sword incapacitated the devil, but did not kill. Taking control of the unclean spirit, Uziel departed the scene.

61.2

"Where is she?" Uziel's rage filled Mount Nebo.

The devil, his disembodied appearance filtering in from shadows of other dimensions, was unable to assume earthly form. Uziel perceived the unfinished levels of the corporal and spiritual composition of the devil.

The head of the devil appeared like an insect's, comprising antennae and compound eyes. Beneath the terrible head, the sloping torso of the thorax and exoskeleton comprised bright feathers and contrasted the heavy hairs of a horse.

"Tell me where she is," questioned Uziel, standing over the ethereal being.

"She belongs to the Prince of Peace, the one who will bring back *koine eirene.*"

"There is only one Prince of Peace," Uziel corrected, placing his mouth close to the devil's head. "Let me make it clear to you: The Prince of Peace is not your angel."

"The one who brings back koine eirene is a god," proclaimed the devil, pealing his elongated mouth back to reveal dirty, jagged teeth.

Bending even closer to the repulsive creature, Uziel asked softly, "Why does he want her?"

"She is of the purest blood. She is from the Castalian Spring. Her blood will finish the elixir."

Rage overtook Uziel. "She is a Nazarite! She is of no use to him!"

In defiance, the devil snarled, "You know little of the truth."

In the fullness of his anger, Uziel pulled the vulgar devil under his sword. "Tell me the truth."

"She is born of a Pythia," spit out the devil. "As you are, son of man."

Uziel staggered backward. The cave spun around in his mind.

Recovering, he gripped the spiritual entity's head. "I'll destroy you, devil," he roared. "I'll torment you into eternity."

"Judge and torment me, Nazarite," continued the devil, "but you'll only torment me for speaking the truth."

Reeling back from the conviction, Uziel reached out to the cave wall to steady himself.

Ariella, my love, you are from the same unclean water as I.

Recovering his balance, Uziel whirled around and once again leaned over the bound devil. "Where is she?"

Chapter 62 Nothing From This Earth

Whoever fights monsters should see to it that in the process he does not become a monster. And if you gaze long enough into an abyss, the abyss will gaze back into you.

—Friedrich Nietzsche

Colonel Lasker sat in his empty office at 1001 Defense Pentagon waiting for the Raven Rock Mountain Complex (RRMC) transmission.

Thirty minutes later, the initial reports started to trickle in.

He didn't believe them.

Twelve dead.

After a second check, he resigned himself to the facts of the report and immediately went into damage control mode. Lifting the DISA (Defense Information Systems Agency) secure phone, he activated the emergency logistics team for MRR1. Within ninety minutes, the damage control team (DCT) took control of the battle site.

Seconds later, DCT locked down the area.

Less than thirty minutes after the DCT arrived, a political assemblage of United States Department of State Officials entered the Office of the Governor in *Babil Governorate* and released a prepared explanation to the Iraqi Government regarding the events.

Contained within the DCT, an internal science team, specially created for corpse removal, took charge of the remains.

All through the night and into the morning, Lasker coordinated the movements of MRR1. By mid-morning, most of the details finished, he felt tired but not hungry.

Lasker never ate breakfast. He developed the habit as a young private. A soldier's unpredictable daily timetable rarely afforded the luxury of eating comfortably, and eating comfortably was the only way he could truly enjoy his meals.

To make up for the sacrifice of his morning meal, he ate a heavy dinner. His eating habits ensured that his body wouldn't feel depleted during the following day's rigorous soldier activities. He'd never been so thankful of his mealtime practices than this morning.

The *shadow alert* from JSOC and DEVGRU came over the secure SATCOM links. The images astonished him.

One by one, he saw the highly trained, expensive SMU hunter-killers killed.

When the real-time footage revealed how the super soldier pulled the RQ-180 and the RQ-170 out of the sky, Lasker closed his cyber sheltered laptop and sat in silence.

It's not possible. Nothing from this earth could do that.

Chapter 63 Nineveh Repentance

And God saw their works, that they turned from their evil way; and God repented of the evil, that he had said that he would do unto them; and he did it not.

—Jonah 3: 10 KJV

The seven high priests intercepted Uziel before he departed Mount Nebo.

"I won't allow you to enter the vapor again," stated deKharouf. "Ariella will survive this tribulation."

Uziel violently shook his head. "You know, she won't survive! I'll go into the vapor and save her."

High Priest deKharouf said nothing.

Uziel studied the priest in anger, before asking, "Why didn't you tell Ariella that her mother was a Pythia?"

Caught by surprise, deKharouf remained calm. He shook his head and answered evenly, "Ariella's mother…wasn't a Pythia."

"The devil said—"

"Now you believe a devil over a high priest?" Disgust poured through deKharouf's question.

Bowing his head, Uziel immediately answered, "No, Master." After a slight pause, he asked, "Her mother…who is she?"

"She's dead," replied deKharouf, abruptly.

Uziel lowered his head in sadness.

"Another doomed woman," said deKharouf, in a distant voice. "Sworn to Apollo and Zeus from her birth, the angels required her at a young age. She rebelled against them and ran away."

"What was her name?"

"Zinovia," replied deKharouf. "When she came of age and became aware that her life belonged to the Delphic angel, she resisted. Her father saw her gift to Apollo as a way for the family to rise in stature. Initially, he demanded her obedience. This led to strife. As Zinovia grew into maturity, her father saw the error of his ways and regretted his decision. He went to Delphi and begged the council to reconsider his daughter's obligation. The angelic gods refused to release her from her Oracle. Zinovia's father chose the only course remaining to her. He helped her run away and begged us for help."

"Did you?" Uziel asked quietly.

"Yes. We succeeded in hiding her, for a time and a season. She started a new life, met a man, got married. When she became pregnant the angels gained knowledge of her whereabouts. A spiritual battle resulted. In the violence, Zinovia died giving birth to Ariella."

High Priest deKharouf told Uziel everything. "Zinovia and her husband dedicated Ariella to the Nazarites."

"Does Ariella know all this?"

Making a sweeping gesture and waving his hand across the room, deKharouf said, "In the normal scheme, yes, of course she would've known, but…" Shaking his head, he looked down. "No. She knows some, but not everything."

His anger growing, Uziel asked, "So the angel of the Oracle…he claims Ariella?"

"The angel believes Ariella is rightfully his through her mother," deKharouf conceded.

"And you sent her."

"To fulfill her nazar," the high priest said.

"To commit suicide!"

Reluctantly, High Priestess Ruth Mara stepped forward. "That's not true," she proclaimed. "All along, we, the Seven, intended to enter into the vapor, not you, and certainly not Ariella."

Surprise overtook Uziel.

Walking over to a rock bench, High Priest deKharouf sat down heavily.

Uziel followed close behind, sitting down next to deKharouf. "Is this true?" he asked, softly.

The high priest's heavy voice cut through the silence. "We never planned to involve anyone else. Delays happened. We needed a diversion." He laid his hand on Uziel's shoulder. "You're so strong. And Ariella's so beautiful and strong. We decided to use her past to give us leverage."

"You used her," Uziel softly said, in anger.

"Yes. We used both of you," admitted deKharouf.

Uziel lifted his head and looked around. "Until today, I wasn't sure if 'the Seven' even existed." Displaying the full humility of a Nazarite, Uziel dropped to one knee before the high priest. Taking deKharouf's hand in his, he pressed the flesh next to his face. "I don't hate you. I know why you did it." In a broken voice, Uziel proclaimed, "You want to bring about the heavenly prophecies. You desire the Almighty to repent. I want this too. I want paradise to come down to earth. Now!"

Placing his hand on Uziel's head, the high priest stroked his hair.

"Master, is my father a part of your plan?"

"No," replied deKharouf, his jaw tightening. In an ancient voice, he said, "When I involved you, he became angry. He didn't want our decisions to bring you harm."

"Did you expect them to take Ariella?"

"No," the high priest answered, without hesitation.

"I'll save her," Uziel declared.

"You'll fail."

I can't persuade him, deKharouf concluded grudgingly. *He's made up his mind.*

"We'll fight together—as one." Rising to his feet, deKharouf commanded, "Come, there is much to plan."

63.2

As a boy, he learned about evil spirits. He learned about the four angels prophesied to emerge out of the bottomless pit.

Throughout his upbringing, High Priest deKharouf explained to him about principalities and spiritual wickedness.

"Why do evil spirits and fallen angels sometimes look like animals and insects?" he asked High Priest deKharouf one day.

"Because they use familiar elements to trick the minds of those they seek to infect. Disembodied spirits are ever seeking a vessel to hold their destroyed essence."

"How did they get that way? Disembodied, I mean?"

"The violent events of the pre-Adamite destruction caused them to be spiritually mutilated in the dateless past."

63.3

The council gathered at the Turkish chalet. Speaking openly to him, "the Seven" acknowledged Uziel's rightful presence in their summit.

"We are the Seven," announced High Priest deKharouf. "High Priest Enoch Chiavona, High Priestess Rhea Korban, High Priest Avi Zanoach, High Priest Munius Spatha, High Priestess Ruth Mara, and High Priest Kilij Marslan. Let us reason together."

"If you enter the vapor, you must know the dangers," High Priest Kilij Marslan counseled Uziel.

Although Master deKharouf incessantly instructed him concerning spiritual wickedness and principalities, Uziel remained silent, waiting for the wisdom of the masters.

"The four angels out of the bottomless pit are invincible on this physical earth," continued High Priest Marslan. "Our objective is to take control of them and once again imprison them in the spiritual bottomless pit."

High Priest Enoch Chiavona spoke firmly to Uziel. "You'll be far from your spiritual source of power. Don't allow your physical senses and emotions to be used against you. This is how the enemy detected you at the palm grove." When the priest finished his admonishment, he reached out and placed his hand lightly over Uziel's heart. "Before you enter Siwa, be sure to cleanse your spirit and overcome the flesh. Purify your weaponry."

High Priestess Ruth Mara stepped forward. Taking his head in her hands, she marked the spiritual sign of the Almighty on his forehead. "This I do," she pronounced, "I do by the power of the Almighty Fire." Pulling back his head, the priestess warned him, "The sign of the Almighty will protect you until you enter the vapor. Once you enter the vapor, the Fire will not follow."

When the priestess finished blessing Uziel, High Priests Avi Zanoach and Munius Spatha ministered to him. "If you stand with the Seven now, you can only be invincible by remaining perfect."

Lying prostrate on the ground, Uziel waited upon the instruction of the high priests.

"As in the prophecies of Jonah," Spatha explained, "Nineveh converted and the Almighty repented from his prophecy. We also war against the vapor to instigate the Almighty to repent from his prophecies. We war to bring forth the Bride of Christ. We fight to bring about the Almighty's eternal earthly kingdom. The Kingdom of Heaven will not support us in this war. We stand alone."

Chapter 64 Into the Vapor Again

Elijah Basra crawled on the ground in pain, perspiration droplets forming across his forehead. His torso convulsed as he heaved, the sounds of his sobbing bounced off the walls of the empty cave.

"Can you hear me?" he called out, his head lowered to the cool rock.

No answer came. The cave remained silent.

The perspiration droplets falling from his forehead landed upon the stone floor a bright red.

I sweat blood, as you did in Gethsemane. You know the pain I suffer.

His anguish filled the secluded cave on the side of *Jabal Qāsiyūn*. His pain lifted to the heavens.

"My son! I cannot lose him this way!" Rolling over on his back, he whispered through the deathly silence, "Oh Almighty, deKharouf's lost his mind. He doesn't fathom you like I do. He's never been removed from your presence…and love."

I will enter the vapor again.

This time I will enter the vapor to save, not to take.

My beloved Hannah, I will enter the vapor to save our son.

Chapter 65 Throne Room

And out of the throne proceeded lightnings and thunderings and voices.

—Revelation 4: 5 KJV

In the early morning, six of the Nazarite Seven escorted Uziel toward the southwest.

Left alone in the neatly ordered Turkish manor, serene quiet surrounded Rhea as she went about performing her throne room duties, a ritual she normally cherished and coveted. On this day, she did not.

All morning and into the early afternoon, she knelt before the altar seeking the face of the Almighty. "Great God," her voice trickled out in heaviness, "please don't turn away from me. I love Othniel, Father! I beg you to forgive him. He's a man of pure heart and has served you his entire life. Uziel, Ariella, Othniel, the six high priests—I love them all, Lord. I beg you, Lord, please understand their actions and forgive them. Please protect them."

Her heavy sobs reached into heaven.

"To enter the vapor...is defilement," she cried, uncontrollably. "Please forgive me, Elah. I beg you to allow me to fight for the lives of Uziel, Ariella, my friends, and the only man I've ever loved."

I can't lose them.

Chapter 66 Pentakis

The hosioi never traveled beyond the lines of the *pentakis.* As a result, when guarding the Pythia, they numbered five.

In their attempt to acquire Uziel, the hosioi sometimes positioned outside the pentakis. In some instances, they even traveled individually or in smaller numbers.

For this reason, only one hosioi encountered Lieutenant Daniels's hunter-killer team in the Iraqi desert, and why Daniels and a few of his killers were able to survive the encounter at the Babylonian ruins.

Nonetheless, the deaths of twelve of the fifteen elite killers within a matter of seconds sent ripples of fear throughout the US military.

Chapter 67 Battle Injury

And when he cometh, he shall smite the land and deliver such as are for death to death; and such as are for captivity to captivity; and such as are for the sword to the sword.

—Jeremiah 43: 11 KJV

United States Secretary of Defense Peter B. Argus sat in his office chair looking cross and apprehensive. Challenged by the eighty percent KIA of an elite hunter-killer team, his single-mindedness focused on cauterizing all openings leading to the details.

"I have a question for you Madam Director," Argus said to the woman sitting directly in front of his desk, wearing a long-breasted blazer over a loose-fitting business suit.

The woman was Abigail L. Rolleston, Director of DARPA.

Argus swiftly gave a glance to the two men sitting to Rolleston's right. The men were Lysander Wilson and Onmus Praetor.

"The question also involves you gentlemen," Argus emphasized.

Pulling her blazer lapel closer to her neck, Rolleston gently cleared her throat and said, "Proceed, Mister Secretary. Our task is to be transparent and precise in answering your questions."

Argus leaned forward. "My question is: What the fuck happened to us in *Al Hillah?*"

Having grown accustomed to the secretary's abrasive personality, Rolleston often reasoned that working with Secretary Argus was equal to working with Doctor Jekyll and Mister Hyde, hot and cold being a matter of timing and mood.

"Mister Secretary," intervened Wilson. "If I may, I'd like to answer the question."

Without hesitation, Argus motioned to him. "By all means do so, Project Manager."

"What happened in Hillah is exactly what we warned about." Wilson said.

The director remained motionless, allowing him to continue.

"What we're dealing with is not a normal human soldier."

Argus, his head down, reviewing the notes on his desk, held up his hand.

Wilson stopped and waited for the secretary of defense to speak.

"Project Manager, why do you suppose DoD has DARPA on the payroll—a generous payroll, I might add?"

In a clear voice, Wilson recited the DARPA Mission Statement. "To create breakthrough technologies for national security is the mission of the Defense Advanced Research Projects Agency. By making pivotal investments in new technology-driven ideas for the United States, DARPA imagines and makes possible new capabilities for overcoming the multifaceted threats and challenges that lie ahead in the modern battlefield."

Argus held up his hand again, stopping Wilson before he went further.

"DARPA's not in DoD's comprehensive R&D diary to give excuses, or even explain battlefield results, correct? There are more capable people who do that for us." Clearing his throat, Argus snarled, "So why in the fuck are you sitting in my office, taking up my time, giving me a fuck'n explanation?"

Silence overtook the room.

Once again adjusting in her seat, Rolleston quietly spoke. "If I may, Mister Secretary. It is I, not my team, who failed this mission. I'm to blame, and I would—"

"*I am* blaming you, Madam Director! I'm blaming you, and then, I'm blaming your team, and then I'm blaming the whole United States Military!" Leaning over his desk, Argus kept his seething voice half controlled. "We're the United States of America! What happened in Hillah cannot happen to us!"

The outburst did not sit well with Rolleston. Noticeably bothered, her skin became taut and her upper body took on a sunken quality that made her appear older.

"Now, as I see it," Argus went on. "We need to utilize the gifts bestowed upon DARPA to curb some of the momentum the enemy has gained and surpassed us in. Not only do I expect DARPA to be brazen in its quest to uncover all of the breakthrough technologies hidden in our soldiery, arsenal, and equipment, but I expect you to take the scientific knowledge we acquire from the enemy corpse and help us figure out ways to combat its power." Pausing, he looked at Wilson. "After going over all the battle reports, do you still assert Daniels's hunter-killer group battled only one soldier?"

A long pause later, Wilson nodded. "Yes."

Argus removed his glasses and ran a hand across his face. "I've never impeded the free thinking—even radical concepts—DARPA's utilized in the past." Clearing his throat, the secretary tilted his head and returned his glasses to the bridge of his nose. "But, disjointed conclusions will lead to even worse catastrophic events. Center DARPA's work on facts and scientific inference, not on religious myth."

"I concur," said Rolleston. "Project Manager Wilson and Assistant Project Manager Praetor paid extra diligence to ensure that all of our corollaries are in sequence. I agree with all of their findings."

"Which is?"

"We're dealing with a single super soldier of supernatural lethality."

Strangely, the statement came from Praetor, not Rolleston or Wilson.

"We're unsure of its origin," continued Praetor. "In all of the SCI Superman Reference Libraries, there's no data to substantiate that an earthly country can fabricate a super soldier of this caliber."

"What are you saying?" asked Argus.

Praetor held the secretary's hard vision before replying. "Our SMU Team ran into only one enemy super soldier."

Visibly upset, Argus once more removed his glasses. "Assistant Project

Manager, did you consider the possibility the enemy planted the body to deceive us?"

"After going over all of the raw data in the Project S Libraries, and breaking down all of the data collected by our team, I don't believe the enemy planted the body."

"Why?"

"We didn't recover any battle evidence to indicate a larger force, even squad size. No equipment. No signs of tracked vehicles. We found only one series of enemy footprints in the battle zone… No other enemy signs…"

Praetor's words stunned the secretary.

"Our scientists examined the corpse." Praetor shook his head. "They didn't discover anything unusual. No weapons, no gear, nothing. For a super soldier of this classification, we should've discovered more than a corpse. Breakthrough weaponry, maybe cutting edge technology. Something on or around the body to tell us about the equipment he used to accomplish his feats."

Argus pointed to a green colored folder on his desk. "According to the battlefield reports, a thick smokescreen covered the combat zone. We couldn't observe what was going on within the fog. Any ideas as to the smokescreen used?"

"We didn't detect any traces of hexachloroethane," answered Wilson. "No magnesium or aluminum traces. We even tested for lithium-combustion technology…" Wilson shook his head. "Nothing."

"Well," Argus leaned back in his chair. "Given the fact that Grey Fox 99 has never suffered this level of battle injury before, we've no choice but to conclude a larger force—platoon to company sized—attacked the hunter-killers at Hillah."

"But Mister Secretary," broke in Wilson, "you mentioned a few seconds ago that DoD does not pay DARPA to think along common military lines, or even logical patterns. We're paid to think outside norms and traditions, not commonality. We're paid generously to think unlike anyone else. We failed in our primary responsibility to the DoD, Mister Secretary, but we wish to recover from our failure and offer DoD an exact solution."

Argus shook his head. "There's too much risk. DoD's primary concern is to determine what nation created this super soldier and what the hell their interests are in Iraq."

Onmus Praetor spoke up, in a quiet voice. "Sir, if Daniels and Johnson survived and destroyed the attacking force, where are the remains? According to all classified accounts, we recovered only one enemy corpse and twelve SMU bodies from the battle site. And sir, the manner in which our RQ-180 and RQ-170 were rerouted out of the sky…cannot be explained."

"I saw the footage from the 180. United States Army Studies and Analysis Activity is itemizing the error and breakdown."

"Sir," broke in, Wilson. "The 180 didn't crash."

Far from convinced about DARPA's findings, Argus forced himself to maintain an open mind. "Project Manager Wilson, Assistant Project Manager Praetor, if our SMU team only faced one super soldier, as you say, then where did he come from? More importantly: Who created him?"

Wilson and Praetor told him what the DARPA team had concluded.

Chapter 68 You Are Invincible, My Son

You are invincible, my son!

—Plutarch, *Nine Greek Lives* 7: 14

The combatants maneuvered in the vapor, fighting for dominance of the ancient ground.

Out of Uziel's mouth protruded a sharpened blade able to cut through flesh, even wound and destroy spirit. Within the thick vapor, a trail of death marked his movements, the dense smoke shielding the corpses and spiritual matter of his victims.

Passing through a heightened entrance, a swarm of disembodied entities materialized through the ancient wall. The attack, swift and violent, allowed little time to react.

Struck on the shoulder, Uziel smashed against the ancient mud-brick and salt, shaking the entire inselberg. Falling to the ground, he barely avoided the sharp point of the enemy's weapon as it grazed his neck and punctured the hard soil.

I must get to my feet! Hurry!

Springing to his feet, Uziel drove his sword into the disembodied evil spirit, cutting it in half.

His energy spent, excruciating agony ripping into his tissue, Uziel slid to the salty dirt. He lay there unmoving, the pain causing him to teeter on the brink of unconsciousness.

68.2

Closely related, Biblical prophecies and the Grecian oracles coincide in many areas.

The dates and the locations are nearly identical.

Biblical prophecies provide the period and the geographical scope, comprising the economic and geopolitical undercurrents and prominent tides that will lead the world down the trail of perdition.

Herodotus specified many of the locations of the oracles along the trail of damnation and conquest followed by Alexander the Great.

"To know the times but not the locations is of no use," lectured deKharouf. "To know the locations but not the times is equally worthless. Recovering the dates of the prophecies and the locations of the oracles will reveal where the conception of the beast will occur. Assuming control of the oracles is the key to hindering the four angels of the purgatory from impregnating the Pythia. According to the revelations given to Alexander at Delphi and Siwa, the spiritual path will culminate through one of the ancient oracles."

68.3

"You are invincible, my son."

Nine-year-old Uziel stood before the master.

"I will teach you the ways of life and death, and instruct you through the thirteen levels of your path," continued High Priest deKharouf.

The early years sharpened his skills, cleared his mind, strengthened his body, and perfected his spirit. The protracted fasts, combined with night marches and dawn runs, increased his spiritual power.

Elevated to a mighty creation, his killing weapons and hardened armor presented a vicious warrior without equal beneath heaven. Where he moved, the earth and hell shook and trembled.

The student, was the master.

On the day of his anointing before the Altar of the Eternal Fire, High Priest deKharouf held the sword to his chest. "Upon this earth, you are invincible, my son."

68.4

On a barren road south of Damascus, Elijah Basra intercepted him.

"What do you want?" he questioned unforgivingly.

"I need to talk to you."

"We have nothing to talk about."

Elijah held up his hand. "Please."

Uziel stopped. Lowering his head, he relented. "Say what you came to say."

"I know what deKharouf is planning for you and Ariella."

Anger exploded out of Uziel's heart. "Don't talk about her," he commanded. "Do you understand me? You lost your right to counsel me a long time ago."

"Uziel, listen to me, please!"

"No!" Uziel pushed back. He went still, unable to rebuff the love coming from his father's broken heart.

"Uziel, what deKharouf is planning is insanity! Your nazar… Ariella's nazar…" Elijah shook his head wildly. "A Nazarite cannot go against the will of God. I know," he cried, as he pounded his chest. "I know because I tried! You mustn't make the same mistake I made!"

"What do you want me to do?" Uziel pointed a finger at his father and shouted, "You left me here! Now, after all this time, I'm supposed to say no to the only father I've ever had?"

"To be a Nazarite is to deny the flesh and embrace the spirit," cried Elijah.

Vehemently, Uziel breathed out conviction, without mercy. "Like you did? You stand there and judge me, after what you did?"

68.5

How much time passed, he wasn't sure. He opened his eyes to the thickness of the vapor. His shoulder throbbed to the edge of his consciousness.

If I don't get up now, I never will.

His spiritual discernment sensed the enemy closing in on his position. Drawing his sword, Uziel commanded his spirit to lead him through the ancient maze.

"The unseen created all that is seen in the dateless past," Uziel heard deKharouf's words blasting in his mind.

"What do you need me to do?" asked the student.

"Be perfect," answered the teacher.

Uziel understood. "Under the blood of the Lamb, I am always perfect."

"When you enter the vapor, you'll remove yourself from the sovereignty of the Almighty," deKharouf explained. "The Divine Law of the Lord declares the vapor—due to the promises the Almighty made in the Garden of Eden— to be autonomous."

The truth materialized in Uziel's mind. "This means…when I sin again—"

"The instant you sin, you'll be subject to the Law, and the enemy's corruptions and wiles." deKharouf said. "Sin will render your spiritual weaponry ineffective."

Entering the vapor, Uziel brandished his spiritual weapon. Walking up the sand path through ancient walkways, Aghurmi Hill ascended above the physical earth and into the paths of the spirit.

Under the enormity and meaning of deKharouf's words, blood oozed out from the pores of Uziel's skin.

Chapter 69 Project Superman

Colonel Ivan Lasker sat in front of the desk of United States Secretary of Defense Peter B. Argus.

GF99's process of discovery was never short and easy. Many times, the scrupulous exactness of the work led to a painful thread of classified code and a covert series of material extractions. In fact, most of GF99's field operations even went beyond the knowledge of the highest offices of the United States military.

The areas of United States military intelligence, surveillance, and reconnaissance (ISR), controlled by GF99, spread everywhere. An intricate web of compulsory deceit, GF99's concealment gave little respect to rank or status.

In the shadowy world Colonel Lasker existed in, he'd grown accustomed to treading lightly, regardless of whose office he sat in, or what title they possessed.

"I just finished meeting with the Madam," began Argus, harshly. "Her people are clueless about much of the details of Project Superman. So is she." The secretary scratched the edge of his precise wooden desk and shook his head. "Quite frankly, so am I."

Here it comes. He's going to try to push his weight around.

These were the games people in high places of government played. In many such difficult situations, Lasker often reverted to a characteristic he'd learned as a young officer.

Humility.

"Project Superman is a complicated program, sir. In which areas were you in the dark about?"

"Well, for one, what the fuck kind of super soldier can pull an RQ-180 out of the fucking sky? Why don't we start there?"

"Sir, the data we've reviewed is raw. We haven't established those facts yet. Time will be required to determine the *Force Protection Condition* (FPCON) of the collection."

"Colonel?" Argus's voice projected across the room and bounced powerfully off the walls. "Do we know where the RQ-180 Shadow is?"

"No."

"Do we know what caused it to crash?"

"We're not certain that it cr—"

"Do we know what the fuck caused it to do what it did?"

"No."

"Colonel Lasker, as Secretary of the Defense of the United States of America, I demand the immediate release of all libraries concerning Project Superman."

"Mister Secretary, I can't do that."

Chapter 70 Judge Absent of Mercy

Do ye not know that the saints shall judge the world? and if the world shall be judged by you, are ye unworthy to judge the smallest matters? Know ye not that we shall judge angels? how much more things that pertain to this life?

—1st Corinthians 6: 2-3 KJV

Dark clouds formed in the afternoon sky, threatening to release their humidity.

Many years earlier, underneath the solemn sky, eight figures walked to the front of the expansive courtyard and stood before the altar whose authority imposed law from heaven to hell.

"Elijah Basra," High Priest deKharouf announced. "You broke your nazar. We, the high priests of the temple, stand as your judges."

Elijah dreaded the Day of Judgment. In silence, he stood and waited for deKharouf to continue.

From the prominences of the clouded sky, the eastern Imperial eagle swooped down as if giving ear to the presiding. The sign gave omen to the hardship Elijah, Hannah, and their child Uziel suffered and continued to endure.

Lowering himself, Elijah pleaded. "In my guilt, I do not ask for mercy. My only request is that my sins not be visited upon my son."

Instantly deKharouf voiced his displeasure. "This is not a trial—this is a judgment of the Seven."

Equally instant, High Priest Simon Gehazi stepped forward. "Under the extreme complications of a child's life and future, I call for a summons before the Almighty and the Stones of the Fire to impose a lifelong nazar."

Anger ignited within deKharouf. He'd anticipated that Gehazi, a close friend of Elijah, might make such a motion.

The lifelong nazar essentially required the sins of the father to punish the son. In return, the advancement of the son's status within the Temple of the Eternal Fire would be assured.

Keeping his anger controlled, deKharouf took a moment to think over Gehazi's summons bid. Looking down upon Elijah, deKharouf agreed to the priest's summons. "Elijah Basra, your son, Uziel Basra, is summoned before the Stones of the Fire to be offered up as a lifelong Nazarite."

70.2

Outside the temple, after the other six high priests retired to their daily sanctifications, High Priest deKharouf confronted Elijah Basra. "You desecrated the temple," deKharouf cried out. "Your despicable affair draws others into its bitterness."

Basra lowered his head. "If it were not for my son, I would—"

"You should have thought of the consequences long before now," interrupted deKharouf. "All this so you could gain the love of a..."

Basra glared at the high priest. "Go ahead, say it."

Needing no further encouragement, deKharouf concluded. "All this to gain the love of a woman of ill repute."

In rage, Basra lashed out, striking the high priest square in the face.

Within seconds, the men fell into a clinch and rolled across the floor locked in mortal combat. From sharp blows parried, to others absorbed, the conflict quickly developed into an impasse.

Gripping deKharouf's neck, Basra snarled his rage into the man's ear. "She's a Pythia. Yes, you're the judge. But you forget High Priest deKharouf—you're not the highest judge."

"Maybe so, but a Pythia has no place before the Fire."

"*Rahab*. Do you remember her, Priest?"

Refusing to answer, deKharouf struggled to escape his adversary's grip. Unable to do so, both men remained locked in a death struggle.

"Rahab, a woman of ill repute, found favor in the sight of the Almighty," declared Basra. "Does Rahab have a place before the Fire?" Not waiting for a reply, he said, "You were my friend, Othniel. A brother I'd once die for." In savage anger, he released deKharouf, pushing him away in distaste. "But you judge absent of mercy."

Chapter 71 No, Mister Secretary, I Will Not

United States Secretary of Defense Peter B. Argus stormed up to the receptionist of General Clarence Dawson. "Tell him I'm here and I need to see him immediately."

Exactly forty-five seconds later, Argus stood before the desk of the general.

"What can I do for you, Peter?"

In the face of the defense secretary's abrasiveness, the general remained calm.

"I just had an interesting conference with Colonel Lasker."

General Dawson motioned toward a leather chair directly in front of his desk. "Please sit down, Peter."

"I don't want a seat," said the secretary of defense, spurning the general's conviviality. "Clarence, I mentioned in the recent Joint Chiefs of Staff meeting my hands-on style. I won't tolerate operating in the models of the past. Colonel Lasker refused to disclose Project Superman's library to me."

"Yes."

"General Dawson, I need the project library. Am I being clear?"

The general spoke with measured care. "Peter, Project Superman is the most dangerous library in the history of this country. The responsibility of protecting the nation from a serious Force Protection Condition (FPCON), the ability for us to respond quickly to attack, falls directly on our shoulders. I can't release its contents until—"

"General, my office is the head of the military edifice you belong to and I de—"

General Dawson responded to being interrupted by also interrupting the defense secretary. "I acknowledge and respect your office, Peter. All I'm asking for is more time."

A tremble pricked the defense secretary's voice when he spoke. "General, you will provide me with the details of Project Superman."

"No, Mister Secretary, I will not."

Chapter 72 Elijah and Mogdos

And it came to pass, as they still went on, and talked, that, behold, there appeared a chariot of fire, and horses of fire, and parted them both asunder; and Elijah went up by a whirlwind into heaven.

—2nd Kings 2: 11 KJV

Outside the tick and spread of Planck time and length, beyond the barriers of the physical world, Elijah Basra was in the cave of his torment—then, he was not.

Forty miles north of the Siwa Oasis, he translated on the *Alamein Road*.

I can no longer exist in the shadow of grief and heartbreak, reliving, into eternity, the memory of a love so perfect.

I lost her…I cannot lose my son too.

More acquainted with the region north of Siwa than the south, he passed through the northern desert and entered the oasis. The dryness of the warm season clung to the air, pulverizing any coolness struggling to push inland from the sea on Egypt's north coast. Nevertheless, even the dryness failed to prevent the vapor from crossing over the land and covering the sea of sand.

The heavy vapor and smoke dominated the vast desert, its opaque murkiness slithering over the faceless terrain of the oasis like a monster seeking to devour its primal magnificence.

After a grueling ten-hour trek, Elijah saw the earthen hill of the haven in the distance. As he got closer, he detected the enemy forces realigning along a northern line near Aghurmi.

I can't enter the hill from the north. I'll need to break through from the south.

72.2

The Shali Resort offered luscious indulgences to intoxicate the senses and provided far more luxury and gratification than a Nazarite craved. Because of the lavishness of the place, in comparison to the modesty of a Nazarite, the resort presented the perfect place for Elijah to hide and remain anonymous.

The resort fit the old façade of the ancient oasis, giving the appearance of mud-brick walls and carved out stone windows. Modern designed pool areas weaved throughout the resort, complementing the traditional Siwa houses fashioned in the old Berber style. Despite the guise of its antiquated frontage the resort's accommodations offered all the contemporary amenities.

"Did you enjoy your trip into Siwa, sir?" The concierge smiled eagerly.

Offering an equally warm smile, Elijah responded, "Whenever I arrive in this paradise, I no longer care about the misfortune I go through to get here."

The concierge appeared to enjoy the remark for he directly busied himself with making all of the check-in arrangements.

Basra waited until the man finished and began providing the details of his lodgings before he asked, "Are there any messages waiting for me?"

Basra hadn't made a prior reservation, making his simple request out of the ordinary. Using spiritual weaponry, Elijah controlled the man's mind.

Without questioning his odd request, the concierge turned and looked in the cubbyhole for suite number fifty-four. "Yes, sir," said the concierge, dully, stiffly handing over an envelope.

Taking the packet, Basra immediately retired to his suite.

The suite, like all the resort, possessed all of the niceties of high-end luxury. Elevated beds complimented sleek end tables and circular lamps, all in the Berber style. The front of the suite gave way to a spacious terrace offering a garden view, further shielding Elijah from any outside prying.

Without waiting, Basra opened the envelope.

My dear friend, Elijah,

I hope your journey finds you closer to the peace you seek. As agreed, at dusk I shall be waiting at the Mountain of the Dead.

Mogdos

72.3

In the early afternoon, the sun lifted high in the sky.

Standing on the terrace, Basra looked out into the garden. In the distance, he heard plates and silverware clanging in the secluded restaurant garden. The smell of *ful medames* and *mashy crump* filled his nostrils and he grew weak from hunger.

He hadn't eaten food or drank liquid in forty days. In addition to the arduous journey he'd just completed, deprivation reduced him to a further humility.

I hunger, Almighty. I beg you to honor my fast and allow me to save my son.

Returning to his quiet suite, he drew the curtains and lay down to rest before the time came for him to depart.

Elijah awoke to the sound of children's laughter and water.

Getting up from the bed, he walked to the window and pulled back the drapes. From the position of the sun, he estimated he'd been sleeping for three hours.

The children's laughter as they played in the pool area recovered his parental thoughts and despondently he returned to the bed. Getting on his knees, he began his devotions in quiet meditation.

An hour later, he left the luxury of his suite and began the march to the Mountain of the Dead.

72.4

Shadows outlined the dusk as Elijah Basra passed through Siwa. In the near distance the hill of *Gebel al-Mawta* appeared. The closer he came to Dead Mountain, the more the physical world melted away.

Translating into the spiritual realm, his unearthly weaponry and armor honed to perfection, his spiritual vision beheld Mogdos standing on the mountain near the entrance of one of the tombs.

"It's been a long time, my friend," said Mogdos.

Elijah returned an equally weary smile. "Yes, a long time."

The men hugged warmly.

In his younger years, Mogdos had been a zaggala, a warrior cast overseeing the barrio of one of the prominent Berber tribes. Like most zaggala, he practiced homosexuality. When he encountered Elijah in battle, his life changed.

After the intense confrontation, Elijah stood over him, spiritual sword drawn.

"Kill me, man of Elah," Mogdos called out, seeing the fearsome sight of death and his impending end. When the deathblow didn't fall immediately, Mogdos closed his eyes slowly. "Kill me," he repeated.

Drawing his sword, Elijah looked down at the fallen warrior.

"What do you want from me?"

"I necessitate your surrender—all of your lusts and desires."

Mogdos slowly got to his feet.

"I want your heart. I want your loyalty." Elijah foresaw the future when he would require the services of a zaggala. "If I give you your life, you'll give me your loyalty."

"It shall be as you command," Mogdos swore. "My life is yours."

In the years to follow, Mogdos married, moved away from Siwa, and raised a family. He lived a quiet existence in *Qantir*, a village situated sixty miles northeast of *Cairo*.

Following Elijah's orders, Mogdos maintained careful watch on Aghurmi through the years, paying special attention to the spiritual forces guarding the hill of the temple.

From the west, the two spiritual warriors—one a Nazarite, the other a collaborator and traitor to his god—moved through the spiritual paths leading to the Oracle. Elijah saw the spiritual city, not the physical city, the spiritual temple, not the physical Oracle, sitting atop Aghurmi.

Because of Mogdos's many years of reconnaissance of Aghurmi, they were able to avoid and circumvent the multitude of guards—spiritual and physical—who vigilantly watched over the earthly and otherworldly paths leading to the Oracle.

In the early night, they arrived at the base of the hill. There, the warriors entered the vapor.

72.5

He remembered the last time he held her.

The memory of her skin and scent pulverized his mind.

I loved being human and loving you.

Elijah followed the grimy passageway leading to the horns of Ammon.

There, they encountered the enemy.

Over 6000 evil spirits exploded out of the remains of their defensive shelter and threatened to overwhelm them.

Elijah swung his weaponry through the immaterial substance composing the devils of the perdition, destroying them before they could assume an attack formation.

Preventing any fiends from escaping, Mogdos cut off their line of retreat, destroying them in their panic.

The night went on. Elijah and Mogdos cut through the heavy fortifications, thousands upon thousands of disembodied entities falling at their feet.

At the returning of time, the warriors stopped to reevaluate the status of their spiritual ground. Mogdos's body felt the weight of the shadow of death. "Coming into contact with such dissolute spirits depleted me. I'm useless to you."

Elijah nodded as he plotted his next move. "We're here. You've accomplished all I've ask of you. If you so desire, you're free of your bond to me."

A glint of anger came over Mogdos. "Master, as we war in perfect battle, do not say such an offensive thing to your friend and eternal slave."

In the dark of the night and the gloom of the vapor, reassurance lifted Elijah's soul. "When I faced you in spiritual battle, I discerned we were of the same blood. I spared your life because I recognized my brother."

Mogdos straightened his back and stood strong before Elijah. The words of his friend giving him strength. "If this is my greatest fight, if this is how I am to be remembered into eternity, then I am content."

Moved by the words of his comrade, Elijah took his concentration away from the field of battle. Gripping Mogdos's shoulder, he said, "My friend, my brother, my blood—I ask you to stay here by my side and make perfect war against the enemies of the Kingdom of Heaven."

The warriors clasped forearms. Tears formed in their eyes and fell upon the unfeeling ground.

In the translation, from out of the smoke and dark, Elijah perceived his son's vitality.

"What?" Mogdos stiffened his back, looking in the direction of Elijah's gaze.

"Uziel…he's here."

Releasing his friend's arm, Elijah turned deliberately. He moved toward the front of the temple, unworried if the enemy detected him.

Mogdos followed close behind his master.

Seconds later, Elijah and Mogdos crossed the threshold of the temple.

Chapter 73 Monster

Colonel Lasker sat before General Dawson's desk.

"General, our research of the bio material recovered from ID 1612 is not equivalent to ID 0143."

Lasker's revelation did not surprise General Dawson. Even though he'd allowed the study and research of the hair samples of ID 1612 to continue, he'd known early on they didn't match. "What do you propose, Colonel?"

"We just lost 12 SMUs," replied Lasker. "We can't afford to resume the project without reexamining our approach."

General Dawson's complexion darkened. "If ID 1612 is a different super soldier than ID 0143, then our priority must be to discover in what ways."

The strangeness of the conversation humbled both men. They were men of action, not words. Waiting was not their métier; their vocation centered on deeds and exploits.

"Very well, Colonel. We'll give the military law of time its due respect. Go ahead, assemble and reconstruct all of the battlefield data from Hillah. In the meantime, suspend all field activity until the research is complete."

For a brief moment, the room went silent.

Out of the silence, General Dawson clenched his fist and pounded his desk. The general's powerful voice ricocheted off the room's walls. "Use technology, use deception, use whatever means necessary. Don't ask today's questions, or seek today's answers. Ask tomorrow's questions. Hunt tomorrow's answers!" The general pounded his desk again. "Colonel Lasker, I need to know who the motherfuckers are who created the monster that killed my men!"

Chapter 74 Alexander the Great, King of Macedon

And I beheld another beast coming up out of the earth; and he had two horns like a lamb, and he spake as a dragon. And he doeth great wonders, so that he maketh fire come down from heaven on the earth in the sight of men, And deceiveth them that dwell on the earth by the means of those miracles which he had power to do in the sight of the beast; saying to them that dwell on the earth, that they should make an image to the beast, which had the wound by a sword, and did live. And he had power to give life unto the image of the beast, that the image of the beast should both speak, and cause that as many as would not worship the image of the beast should be killed.

Revelation 13: 11-15 KJV

The luxurious atrium of Zappeion Megaron Hall in Athens radiated prominently in its spacious beauty.

The all-day event in the lavish vestibule to discuss trade relations began in the morning with the EU Meeting of Ministers for Foreign Affairs. Entering the reception area through the high arching columns, the ministers sat nervously, understanding the importance of the summit to the country's future.

The conference brought attention to successful models of trade and business within the EU.

In the early afternoon, a luncheon took place in the *peristilio,* under the bright sunlight. From there, the official event moved to the commodious atrium, where the golden lighting cascaded to every table.

The event was a special occasion for SHU International. The Grecian Government, regarding the importance of trade, honored the company's status in the EU model of commerce.

Although the event's basis came from a politically driven source, its internal momentum hit far closer to home. A grand ceremony held for Sevilo De'Esanatasos, the hometown favorite, included the city of Athens presenting him a laurel leaf ceremony for his achievements.

The Megaron, or palace, built in 1888 in a classical style, was a significant government building used to host many momentous events in Greece's modern history. Surrounded by thick trees, the grand building stood separated from the city, like a beacon—portentous and magnificent—speaking of a younger time in Greece's history. Nearby, the temple of Zeus reiterated the message of a glorious past.

Deeply troubled, Greek Minister of Economy and Finance Philip Kritolaos picked at his Portobello mushrooms & creamy feta spinach. Normally, he enjoyed sampling all of the fish mezzés, immersing his taste buds in the numerous delicacies served up throughout the multiple course meal, from the Catalan squid croquettes, to the smoked mackerel crostini.

On this evening, the mackerel, the crème fraiche, the capers and lemon were not enough to entice him. Not even when the servers brought out the *taramosalata* course did his appetite awaken.

Janessa, oh how I wish you were here tonight.

Nearly inseparable in eleven years of marriage, a family matter called Janessa away and she'd been unable to be by his side consistently the past three months. Three months where he'd faced the most severe adversity of his political career.

"I'm so sorry, Philip," she said on their last phone conversation. "Papa's still mending from his latest gall bladder operation and he can't care for her. I will try to finish my caregiving of Sonia in the next few weeks. I promise, darling."

Her cousin Sonia moved in with Janessa's widowed father after she suffered a work-related accident. Her slow recovery and recent relapse left her dilapidated and unable to manage after her needs. When Sonia's seizures occurred, Janessa felt an obligation to act.

Ripping his mind away from his personal dilemma, Philip struggled to focus on his business issues.

What troubled the Greek Minister of Finance was how much the message he'd give to the ministers diverged from the truth. *Sovereign default*—an economic maneuver he abhorred—seemed unavoidable.

"But I am the minister of finance," he argued. "I wish to be of service to my country, not be its destroyer."

Tyrimmas Archelaus disregarded his words. "Do not try my patience, Finance Minister. I demand your obedience!"

Convinced Archelaus was not a man, Kritolaos lamented, *He is our god, oh Greece. Our god has come to destroy us.*

All of his life, his mind, progressive and modern, seemed far above such antiquated religious persuasions. Raised by parents who taught him to question everything at the scientific and mathematical level, his consciousness did not have the capacity to confront ancillary events outside his limited subjectivity.

He remembered the episode from six years earlier.

"What the…? How did you get in here?" Kritolaos, agitated and startled, stared at the powerful looking man standing in front of his desk, in the empty office.

Strangely, Archelaus did not immediately answer him, preferring to stand in silence and study him.

"Who are you?" questioned the minister of finance, starting to rise from his chair. "And how did you get past the *Proedriki Froura?*"

Kritolaos looked toward the office entrance. *I didn't hear anyone come in,* he resolved in his mind.

Archelaus spoke in a commanding voice, absent of human quality. "Sit down, Minister of Economy and Finance."

Measuredly, Kritolaos returned to his chair.

Why don't I call out to the presidential guard? Who is this stranger who controls me, without consideration or respect for my authority?

As if in reply to his mental inquiry, the man said, in a confident voice, "My name is Tyrimmas Archelaus. I have urgent business to discuss."

"Make an appointment with my secretary and I'll be happy to—"

"Silence!"

Trying to maintain his composure, Kritolaos said, in the most even voice he could muster, "I can no longer tolerate your behavior. I will summon the Proedriki Froura." Reaching for the alarm pad hidden underneath his desk, he pushed the three-button sequence to issue a presidential distress.

"There's no need for that, Philip Kritolaos."

Speak to me like a commoner, no mention of my presidential cabinet title. This goes too far!

Eerily, the man walked toward the office door.

Confused and uncertain, Kritolaos looked after him.

Opening the door, Archelaus called out in an authoritative voice, "Come in here, immediately."

Almost instantly, five presidential guards entered the office and took up positions in the four corners of the room. One of the guards stood alongside of Archelaus.

"Now," started Archelaus, "there won't be any need for you to further distract our conversation. The presidential guard you were anxious to summon is here."

In shock, Kritolaos sat back in his chair.

He controls the presidential guard too. A normal man cannot do such things.

Calmly taking a seat, Archelaus began to recount Kritolaos' financial actions up to that point in his tenure as financial minister. When he finished, Archelaus said, "You performed virtuously in your seat as Minister of Economy and Finance. You brought Greece back from the brink of collapse. I commend you."

Kritolaos sat silent and unmoving.

"I directed my financial network to negotiate the internal IMF document which reported Greece's debt levels 'unsustainable.' I'm now creating more official reports to explain why you'll advise Greece to restructure its debt."

Kritolaos began to object.

Archelaus talked over him. "Minister of Finance, you will do this or give up your position of authority and we will seat another in your governmental seat who *will* execute our commands."

Kritolaos, desperate to hold on to some semblance of control, tried to fight off his fear as he once more asked, "Who…are you?"

Archelaus scratched the side of his neck. Pulling on the lapel of his shirt and adjusting his suit, he answered, "You know who I am, Financial Minister."

Somewhere within the cerebral habitations of the financial minister's higher learning, he sensed the identity of the man before him. Nothing short of his acquiescence would be acceptable. "No," he shook his head, "I don't know you, sir."

"Look closer, Financial Minister. Look straight into my eyes."

Kritolaos obeyed the man. Seconds later, his face went ashen. "You. You're the…"

74.2

Six years passed. With each passing day, he came to realize that Tyrimmas Archelaus was not a man.

Kritolaos glanced up from his dinner and saw Archelaus walking toward him. Next to him, Sevilo De'Esanatasos.

"Minister of Finance, allow me to introduce you to the man of honor." Addressing De'Esanatasos, Archelaus said, "Sevilo De'Esanatasos, this is Philip Kritolaos. As you know, he is the financial minister of Greece."

"Pleasure to make your acquaintance," Kritolaos said, as he arose from his seat to extend his hand.

"The pleasure is all mine," the powerful looking De'Esanatasos responded, warmly. "Are you enjoying the cuisine?" De'Esanatasos asked cautiously. Despite this, an underlying charm made him accessible and friendly.

Although his plate betrayed him, Kritolaos nodded politely. "The food is delightful."

Smiling warmly, De'Esanatasos did not challenge him. "Good. Taste is a paramount compensation of our senses."

Although he found the comment peculiar, Kritolaos ignored its oddness, going back to picking at his smoked fish and olive oil with herbs.

"Mister De'Esanatasos is aware of the economic strategy you've been using to lead Greece through."

In shock, Kritolaos instantly objected. "But Mister De'Esanatasos is a private citizen."

Raising his hand, Archelaus motioned him to silence. "Finance Minister, you don't understand. Mister De'Esanatasos is not who you believe him to be."

Kritolaos stopped and turned to scrutinize De'Esanatasos' face, trying to see what his physical eyes could not.

"Mister De'Esanatasos is the one whose instructions you've been following for the past six years," Archelaus went on.

Kritolaos turned ashen and grayish. Terror gripped him and he went mute.

"Do not be troubled, Minister of Economy and Finance," pacified De'Esanatasos. "I am not a stranger after all. You know me. Look closer, Mister Kritolaos," he commanded.

Kritolaos strained his eyes. The world began to lose focus. In his mind, the world faded away and only the three men remained.

"I know you, Philip," De'Esanatasos calmly whispered. "And you know me."

Kritolaos went numb.

"I know your family," went on De'Esanatasos, his dark eyes penetrating Kritolaos' soul. "I know your parents. I know your two sisters and half-brother. I advised you in high school, and taught you in college. In college, when you attended Athens University of Economics and Business, I took a more pronounced interest in your education. You've been led to this point in your life to perform your duty not for your country—as you've often believed—but to serve your god."

Kritolaos sat paralyzed, unable to speak. He frenziedly searched De'Esanatasos' face. Mysteriously, the man's identity became more familiar to him.

"I've placed you here, in your position of authority, to do exactly as Mister Archelaus has instructed. I've molded your mind for this exact purpose." After a slight pause, the man asked, "How's Janessa?"

Kritolaos nearly choked on his food. *Janessa? How the hell does he know my wife?*

De'Esanatasos went on without consideration to Kritolaos' discomfort. "She's an amazing woman, Philip. Such dedication to her family is rare these days, and speaks highly of her character."

Kritolaos, in agitation, said, "Sir, do not presume to speak of my wife as if you know her."

Not dismayed, De'Esanatasos responded calmly, "Philip...I know everything about you."

Kritolaos tried to speak, but words escaped him and he sat in silence.

Breaking into his thoughts, De'Esanatasos declared, "When you were born, I became your father and ruler. In your school days, I assumed the role of teacher. In marriage, I selected Janessa for you and oversaw the union. In religion, I commanded you to forsake all others. I am your god."

Kritolaos looked at the man in unbelief. Dark memories congested his mind, remembrances dismissed as dreams. "I always considered you to be a hallucination. I never believed the night dreams I dreamed, were real."

"To admit my existence would go against the logic your parents instilled in you," De'Esanatasos gently comforted him. "If you hadn't been raised atheistic you would've been of no use to us in your seat of authority. Simply circumstances and details."

Kritolaos reached for his Metaxa Amphora 7 Star Brandy and downed the glass.

De'Esanatasos motioned for the server to replenish Kritolaos' glass.

Reading the growing distress within the man's soul, De'Esanatasos persisted in consoling him. "Do not be hard on yourself, Philip. Certain people within the parliament needed to perceive you without the complications of pious convictions."

Kritolaos fell into despondency. De'Esanatasos brought clarity and totality to his life. Everything came into focus and made complete sense. Hidden memories in his brain, concealed secrets he now remembered clearly.

"My parents knew about this?"

De'Esanatasos nodded. "Yes."

"My wife?"

"Yes."

Kritolaos downed the glass of Metaxa Amphora again. This time De'Esanatasos did not signal for the server to refill the glass.

Giving Archelaus a side-glance, Kritolaos cleared his throat and reached for his napkin. The nationalistic music flooding the open space seemed to be coming from far away. Turning back to De'Esanatasos, he asked, "You want me to do something?"

"Yes."

"What?" asked Kritolaos weakly.

De'Esanatasos answered matter-of-factly. "Our first objective is to force Greece to withdraw from the euro zone. I've completed most of the initial work. What we require of you is to be the economic conductor. I'll orchestrate this global event."

Giving a slight nod and shifting his body, Archelaus confirmed De'Esanatasos' words.

"The benchmark interest rate set by the European Central Bank is to our advantage, especially now that the central bank of Greece shows the primary surplus reaching €2.6 billion this year. Compared to last year's deficit of €3.1 billion, this is a significant enhancement." De'Esanatasos paused to survey Kritolaos' discomfort. "This will be the first time in more than a decade Greece will secure a primary budget surplus for the year."

Kritolaos managed a nod.

De'Esanatasos placed his hand over his heart. "The predetermined, historical debt to GDP ratio; the primary surplus as a share of GDP; the real interest rate on government bonds; the growth rate of real GDP—these are the four factors that determine solvency and the sustainability of government debt. While these four factors aren't independent of each other, with the exception of the primary surplus, they are outside the direct control of governments. I tell you truly, there is another economic area government has limited control over."

Thunderous explosions went off inside the mind of Kritolaos. The meaning of the man's words terrified him.

"The long negotiations alongside the troika will continue. We'll introduce certain negotiators into the conferences who will cause disruptions."

The troika—the European Commission, the European Central Bank, and the International Monetary Fund—were the central figures in the desired economic salvation of Greece.

"Freeze the natural reserves beneath our feet. Greece is rich beyond the levels of everyone in the EU. We'll conserve these natural assets for our use."

"Our use?" Kritolaos feigned confusion, even though he understood the man's meaning perfectly.

"The Greek crisis," responded De'Esanatasos, "up to the economic collapse, and beyond, to the financial recovery, is part of a carefully crafted global strategy."

The sight of the sumptuous cuisine repulsed Kritolaos.

"Savings—individual and otherwise, personal and corporate—is the key," De'Esanatasos said, waving his hand across the table, dramatically.

The man's intonation—baleful and menacing in his ears—contrasted the succulent residual zest of the garlic and mushroom in Kritolaos' mouth.

"Take away the whole rotten government structure and everything it sits upon, and holds up, will crumble," asserted De'Esanatasos.

Oh Greece! Our god is angry! Our destruction is imminent!

"When this happens," De'Esanatasos said, his expression turning to stone, "your final task as minister of finance will be to slam the doors of escape shut and not allow the Greek Government to escape its doom!"

In the mind of Kritolaos, De'Esanatasos' voice rose over the sounds of the entire world.

"Using internet-based electronic warfare, and hidden international financial operatives and government spies, every commercial and private treasury platform holding up the Greece economy will be destroyed! An organized and methodical electronic run will cause the Grecian banking houses to default!"

"Electronic run on Grecian banks?" Kritolaos stammered weakly.

"At a prescribed time, thirty billion euros will be withdrawn from reserve accounts throughout the banking networks of Greece simultaneously."

"Oh my…" Kritolaos stammered; his words stuck in his throat.

"Use all your intelligence, all your influence, to further destabilize Greece's economy. When Greece is distressed and economically dead, Macedon will emerge and revive it."

"Why," Kritolaos gasped. "Why would you do this?"

De'Esanatasos used his arm to make a sweeping gesture. "The sacred tribe will possess the blessed land. Central Macedonia is ours. Greece to follow."

"But your country—modern Macedon—isn't even Greek. Greece won't accept its aid."

Both men smirked.

"Yes, that's what Demosthenes told Philip the Great in the times of the kings," Archelaus interposed, sharply. "Do you recall Philip's response?"

Kritolaos nodded his head slowly. "I do," he whispered.

"I assure you—Macedon is Greek. Salvation is the teacher of Greece."

"But the leader of Macedon, he will not comprehend the financial—"

"Silence," De'Esanatasos softly commanded. "Leave the instruction of the Macedonian President to me." As if reading Kritolaos' mind, he concluded, "The man who occupies the presidency now is the vehicle to prepare Macedon for the return of its rightful king."

"What do you mean, sir?"

Sevilo De'Esanatasos bore his eyes into Kritolaos, imparting his thoughts and words into the man's mind.

"Oh no," Kritolaos cried out, in reaction to the images placed in his mind by De'Esanatasos. "Please…no."

"The prophecy must be fulfilled," countered De'Esanatasos.

After all the work he'd put into Greece's economic recovery, Kritolaos loathed the idea of a default. "But we've produced a primary surplus. There are other options," he pleaded, weakly.

Disregarding the man's pleadings, De'Esanatasos turned and gazed up toward the sky. "Pella will rise again. Out of the ashes, the throne of the god will reside there."

In the distance, Kritolaos heard the sound of the Proedriki Froura marching, a common rotation of palace forces. In his mind, everything faded away.

In his mind, only the image of the king endured.

He shuddered in fear.

The ceremonial movements of the Evzones brought Kritolaos back to reality. The image of the king becoming clearer in his mind.

The crudeness of De'Esanatasos' voice detonated into the spaciousness of the Peristilio. "And upon the throne of the god will sit Alexander the Great, King of Macedon."

Chapter 75 O pai Dios

"Alexander the Great advanced his military campaign to destroy Persia. Rather than continue, he deviated into Egypt. This could be a necessary military step to protect his rear, and to a point, I agree. But then, after all of Egypt and its riches were handed over to him—his military stationed at Memphis—he deviated again. He led his companions and friends, and a small contingent of soldiers and guides, to Siwa the Oasis." Nabil went silent for a moment, before asking, "Why?"

Merlin held his folded thumb to his chin, deep in thought.

"No military purpose or reward existed to make such an arduous and dangerous journey to Siwa. The oasis is separate from his military operations." Nabil held up a hand. "What's even stranger than Alexander deciding to travel to Siwa, are the details described by the ancient historians about the trek across the vast desert."

"Give me as much of the details as you can."

"Within a few days, Alexander and his small party ran out of water." Nabil squinted against the fading sunlight. "In this part of the desert, known as *Sekket Al Sultan,* many perish because of its dryness. Death is inescapable. And then, out of nowhere a powerful rainstorm developed and saved them."

Merlin shrugged his shoulders.

"Next, a massive sand storm swirled around Alexander and his small group and they became lost. Again, death appeared inevitable. As before—in a pattern occurring regularly in Alexander's life, whenever sure destruction is upon him—

a miracle occurs. Incredibly, two snakes appear and guide Alexander and his small assembly to safety. In other accounts, two birds appeared before them and Alexander commanded his men to follow them, saying the fowl were messengers from Ammon. Regardless of who the messengers were, they led the way to the Oracle. Because of these inexplicable events, the ancient historian Arrian is convinced Alexander's mission to Siwa was divinely inspired."

Merlin sat unmoving.

"So, this brings us back to the question: Why did Alexander the Great interrupt his military campaign against Persia to make the dangerous trip to Siwa? The campaign against Persia was his lifetime quest. Not only did he hate Persia, so did all the Greek city-states. He wouldn't suspend the conquest of Persia to journey to some old temple in the middle of the desert, unless…its importance overshadowed his life's mission. Or, his life's mission was to go to the temple, and everything, before and after, was a direct result of the prophecies given to him."

"Why did he go?" asked Merlin.

"Because of Zeus-Ammon," replied Nabil, unequivocally. "Alexander needed to confirm his father…Zeus-Ammon. The ancient Grecians represented Ammon as a god in the form of a man possessing ram *horns,* and associated him with Zeus. Alexander the Great—*Zulkarnayn*—is persistently linked to horns."

"I recall this legend and facts regarding Alexander the Great's temple visit."

"Zeus-Ammon is one of the four mighty angels incarcerated in the bottomless pit for nearly two thousand, and five hundred years. Alexander went to Siwa to ask the Oracle a list of critical specifics, all of them regarding his lineage, his military campaign, and his future. Historians say the high priest greeted him as *O pai Dios,* which translates to *oh, son of Zeus.*"

Merlin gestured loosely. "Many historians believe this a slip of the tongue by the priest, who wasn't fluent in Greek."

Nabil seemed unfazed by the genetic engineer's remark. "Of course," he said. "Many modern historians refute the historians of antiquity concerning Alexander the Great's life, even when the ancient historian lived in a different time period than Alexander, and had no reason to fabricate. Look, after what we've been discovering in the Project Superman Library, let's agree that what we're dealing with is not of this earth. Only an unearthly explanation can provide evidence."

Merlin looked away for a moment. "Didn't Alexander the Great go into the temple alone?"

"Not the temple. He went into the inner room by himself," corrected Nabil. "*Diodorus Siculus* gives account of the secret prophecies Zeus gave to Alexander." Nabil adjusted his thick glasses and relaxed his forehead. "To answer your question: I know what the angel told Alexander in the inner room."

"How do you know?"

"Combining the prophecies of the prophets Daniel and John, with certain events in Alexander's life, as well as the finish of his conquests, I know exactly what the mighty angel Zeus prophesied to Alexander in the inner room."

"The god the Greeks worshiped..." Merlin stopped to deliberate for a few moments. "Zeus is an angel? One of the four angels?"

"Yes. The Greek accounts of their gods and their *mighty men* parallel the Biblical accounts. The gods of the Greeks were, in fact, spiritual principalities dominating the country and culture of Greece. Angels—good and bad—govern all of the nations, realms, provinces, and people of the world."

"What did Zeus tell Alexander in the inner room?"

"The angel gave him the list of countries he would conquer in his lifetime, when he would die, and where his bones would be kept."

Merlin wrinkled his forehead. "His bones? What's so important about his bones?"

"Alexander the Great's bones are important because God forbids angels from mating with earthly women anymore. The bones contain the genetic information."

Understanding came to Merlin. "Are you saying—?"

"The bones of Alexander are needed because of the *aDNA* within them."

"What do they need ancient DNA for?" asked Merlin.

"The abomination of desolation will attempt to usurp God's power over life and death."

"In what way?"

"The abomination of desolation...will be a clone of Alexander the Great."

Chapter 76 Master and Brother

In the desert salt existed *Marmaricus Hammon,* the *Field of Palm Trees,* the place of the fruit date.

After many years away, the master returned to the oasis.

Aghurmi called out to him from the past and he remembered every archway of the temple. Dressed in his priestly mantle, he passed a group of children playing in the dirt street. Their laughter filled the old thoroughfare.

Arriving from *Sekket Al Sultan,* deKharouf moved southwest. Having consulted the *Siwan Manuscript,* he decided on the specific location where he would enter the vapor.

Passing in and out of the broken dwellings north of the stony, outermost crag, deKharouf breathed in the hot afternoon air. In the northern section of the defense line, a spiritual blind area occurred. He'd purchased the weakness long ago, through the subjection of four devils.

Nearly one hundred years earlier, he encountered a swarm of evil spirits holed up in the countless otherworldly territories in and around the region east of Mesopotamia. He destroyed most of the evil spirits. Only the four, aforementioned, remained.

"Man of the Almighty!" the devils screamed out to him. "Do not destroy us! Tell us who you seek."

"I seek a Nazarite. His name is Basra—Elijah Basra."

"We know your brother," the devils admitted. "He dwells in the region north of the Valley of Devils."

"If I spare you," deKharouf said, "I demand your obedience. On the day of reckoning, you will surrender your defensive position to me at Siwa. This is the price of your life. Do you accept?"

From the information given to him by the devils, deKharouf located Elijah and his wife Hannah in an earthen shanty. Shaken by his sudden appearance, shock and truth permeated their faces.

"Your spiritual weaponry and armor are dull and broken," declared deKharouf. "You failed to discern my spirit?"

Elijah did not respond.

Without showing mercy, deKharouf judged their affair straightaway. "You must answer for the child, Brother Elijah. And for the woman."

Anger engulfed Elijah. "There's no judgment outside the Fire, Priest," he prompted. "Do not stand before me as judge."

"You know we are commanded to judge all things earthly."

Without warning, Elijah delivered a kick to deKharouf's chest, smashing him against the wall. The shanty shook tremendously.

The retaliatory strike from deKharouf sent Elijah reeling to the ground. Like a large cat, he landed on top of his fallen brother.

The men rolled across the floor in a violent rage.

"Stop it! You're scaring the child!" Hannah's screams lifted above their rage and the baby's cries.

Releasing their grip on each other, the men rose to their feet.

Without further violence, deKharouf declared, "You are required to return and stand before the Eternal Fire, and answer for your broken vow."

76.2

After nearly a hundred years, on a cold winter's day, deKharouf appeared out of thin air in front of the evil spirits he'd commissioned to allow passage into Aghurmi.

"Is it you, Man of God?" the evil spirits cried out, in terror.

"It is I," replied deKharouf.

He intercepted the roaming unclean spirits in the sandy desert fifty miles south of *Marsah Matruh*.

"What have we to do with you, Man of God? We abandoned the house wherein we dwelt and are walking through dry places, seeking rest."

"Did you find rest?"

"We found none."

"You're contemplating bringing more spirits to your old house to help you overcome the owner of the home."

"Yes, Master."

"Do what you will," said deKharouf, holding up his hand. "But first, are you ready to live by your covenant? Or do you wish me to torment and destroy you here and now?"

"Son of the Almighty!" cried out the polluted devils, fearful of their destruction.

"Silence," deKharouf commanded, ominously.

Bowing in reverence before High Priest deKharouf, the amazed devils responded in unison, "We will keep the pledge we made to you, Master!"

The impure devils waited for his commands.

"I come to secure my entrance into Aghurmi."

Bowed before deKharouf, the incorporeal entities quickly offered their obedience.

Having full control of the devils, deKharouf outlined the event of his assault on Aghurmi's most valuable treasure: The Oracle.

Entrance from the north—extreme and unexpected—gave deKharouf advantage. After the devils permitted him entrance into the thickness of the smoke and fire, he passed the northern dwellings and entered the highest echelons of the hill quickly, encountering little resistance.

Nearing the temple entrance, through the dense vapor deKharouf recognized the minaret standing high in the smoke and fire.

The time is now to kill the evil seed and stop the disaffected angels from defiling the image of the Almighty.

Brandishing his sword, deKharouf marched boldly to the Oracle entrance.

Without hesitation, he crossed its threshold.

Chapter 77 Aghurmi Hill

Upon the ruins of an ancient temple and perverted ground, the Nazarites came to war against the four mighty angels of the perdition.

They—the judges—came to judge.

At Siwa flowed the battle to prevent the angel of the Oracle from planting the seed of the beast within the womb of the Pythia.

At Aghurmi Hill, the decrepit temple, neglected for so long, awakened to its evil end.

77.2

The ascent through the Aghurmi Hill residences went from ferocious combat to peaceful acquiescence, all depending on what section of the dwellings Uziel and his angelic host attempted to conquer.

Destruction needed to be swift and absolute, to prevent any surviving elements of the enemy spiritual forces from having the opportunity to report the incursion.

Well into the night, Uziel and his angelic forces reached the highest level of the temple plateau. Behind them, an enormous mound of devils released a glob of toxic wickedness, splattering out of their spiritual remains. If not for High Priest deKharouf's lifelong Nazarite dedication to his spiritual and physical conditioning, he would've perished in battle.

In exhaustion, Uziel's exaggerated slowness came to a near halt.

Likewise, his angels, hampered by the toxic irreverence originating from the dead spiritual matter of the devils, exhibited a peculiar sluggishness.

We're done. We can't dislodge them.

In his lowness, the image of Ariella stirred him. Pressing onward, they approached the temple. Nearing its entrances, he discerned a spirit that stopped him in his tracks.

Dad? Is that you? What are you doing here?

"When you enter the vapor, test the spirits more intensely," he recalled deKharouf's instruction. "Don't place any trust in your physical senses. Question everything you see, hear, and feel."

Guiding his angelic forces up the slightly curved stairway leading to the temple's entrance, a sobering thought gave him pause.

I must search out his spirit before I believe he is here.

A whirlwind of movement broke the spiritual barrier between the smoke and vapor outside the temple and the thicker vapor engulfing the inner of the shrine.

Familiar to him, Uziel observed the powerful violence of the whirlwind crash into the temple entrance. In the spiritual windstorm, Uziel penetrated its density and discerned his father's soul.

A mighty surge of emotion pushed out of his weary spirit, detonating his flesh with a charge of energy. Without thought for his personal safety, he stormed the gates of the temple, his angels, who had charge over him, fast behind him.

Chapter 78 Nazarite Seven

Instructed by deKharouf to remain behind at *Mount Yeroham*, Rhea did not accompany the five high priests who entered Aghurmi and followed the path of the perdition.

Entering the temple, the priests searched the first chamber. Fiercely, out of a thick smoke, six legions of unclean spirits attacked them, the intensity of the attack leaving the priests besieged and fraught to prevent the evil forces from overrunning their position.

From out of a *Planck mass void*, and a *Planck energy vortex*, two of the four angels out of the bottomless pit—the angels of Syria and Turkey—attacked them.

Despite the priests' tenacious defense, the angels tipped the balance of the battle, killing two priests, Munius Spatha and Ruth Mara, in the initial combat.

Gallantly, the priests fought on, against overwhelming odds and numbers.

"This is a planned deception!" High Priest Enoch Chiavona called out to the two remaining priests, Avi Zanoach and Kilij Marslan. "They allowed High Priest deKharouf to pass through to the second chamber but we will be tested!"

Led by the two angels, another legion of devils madly tried to rout the three remaining priests.

Over the uproar of the crazed devils, High Priest Kilij Marslan replied to High Priest Chiavona, "You're correct, Enoch! Fight on to the end! The longer we detain these forces here, the better chance our brother can accomplish our mission!"

Chiavona, Marslan, and Zanoach fought intrepidly. In the end, fatigued and aggrieved by injury, the three priests succumbed to the enemy's persistent attacks.

Gaseous waste swirled around them, and the destruction of the ethereal material of the unclean spirits built up in the vaporous air.

"Nazarites!" called out Chiavona. "Fight the good fight to our end! Submit our spirits to the Almighty!"

To their deaths, the priests' fearless sacrifice gained deKharouf and Uziel valuable time.

Chapter 79 What Are You Doing Here?

And, behold, there came a voice unto him, and said, What doest thou here, Elijah?

—1ˢᵗ Kings 19: 13 KJV

The sanctuary comprised three consecutive chambers. Stretching beyond the temple rooms, the spiritual vapor bent and distorted the fabric of space, creating an *event horizon* powerful enough to seize all matter, energy, and time in an overshadowing energy field and pull them toward and into the bottomless pit.

In the supernatural ferocity, space, matter, energy, and time lost their values in the emptiness of the vapor. The nothingness of the outer hall of the sanctum, caused an eerie quiet to bounce off the steep inner walls.

In the absence of time, a wave of unclean spirits assaulted deKharouf's position. Driving him from the temple, he retreated into the split of the sanctum's front gateway.

Unleashing a deadly counterattack, deKharouf savagely ripped the attackers to pieces, leaving tens of thousands of devils strewn across the ancient sand. By his vicious sword—a refined and perfect line able to cut deep and destroy spirit and flesh—the master purged the first chamber of the Holy of Holies. Slashing and cutting through the evil forces, he distinguished a stirring in the spiritual air.

Her spiritual loveliness floated like an ephemeral waft in the breeze. The thick vapor and dense smoke failed to quash its loveliness.

Breathing in her exquisite fragrance, a sweet transcendence swept over deKharouf.

My darling, Othniel!

Rhea? deKharouf called out to her, in astonishment. *My love, what are you doing here?*

Sensing weakness, the devils ferociously attacked, assailing deKharouf.

I came to fight by your side, Rhea answered, in her spirit.

Torment ripped deKharouf open. *Rhea, stay where you are. I will fight my way to you.*

His strength renewed, deKharouf unleashed savagery upon the host of his enemies. Tens of thousands of devils littered the outer room of the temple.

Chapter 80 Child We Never Had

Can a woman forget her sucking child,
that she should not have compassion on the son of her womb?

—Isaiah 49: 15 KJV

From out of the dateless past, beyond the barrier of the *Planck constant*, Rhea's spirit knew the ancient oasis in the desert. Standing upon ancient *Gabal El-Mawta*, she looked disgustedly toward the palm groves and barrios.

The spiritual vapor enveloped and shrouded Aghurmi Hill in a mysterious sheath.

Passing through the thick spiritual smoke, she saw shadows of her past—old images and happenings still affecting her mind and directing her spirit. Feeling the massive weight of the evil event horizon, Rhea understood the calculation and sum of her faith.

Due to the galactic supremacy of the vapor over the Siwa Oasis, it took her three hours to reach the outer edge of the heaviest vapor. In the dusk, she thought back to when she'd traveled to the forest covered highlands of Syria to learn of the oasis.

Ninety-five years ago.

"I see bad days coming. I'm certain you do too. Will you help me?"

Rhea travelled to the Alhulu West Forest unsure what to expect. For a Nazarite to speak with a Pythia was extraordinary, yet, Rhea felt empty of choices.

Hannah failed to cover her surprise, even as she invited the prophetess into her cottage.

Hannah furnished an intricate porcelain teapot and cups containing an aromatic chamomile flower tea. "Does anyone know you're here?" she asked Rhea.

Rhea shook her head. "No."

Hannah poured the tea. "How can I help you?" she asked carefully.

Tenseness appeared on Rhea's upper lip—a negligible tremble issued through her spine. She brushed her long hair away and asked, "Siwa… Can you tell me how to enter the Temple of the Oracle?"

"You can't. Only the Pythia and the god's prophets and warriors are allowed entry into the temple."

"Not now, in the future," she quickly responded.

Closing her eyes as a rush of pain gripped her tired body, Hannah opened them to study Rhea. "I won't live much longer," she said, giving a nod toward the crib in the corner of the living area. "My son, he'll need all the help he can get. My family in Delphi were angry when I abandoned the Oracle." Forlornly, she shook her head. "They don't want to have anything to do with me or my baby."

Rhea didn't know what to say so she said nothing.

"If I help you…promise me you'll help my baby."

Buried in her thoughts, Rhea regarded the crib and listened to the quiet noises of the small child. "Elijah?" she questioned. "Where is he?"

"You don't know?"

"No," answered Rhea, shaking her head.

"The Holy Spirit led him into the wilderness. He's in exile; I don't know where."

Rhea didn't know what to say to ease the woman's hurt. "What's the baby's name?"

For the first time, the hint of a smile formed on Hannah's lips. "His name's Uziel."

The baby smiled and made happy sounds.

"How can I help?"

"I want Uziel to follow in his father's footsteps," Hannah replied. "I want him to be raised a Nazarite. Help me gain an audience before the Fire. Give me a chance to petition the Almighty on behalf of my baby."

For a while, only the sounds of the baby and the wind hitting against the outside cottage walls filled the room.

Delicately, Rhea reached down and touched the baby's little hand.

In tears, Hannah said, "I felt something special when I carried him inside of me. In my lowest times, he leapt inside my belly, and made me happy."

Rhea's spiritual discernment perceived the child's positive energy—compelling and uplifting.

"My man-child can be a great Nazarite warrior," Hannah said. "Like his father."

Rhea looked away from the baby and turned to Hannah, deep hurt evident across the woman's features. For years, Rhea considered the woman an enemy, and believed she had seduced a Nazarite. However, when she learned more about Hannah she developed a deep respect for the woman.

With her lover sent into banishment, her child would soon lose the only person who could care for him. Rhea felt sorry for the woman.

She may never see her man again.

A strong gust of wind pushed down from the mountain and slammed against the walls of the cottage.

"Do you, want to hold him?" asked Hannah, smiling gently.

Rhea nodded. "Yes."

Hannah weakly tucked the blanket around the child, who nestled up to Rhea's neck. "He likes you," she remarked, managing a frail smile.

Giving the baby a gentle hug, Rhea said, "He's adorable."

Rhea's visits to Hannah increased in the coming months. Having realized early on in her life that she would never bear children, nonetheless, she prized the opportunity to take a more active role in helping to care for the child.

Upon Hannah's death, Rhea offered up a benediction and prepared her body for interment. Assuming the mother figure role in the child's life, forthwith she confirmed the magnificent fire kindling in the infant's spirit.

Othniel and I will never have children together. Uziel is the child we never had. We'll raise and love him as our own.

80.2

Breaching the perimeter, Rhea quickly cut through three evil spirits guarding a group of dwellings on the western verge of the ridge. Stopping on the crest of the lowest gradient, she waited, looking for signs of movement. When she observed none, she advanced past the dwellings filling the rim of the settlement.

"Just as in the physical realm, there exist secret portals, in and around the temple, where spirit can pass through and enter into the Holy of Holies. But be careful," Rhea recalled Hannah's warning. "Once you enter, you won't be able to pull away and escape from the vapor."

Rhea knew the spiritual passageways of the air were different from the spiritual portals the Nazarite's used to translate.

"The portal is the bridge from the spiritual to the bordered shadows between spiritual and physical," continued Hannah. "Elijah experienced pain when he entered the vapor's limited reality of *proportions, magnitudes, and measurements.*"

Hannah's face clouded over.

"What's the matter?" asked Rhea.

"That's what the angel, Zeus-Ammon, is trying to do. He's merging spiritual with physical. He promised Alexander the Great immortality." Hannah's dark eyes opened wider. "The angels of the bottomless pit desire to make a human immortal through their power and authority, and make God a liar."

80.3

Rhea's countenance reflected the moon light. The glint in her eye intensified the brightness of her killing spirit. Taking the high ground, she observed the enemy's movements and considered her actions. In the coolness of the foul crepuscule, she carefully searched the iniquitous air for the portal. Crossing an archway adjacent to the temple entry, an asphyxiating coldness spread through her spirit.

This is the portal, Rhea determined. *This is the entry where the angels pass from spirit to flesh.*

A warm breeze moved across Siwa.

Pushing out her spirit, Rhea felt the disembodied elements of the evil spirit. Confident she wasn't facing an angelic entity, she quickly drew her spiritual weapon.

Viciously, she swung her spiritual sword. Her long, elegant hair tossed to the right as she felt the spirit fall to her left.

With her spiritual sight, she searched the evil smoke for any counter attack from the enemy.

The night stillness remained unbroken.

I won't let them murder him. I've loved him for a lifetime and I refuse to let him die here.

In battle stance, Rhea inched closer to the temple entrance leading to the abyss, wherein the ancient altar stood. Enhancing her power and fierceness, her exquisite lengthy tresses blew in the night, a sign of the Nazarite.

Chapter 81 Heaven's Might

But will God indeed dwell on the earth? behold, the heaven and heaven of heavens cannot contain thee; how much less this house that I have builded?

—1ˢᵗ Kings 8: 27 KJV

Uziel smelled the sugary fragrance of the angelic prince of Macedon. Distinguishable by its mellifluousness, the angelic scent filled his nostrils with a rich honey and date fruit fragrance. Because of the angel's sweet aroma, various sources throughout his lifetime spoke of a sweet scent emanating from the body of Alexander the Great.

Detecting the primordial earth shifting under his feet, he moved through the archways of the sanctorium grounds, coming near the temple entrance. In the wake of his spiritual wrath, untold demonic entities were destroyed.

Encircled within the abundant vapor, he smelled another fragrance, a perfume of innocence and freshness, tenderly familiar to him.

Jasmine, lilacs, rosewood—her favorite scents.

"Do not be deceived," he heard Master deKharouf's voice in his memory. "What you hear, what you see, cannot be trusted. Guard your emotions and your senses."

Uziel! I need you, my love!

The temple convulsed from the power of the four angels. Smoke emerged from the temple adyton.

Although frantic to save Ariella, Uziel recalled another instruction deKharouf repeatedly drummed into his mind.

"Do not confront any of the four angels, even if you manage to arrange an individual battle. In power, they're surpassed by few warriors on earth."

His early years of Nazarite training consisted of endless days and nights of physical drilling and mental conditioning. Persistently, deKharouf schooled him in the exploits of the four angels.

"Every war, every battle in antiquity was sword to sword, spear to spear. In the war between Macedon-Greece and Persia, the kill numbers are staggering," said deKharouf. "Using the war breakdown of *Plutarch* and *Arrian*, Alexander's force of approximately 40,000 to 50,000, faced Persian forces upwards of a million men, or more. There are many who claim the reports are inflated. They insist the numbers are closer to half or a third of this number. Their wrong. Both writers lived long after Alexander lived. What would've been their motive for exaggerating the reports? Nonetheless, let's use the lower figures. Let's say 350,000 Persian soldiers fought against 40,000 Macedonian-Grecian soldiers. The numbers are still around ten to one. Let's say he lost twenty-five percent of his forces. This comes to 10,000 Macedonians killed or wounded…opposed to, let's say sixty percent devastation." Holding up a hand, deKharouf said, "In actuality, Alexander the Great's Army inflicted far worse damage, upwards of seventy, to even as high as eighty percent Persian losses. This means the number of Persian dead totaled around 260,000 to 280,000, making the kill numbers anywhere from twenty-eight to thirty to one."

Uziel remained silent, his young mind racing through the astonishing statistics.

"So you see, the awesome, unearthly power we are up against is absolute and leaves little margin for error."

81.2

"Uziel! Darling, please! Help me!"

Across the temple's entryway, the splendor of Ariella's silhouette highlighted the waterfall of her flowing hair.

Stunned by his emotions, Uziel exploded out of his defensive posture and advanced toward the temple entrance. From the denseness of the vapor, another form familiar to him materialized. The image lived in his dreams and nurtured him in his early days.

Father!

To Uziel, the image of his father compared to a rushing wind.

81.3

He came to the temple to save the love of his life.

Everything changed when he saw his father.

Straightaway, Uziel blasted up the steps of the brief enclosure leading up to the temple's entrance gate. Entering the temple's first chamber, he perceived the extended scope of the temple's chamber, wielding his spiritual sword with godlike power.

Heaven's invincible might entered the hellish temple.

Chapter 82 Rhea

Darkness engulfed the temple's inner chamber. She imagined it gloomy inside, even black.

What she saw astounded her.

Brightness radiated around her like a swirl of water and bounced off the walls and floor, the welcoming peaceful light guiding her deeper into the hidden rooms of the temple. Strangely, the light calmed her, reminding her of childhood and the warm feelings she'd experienced as a little girl. The feelings grew stronger, until elation flooded out of her.

How can this be?

A dedicated Nazarite and deliberate thinker, Rhea habitually interrogated her thoughts and didn't fool easily.

"Come in, Rhea. We've been waiting for you."

The words startled her. Instantly, she repositioned her spiritual weapon.

"You won't need your weapon, Rhea. We don't wish to hurt you."

"Who are you?" Her words deliberately poured out of her mouth.

"I'm the peace you seek. I'm your exceeding reward."

She quickly denounced the assertion. "I only seek the Prince of Peace. He's my exceeding and great reward. You're not Him."

"Rhea, Rhea, why do you not trust and believe?" The voice soothed her, overwhelming her with its tranquility.

Rhea weakened her grip on her sword, only for an instant, but enough to make her vulnerable.

"You… You can't be…Him."

"Yes, Rhea, I am the Savior and King."

The shockwave caused her to drop to her knees, her soft, long hair falling across her features, briefly shielding her from the light's brilliance. For an instant, Rhea's heart broke free from the light's influence.

Lord, call to me. I'll come to you.

There came no call and Rhea realized the deception of the false light in the temple. The ruse succeeded in weakening her power. She struggled to focus on her exact location.

I must recover my spiritual vision or I'll die here, Rhea cried out to the Almighty. *I don't have the Holy Spirit to cling to in this evil vapor.*

Her flesh became lower than the ancient sand and her spirit swelled in power. Even in the thickness of the deathly vapor, the pureness of Rhea's heart came before the Lord, thus, her sword's sharpness retained its full killing force. Employing deadly exactness, she swung her sword to the left and right, her long hair splashing across her shoulders. In the form and incarnation of violence, she savagely fought her way to the edge of the first chamber.

In her recovered soul, her eyes opened and she once again witnessed the unseen.

In amazement, she observed the temple's outer compartment unadorned and bare, not garlanded and bright.

82.2

Swinging her sword, she cut open the killing ether.

The vapor bled out of its cold flesh.

Her long hair, stained with the blood and spiritual residue of her victims, streaked the deathly liquid across her fierceness.

Approaching the inner sanctum, she discerned Othniel within the whirlwind churning at the center of the innermost reliquary chamber. Inside the clutches of the angelic forces who ruled the inner temple, Rhea distinguished the spirit of her greatest love.

Othniel! My beloved friend! I will fight by your side and take captivity captive.

Chapter 83 How to Kill It

Colonel Lasker walked down the long hallway of the United States Army Research Laboratory (USARL). Opening a door at the end of the corridor, he followed a narrow stairway leading down to a series of lower level laboratories.

Kept secret by USARL, Lasker walked past a series of doors marked with the acronym LSSP. He entered the laboratory door labeled LSSP 6.

Inside stood a thin, lanky man wearing thick glasses and a heavy white lab coat with blue trim around the arms and waist. The man's name tag read Wendell Epstein.

"What's the comparison measure?" asked Lasker, skipping all congenial formalities.

"There are salient parallels in the authentic brawny tissue, but the parallels disintegrate at the conversion to energy ratio, where the abnormalities are quite distinguishable."

"You studied the follicles?"

"Yes, I did," the man confirmed. "The follicles aren't analogous." Epstein walked over to the first lab table where the body of a man lay. "ID 0143 is the only specimen I've studied whose hair consolidations encompass the potencies we've discussed." Epstein gave a slight nod and pushed a small white button on his desktop next to the table. "Here, let me show you something."

A schematic came over a large screen next to the desktop.

"Observe this cross-section of a normal active follicle," Epstein said, pointing to a spot on the diagram. "Now compare the active follicles of ID

284

1612 and the old follicles of ID 0143. See the diverse dimensions?"

Lasker followed the man's directions.

Epstein hit another button and a different cross-section appeared on the screen. "This is what is most peculiar of the active follicle of ID 0143." Pointing to a segment of the cross-section of the hair follicle, he said, "From the *sebaceous gland*, to the *arrector pili muscle*, even to the *germinal matrix*, there are inconsistencies throughout."

"The same anomalies discovered for the past sixty-two years of study?" questioned Lasker.

Epstein turned away for a moment, before replying, "Yes." He pushed the small white button and another image came over the screen. "Here's a cross-section of a recovered follicle of ID 1612. The complexity of ID 0143's doesn't match. What's interesting is that while the convolutions don't match, there are many similarities between the two. For instance, observe the silvery appearance of the cells in the sebaceous gland of 0143's follicle. It's normally foamy; whitish, not silvery."

"What does that mean?"

"I don't clearly know. However, I can tell you the end result. The foamy look is because of the cells' high lipid content. When the cells disintegrate and the waxes and triglycerides undergo breakdown, they separate into hydrocarbon chains of random lengths. What I surmise is the silvery build up is the substance giving ID 0143's hair its incredible strength and longevity," Epstein quickly said, excitedly. After a slight pause, he asked, "ARL's been studying and testing ID 0143 for sixty years?"

"Sixty-three years," corrected Lasker.

"Right," reacted Epstein. "And nothing's been done to preserve the body?"

"No," answered Lasker. "ARL's research of ID 0143 proposed more advantages to military study if they didn't preserve the corpse."

"You mean, because of the lack of decomposition?"

Lasker nodded. "According to early portfolio entries, the rate of decay of the corpse is negligible. ARL conclusions believe this is not only a super soldier, his technology can provide a scientific breakthrough. A technological game changer." Lasker continued to study the cross-section documentation.

"For many years, the US Military kept the entire portfolio top secret. They released it to certain agencies, including DARPA, to gain military tactical application and advancement."

"We're the first to conduct a far-reaching analysis on the hair?"

Lasker nodded. "A battery of ARL studies took place thirty-five years ago. Because DARPA's most recent research identified the specimen, to some degree, it seemed practical to look at the hair more closely."

"You believe DARPA's discoveries?" asked Epstein.

Lasker didn't answer.

The US Military, for decades, closely studied the super soldier research of the Nazis and the former Soviet Union. Project Superman based its preliminary understanding upon the research of these two nations.

"Doctor," began Lasker, in a marginally supercilious manner, "let's concern ourselves with your discoveries. What are your conclusions on the hair of ID 0143?"

Epstein adjusted his glasses, trying to avoid Lasker's hard look. His eyes landed on the cross-section slides still shuffling through his desktop. "The follicle's not separate of the muscle tissue. The follicles appear to be secreting an especially potent derivative of *sebum*. The sebum doesn't seem to be for moisturizing the hair and skin, but rather for providing nourishment…and stimulation to the muscular tissue and nerve train."

"Do you realize what you're telling me?"

Epstein gave a slight nod.

"Deconstruct him to the absolute," Lasker commanded the man in the white lab coat. "Study him to the cellular. Rip him apart and go over every cell, one by one. I need you to verify the conclusions you've presented to me." Squaring his shoulders, the military man focused his full attention on the scientist. "I need to know how dangerous the superman soldier is to my men, and if we can duplicate his power. Doctor, I need you to show us how to kill it."

83.2

Life Sciences Superman Portfolio (LSSP) of USARL was as old as all other portfolios and folders in its library.

When ARL first created the series of top-secret labs, they placed them on secondary status and on an indefinite time schedule. Through the decades, they remained on secondary status until the most recent events throughout the globe pressed ARL to upgrade LSSP's primary rank.

The delay proved to be a serious mistake on ARL's part.

It became a question of when, not if, the consequences of the error would cost the lives of US soldiers.

Chapter 84 Free from the Vapor

Forgive me, Father. I've entered the vapor again. All the years alone, separated from your love, and here I am again.

Elijah's zealousness and passion caused him to take chances he normally wouldn't take.

"Master," Mogdos cautioned, "above all, be careful."

In response to the zaggala's warning, the temple chamber exploded in movement. The angel of Macedon came at Elijah with the rage of hell, in a fierceness bristling of the perdition and the thick smoke of brimstone.

Earlier than the Planck measurement of time, Elijah gave ground and repositioned with unearthly speed. Lesser than the Planck length of measurement, he moved faster than light. "Right thrust," he commanded, calmly. In answer to his spiritual command, a mighty violence struck the attacking angel.

Half parrying Basra's spiritual blow, the Macedonian angel whirled around and unleashed his ferocity against the Nazarite's legs.

Fearing his legs broken, Elijah threw himself to the side even as some of the assault smashed into his flesh. Elijah's body went flying across the temple ground, stopping near the southern wall.

Mogdos thrust his sword into the back parts of the angel, his blow redirecting the cherub's violence. If not for this, Elijah would certainly have perished right then.

Legions of unclean spirits assailed the men in wave after wave of offensives.

The men's will to war began to weaken.

"Master," called out Mogdos, the strain of warfare devastating his spirit and body. "I feel the weight of the mountains upon my shoulders. I can fight no more."

"Your life is mine!" responded Elijah, a lion's heart beating in his chest. "I command you to fight!"

Nearly overcome by exhaustion, Basra and Mogdos paused to rest, before confronting the bright lights radiating inside the third chamber.

84.2

"I want him to have your good heart. Yours is pure. Mine is…"

"Honey?" Hannah pulled his face toward hers.

He remembered how warm her hands were during her pregnancy. The recollection opened wounds in his heart.

Elijah allowed the cascade of humanity to clean his impurities. His oldness washed away, and in the sunlight, he was reborn. "I've never trusted anyone like I trust you. I believe you'll allow God to create our healthy child in your belly."

She placed his hand over her abdomen. "Feel him move, darling. This is our love inside of me. I want him to be like his father. I want our little man to take after you, my husband."

God, I miss you, Hannah. My love for you will always grow.

A spiritual perfume interrupted his thoughts. He discerned a woman of refinement and justice.

Rhea? She's here?

In shock, Elijah's spirit searched for her.

She's ahead of me, he determined. *She's in the inner sanctum!*

Emotions swept over him and he almost fell backward.

Oh deKharouf, you poor soul! You're at the mercy of a woman, as I was. An uncompromising man such as you cannot survive such dependence and vulnerability.

A newness of strength rejuvenated Elijah.

Raising his sword, he called out in the voice of a mighty man. "Mogdos! When we're weak, we're strong!"

Advancing forward, the men saw the horizon beyond the inner sanctum. They understood the good and the evil. Fighting with rehabilitated zeal, they fought to the edge of time. A flash of angelic brightness pushed out from the third chamber and the battle raged, threatening the defeat of the undefeated angels.

A series of reversals led to a heavy concentrated attack from the Macedonian angel and his host of spirits. Pushed to the limit and spiritually worn out, Elijah and Mogdos could not pay correct heed to their left flank.

Out of a ghastly whirlwind, the angel of the morning star appeared on their left. Savagely, brutally, the angel ripped open Mogdos right where he stood in battle stance.

A hole appeared in Elijah's heart when he realized the death of his last earthly friend. *I will be next.*

A cruel blow pierced his heart. Falling to the ground, his life force spilt out of him.

In a flash, he saw Hannah in the sunlight. Joy filled his heart as he saw his son, and his son's son, existing amongst the stars.

As the Angel of Death recovered his soul, he ascended above the Temple of the Oracle and lifted into the clouds. In the commencement of his afterlife, he discerned the spirit of his son and knew he still lived.

He's still alive! Oh Lord, I beg you! Save my son!

Chapter 85 Temple of the Oracle

He was the supreme soldier.

At the edge of the first temple compartment Uziel encountered a contingent of unclean spirits.

He destroyed them instantly.

After his fury subsided, he located the physical remains of the five Nazarite high priests, strewn across the old temple ground.

He wept.

They nurtured me. They were my family. I loved them!

The unclean spirits and the angels of the Temple of the Oracle easily detected the release of his emotions.

The attacks ensued soon after.

They numbered in the hundreds, and promptly Uziel moved against them, destroying them quickly.

Returning to each body, he gave each priest a separate benediction. He contemplated doing more for the bodies, but feared he'd delayed his progress long enough.

I'll return to retrieve their remains.

The spiritual air in the second chamber churned thicker, and Uziel paused to acclimate to its vileness. Moving along the north inner wall, in a sweeping pattern, he worked his way to the north center of the chamber.

Due to the pressure of the intense spiritual vapor, earthly dimensions twisted and convulsed, causing severe distortion. Up became down, down turned into up. Left turned into right, right turned into left.

"The entire temple's a north base. This means the entrance into the inner shrine, via the spiritual conduits, begins at the north wall," deKharouf often explained to him. "The best way to maneuver is from the east."

The battles were heavy.

Fearsome and tenacious, the devils and disembodied entities slowed his advance. Uziel annihilated tens of thousands of unclean and impure devils by the time he reached the inner chamber.

Where are the four angels?

He'd advanced too far to adjust his progress. Without an alternative, Uziel proceeded to the boundary between the second chamber and the innermost shrine. Here, the thickest smoke and brimstone ascended out of the abyss. Obscure and smoky, the dullness of the vapor gave way to brightness coming from the inner reliquary containing the relics of long ago.

"The inner sanctum will be occupied by the angel of Egypt, and the angel of Macedon," High Priest deKharouf's voice resounded in Uziel's ears. Originating from out of the shrine, he saw bright, heavenly lights.

"Besides the other two angels—the *Princes of Syria and Turkey*—there's one more angel who will also occupy the chambers of the temple, even the inner sanctuary. That angel is the prince of the power of the air, the spiritual king of Tyrus."

"The king of Tyrus...is Lucifer," said Uziel.

"Yes," replied deKharouf. "In the Temple of the Oracle, the deception of Lucifer will be a great danger to you. The four angels out of the abyss are far more proficient at destroying than deceiving. The *king of Tyrus* will rely on deception."

On the horizon, bordering the second chamber and the gateway into the third and most sacred room, a peculiar light flashed in abnormal intervals.

The soft light of the angel of the morning bathed the ground where Uziel stood, sword drawn.

In the soft light, Uziel saw the body.

Father!

The sight of his father's wrecked body near the gateway into the inner room of the temple brought Uziel back to his training. He crouched down lower, scanning for the enemy.

Kneeling next to his father's body, horrible despair pounced upon his soul and Uziel wept quietly, violently stunned by emotions.

Anger mixed with sorrow as he rose to his feet. Leveling his sword, he readied for battle.

In the form of earthquakes and floods, the vapor haunted him with images of wickedness and suffering. Legions of unclean spirits exploded from out of the ancient horror underneath the base and foundation of the morning light.

Uziel released his wrath upon them, destroying them by the tens of thousands.

The five angelic whirlwinds swirled in the inner room, causing the old altar to shake and tremble. A stream of beautiful color and lovely imageries bathed the inner sanctum.

The appearance of one beautiful image paralyzed Uziel.

It can't be. Almighty God, it can't be.

Adorned in a flowing gown, the graceful image of his mother moved within the beautiful colors permeating the chamber.

Momma.

The smoothness of her skin, the aroma of her soft, lithe hair, struck him in the most vulnerable places. He moved closer to her, coming dangerously close to the altar.

Dizziness came over Uziel. A clear light drenched the image of his mother and moved toward him. He welcomed the wholesome light, the spiritual force drawing him toward an outward pureness. Deep in his spirit, the magnificent colors and seemingly pure light were not what they seemed.

Uziel! Break free, Uziel!

From the deepness of the vapor, the colors surrounded him. If not for the spiritual call of Master deKharouf, Uziel would've succumbed to the deception of the king of Tyrus.

Uziel saw them in the unearthly light of the inner chamber, in between the flashes of death and perdition.

Ariella! High Priestess Rhea! Master deKharouf!

The sinister light of the vapor bathed Ariella spectacularly.

By his spiritual gift of discernment, Uziel immediately discovered her spotlessness.

She hasn't been defiled!

Elation came over Uziel.

In the next moment, he witnessed the actions of High Priestess Rhea fighting her way to the altar.

Offering her support against the angel of Turkey, deKharouf engaged in a colossal battle with the angel of Syria, to one side of the altar.

In a flash, Rhea attained the ground around the altar.

85.2

His killing proficiency exuding out of his spirit, Uziel reached the zenith of earthly invincibility.

Before him, the battlefield extended.

The sheer violence of Uziel's assault caused the enemy to give ground.

A small gap opened in the enemy lines providing Rhea all the space she needed. Uncaring for her safety, Rhea drove into the opening. Frantically, she freed Ariella from the spiritual binding holding her to the altar.

Ariella fell to the ground, too weak to stand on her own.

"Stand or die!" Rhea screamed, pulling up Ariella. Courageously, she took a defensive position in front of the altar.

Without delay, the angels of Egypt and Macedon beset her.

The attack of the two angels, in addition to the violence she still faced from the angel of Turkey, caused her to fall backward.

Like the mighty men of old, Uziel brandished his sword with a perfect brutality, and leapt in front of the women. Outside the span of time, tens of thousands of unclean spirits perished in his awakening. The smoke and brimstone of the heavy vapor shrouded the remarkable sight of Uziel's long hair, whipping this way and that, as he swung his killing blade.

Uziel's support prevented the three mighty angels from overcoming Rhea.

Still pushed back by the three angels, Uziel and Rhea fought to stabilize the ground around the ancient altar.

"Ariella!" Uziel called out to his love.

Ariella slowly recovered her senses and equilibrium.

In desperation, deKharouf entered the fray. Immediately, the three angels of Egypt, Turkey, and Macedon were thrown back. In the brief respite, deKharouf shouted out to Rhea, "What are you doing here, my love?"

"I couldn't lose you," she answered. "We've lost so much already."

Whirling to address Uziel, deKharouf yelled, "Get Ariella out of here before the next attack!"

Losing his father and the five high priests strengthened Uziel's resolve. "I can't leave you and the high priestess. I will stand and fight with you."

Both deKharouf and Rhea violently shook their heads. "No!"

"You must go!" deKharouf desperately yelled out. "We'll stop the enemy from acquiring you! Translate now! Go!"

Time ended. Uziel made the decision to obey the directions of his master. His undisciplined spirit quieted.

No man is an island. I am obliged to submit to the will of the Almighty, if I am to live in a manner that pays homage to…Mom and Dad.

Ariella, still unsteady, leaned on Uziel for support. Perfectly, they translated through the whirlwind. Passing through eternity, they heard the fallen angels and their legions of unclean spirits howling outside the whirlwind, clawing to break through the celestial threshold and prevent them from escaping.

They failed.

Uziel and Ariella escaped.

Full of rage, the three angels and their host of devils once more turned their vile attack against the only remaining Nazarites, Othniel and Rhea.

Chapter 86 Companions on a Battlefield

They were companions on a battlefield.

They were one flesh, one mind, existing in an endless spiritual union.

They'd loved each other for 145 years.

Plunging his sword into the spiritual powers arrayed all around, deKharouf felt the agony of endless love.

You cannot die. I will die for you, my love.

Translating behind enemy lines, he then appeared on the enemy's flanks. Moving heaven and earth, hell shook beneath deKharouf's spirit.

The evil spirits gave ground.

The spirits give ground to pull me closer to the enemy angels who command them.

Chapter 87 No Greater Love than This

He that dwelleth in the secret place of the most High shall abide under the shadow of the Almighty.

—Psalm 91: 1 KJV

Standing as one against the spiritually unclean, the companions took up a battle position across the sanctuary from each other.

Before long, the enemy surrounded each of them.

The weighty substance of the vapor prevented them from translating.

Pulling lightning from the sky, the prophētai redirected the energy and wielded its power.

Sensing the flash across the heavens, deKharouf launched his body into a stone opening. Landing on the crusted limestone, he barely avoided the lethal strike.

The chamber went still.

I can't sense them. They're hiding in the vapor. I can't let them seize the initiative.

Exploding toward the inner chamber's entrance, deKharouf attained the elevated spiritual levels leading to the altar of the beast. There, he discerned Rhea's weakened condition, his concentration and energy diverted for a Planck time interval.

The prophētai exploited the interlude, the lightning bolt slamming into the chest of deKharouf.

"Othniel!" Rhea's scream pulsated across the old limestone mound.

Allowing the power of the lightning bolt to drive him through the opening of the altar's elevation, deKharouf slid across the salt and ancient dirt. Writhing on the ground, deKharouf madly drove his body behind the heavy wall.

Leave me! deKharouf's spirit cried out to Rhea's spirit. *I can fight on my own!*

Fraught, Rhea threw her body over an embankment, just as the lighting flashed by her. She no longer cared for her safety.

I've loved you since I was a little girl! I'm 151 years old, and yet, you still make me feel clean and pure like a child. I cannot lose you, my magnificent man!

87.2

Searching through the ruins of the Oracle, Rhea discerned the prophētai lurking in the vapor behind the deadly hosioi.

The hosioi shielded the mighty power of the prophētai, who stole the lightning from the thunder and hurled bolts of fire through the dense smoke.

Behind them, out of the dreadful valleys of death, she perceived the mighty angels of the temple.

In a blur of speed, Rhea slashed through the devils who fought alongside the hosioi. Upon reaching the hosioi, she wielded her sword and spoke the word of the Spirit, hoping she still possessed the power of the Almighty.

She did not.

I'm in the vapor, Rhea scolded herself. *The only sword I have is mine.*

Adjusting her position, she concentrated her spiritual force and destroyed the hosioi where they stood.

Intertwining their spirits, the spiritual beloved expressed their violence from the deepest reservoirs of their souls.

I love you, my darling, Rhea said within her heart, swinging her sword with effortless violence.

I love you, my dove, Othniel said within his spirit, swinging his sword with tremendous might.

They did not fear the terror by night, or the arrow that flew by day, or the pestilence that walked in darkness, nor the destruction that wasted at noonday.

Alongside their angelic host, Othniel and Rhea fought like judges and destroyers.

1,000 devils fell to their left; 10,000 evil spirits fell to their right.

Even the vapor succumbed to their ferocity.

Nevertheless, before long, the devils began to push back on the Nazarites.

"Rhea! Withdraw!" deKharouf called out, seeing the enemy advance. "I'll hold them back until you escape!"

"I won't leave you!" Rhea screamed.

"This is my nazar, not yours! Now go!"

Repentance filled deKharouf's heart. Reexamining the events of his life, he saw things with a contrite spirit and a broken heart, and repented his nazar.

Sensing his change of heart, a fresh thought developed in Rhea's mind. *Maybe, finally, we can live the remainder of our lives free from this heavy burden.* The thought gave her hope and rejuvenated her.

Expertly, Rhea succeeded in pulling back from the enemy attacks, taking a position far back from the fighting. Viewing the raging battle, she observed the vision of a spiritual warrior.

Out of the swirling vapor, the angel of Syria, and the angel of the morning, Lucifer, attacked from the left flank. The angels quickly overwhelmed deKharouf.

The two remaining angels! Terror struck Rhea as she saw the enemy forces completely encircle Othniel.

The angels are using the prophētai and the hosioi to disguise their attack!

Blasting out of the sky, another lightning bolt streaked toward deKharouf.

He doesn't discern the lightning from the heavens!

Without hesitation, Rhea gave up her Nazarite vow. No longer a sharpened weapon of God, she was simply a woman in love with a man.

Vulnerability, ache, and need consumed her. Love controlled her and she could not resist its commands. She loved her man too much to allow him to die when she could save him.

Far off beyond the lofty heavens, where dwells the Almighty, resides the purest love. From out of this secret and holy place emanated Rhea's love for Othniel.

Emotions bled out of her heart and she erupted out of her cover. With all of her strength, she threw herself between the deadly lightning bolt and Othniel!

The lightning bolt struck her between her breasts!

Pulverized by the savage blast, Rhea's lifeless body smashed into the southern wall of the innermost shrine!

She lay unmoving.

Great alarm and sadness overwhelmed deKharouf.

Instantly, his spirit cried into the universe.

My one and only love! I've loved you further than the ecstasy! I've dreamed of you in the softness of the night! I've drank from your placid springtide!

Losing all control, deKharouf gave himself up to his vengeance and rage. Defending against the enemy's thunderbolts and ferocious lightning, he drove his spiritual sword against the wicked principalities within the vapor.

Shredding the fabric of the cosmos to the distant heavens, deKharouf fought with the might of love.

I will not lose you! I will destroy the foundations of the earth before I allow them to take you from me!

Instantly healing the wounds and broken limbs inflicted upon his body by the enemy, deKharouf became like a roaring lion. He fought with the perfection of the invincible warrior, ready to defend the only woman who possessed his excellent secrets within her heart.

Driving a wedge between the enemies in the vapor, he forced the angels to give ground to the fullness of his hate.

Rhea! I'm coming to save you!

Pushing the enemy to the edge of the vapor, deKharouf pressed through the thick smoke and fire, getting closer to Rhea's body.

Chapter 88 Revelation

But thou, O Daniel, shut up the words, and seal the book, even to the time of the end.

—Daniel 12: 4 KJV

"DoD is decommissioning DARPA."

Merlin's revelation didn't surprise Nabil. "Not for long."

Merlin sat across from Nabil in the empty cafeteria. Giving him a half-smile, he said, "You're the prophet."

Nabil smiled back and took a sip of his tepid coffee.

"It'll be down for a few months. After DoD reconstructs DARPA, it'll be back in business, better than ever." Merlin's coffee smelled fresh and hot. He sipped it carefully.

"DoD will always need DARPA." Nabil lowered his head. "I just wish DARPA didn't need DoD equally."

Merlin's respect for Professor Nabil—no longer given reticently—mixed with admiration. "DoD intends to remake DARPA and attach a dedicated super soldier research team to it."

"New and improved," whispered Nabil, looking into Merlin's eyes. "War gets a makeover, the world's militaries get a more efficient warrior, peace gets...nothing." Nabil traced the upper edge of the cup with his finger.

Seeing the futility of it all, Merlin dropped the subject. "What will you do now?"

Not having an answer, Nabil lowered his vision.

"We could use you, you know?"

Nabil returned his attention to the man. He stayed silent, thinking through Merlin's words. Raising his cup to his lips, he stopped and put it back down. "I think we both know DoD knew what they were dealing with long before they assembled our team."

"Maybe so, but they place value in our confirmation. They wouldn't be retooling DARPA if they didn't."

Nabil finally took a drink of his cooled coffee. "They want you to head the super soldier research team?"

Merlin nodded slowly. "There's an exhaustive library to work from. They believe I'm the best option right now."

Nabil, full of reflection, looked out the window at the sun's descent behind the horizon.

"So, what do you say, Prophet?" asked Merlin, carefully. "We need you. Your country needs you. Will you be a part of our DARPA team?"

Chapter 89 Eternal Kiss

Let him kiss me with the kisses of his mouth: for thy love is better than wine.

—Song of Solomon 1:1 KJV

The woman he'd loved since childhood lay motionless on the ancient ground. Through the abundant smoke, he saw her beautiful hair. Her eyes sealed and closed, he trembled at her peacefulness.

The sight of Rhea's lifeless body stabbed deKharouf in his heart.

Tens of thousands, upon tens of thousands of devils fell before the ferocity of his sword. His hair whipping this way and that with every thrust and slash of his mighty blade, deKharouf cut through the enemy forces, getting closer to where Rhea's body lay unmoving.

Littered across the temple's inner chamber floor, the remains of the innumerable disembodied spiritual remnants spoke of deKharouf's ferocity. Only the angels of the bottomless pit and the angel of the morning remained, accompanied by their evil spirits.

Upon the elevated stone platform, wherein resided the altar, Rhea's body lay unmoving. Around the altar, the enemy forces of the angels of the perdition stood between her lifeless body and deKharouf.

I can't save you, my love. I tried with all of my might but I've failed both of us!

No other alternative left to him, deKharouf dropped his sword. Falling to his knees on the noxious ground, encircled by the rancid vapor, he relinquished his will to the will of the Almighty. Lowering his head, he prayed to God and committed his soul into the hands of the Lord of hosts.

If I am to fail, then Father, please…let us both enter paradise together.

I beg you, Almighty God…let me die with her.

In divine translation, a mighty whirlwind swept across the temple.

Outside the Planck time barrier, beyond the Planck length measurement, the heavenly whirlwind carried deKharouf away, placing him to the side of Rhea's unmoving body.

Opening his eyes, deKharouf realized what had occurred.

We've both been translated!

The four angels and their accompanying devils were no more.

Rushing to Rhea's side, deKharouf touched her face gently.

She did not respond.

"Awake, my love," he whispered kindly.

Nothing.

Lowering himself closer to her, he discerned movement behind him.

The hosioi! They remained!

Throwing himself to the side, deKharouf lashed out and drove his fist through the hosioi, killing him instantly.

Discarding all caution, deKharouf pierced the gap between the four remaining hosioi. No longer inside the evil vapor, his spiritual sword materialized out of his mouth. Lashing out, his ferocity caused the hosioi to give ground.

Concentrating his spiritual energy on the nearest hosioi, deKharouf instinctively called out, "Die."

In answer to his spiritual command, his killing words blasted out of heaven and destroyed the Delphic combatant instantly.

I possess the sword of the Spirit, he resolved, in astonishment. *But how?*

In galactic proportions, deKharouf's fury reached thunderously into the angry sky.

The three surviving hosioi, seeing the futility of giving battle against his wrath, yielded to his rage and death and departed into the darkness of the night.

Taking advantage of the respite, deKharouf returned to the Rhea's lifeless form. Reaching down, he lifted her in his arms.

In a twinkling of an eye, the spiritual helpmates translated through the transcendent paths of eternity.

In timelessness, deKharouf prayed for his eternal love.

She's all I have, Father. Besides you. Please...take me instead. Don't take her!

A mighty angel appeared in dazzling brightness, pushing back eternity.

Thank you, Father, deKharouf said in his heart. He reached up and grasped the radiant being.

Across the span of forever, beyond the perception of time, the angel brought deKharouf and the lifeless Rhea to the secret place of their youth.

89.2

From the height of a plateau, they observed the greatness of the *Abarim Range*.

He remembered the overlook where he'd first pronounced his love to Rhea.

She had just turned seventeen, he nineteen. The world seemed so much bigger then.

"I've known you since we were children. Your smile...the color of your hair...I loved you in eternity before we were born. I'll love you into forever."

Moving away slightly, she looked out over the land below. "How can we love?"

Clouds hung in the sky, intermittently blocking the sun's rays. A streak of sunlight broke through and kissed her face.

Bypassing her question, deKharouf's youthful vigor took possession of his mind. "With faith, we can do all things. Do you love me?"

When she turned, he sensed warmth.

"Our vows. We are sworn...to God."

"Do you love me?"

She made a slight movement toward him.

He held her hand, a man hungry for something greater than food.

"It's not that easy," she whispered, sounding out of breath. "I'm afraid."

A man of action, the simplicity of her voice assured his manhood. "I won't hurt you. I promise I'll treat you right."

She pulled back. "Why me? Why am I special to you?"

Although still a young man, wisdom resided in deKharouf's spirit. He stepped closer to her. "Because even when I translate to the farthest galaxy, I feel you there. And when I am near to heaven, you are there. If not you, there can never be anyone else. Ever."

89.3

Gently, deKharouf dropped to his knees and lay Rhea's lifeless body on the ground.

Rhea's head fell back, her long hair cascading down to the sacred ground of the *Abarim Range*.

"Come back to me…please…"

His hands shook as he tenderly placed her head on the many-hued blanket.

I've loved you in the years of my youth, through the bedlam of my manhood, into the maturity of my years.

"Please," he spoke aloud. "Don't go."

Rhea remained still, unmoving.

Confronted with the finality of death's dark shadow, deKharouf called out, "Look down upon me, Almighty God. I beg you to hold her blameless before your throne." Tears streamed down his face. "It was me. Blame me," he cried out. "I dared to try to prevent your prophecies. I'm guilty, not her."

Lovingly, deKharouf placed his mouth over her mouth.

He breathed his breath of life into her body.

I will raise her from the dead.

The breath was a kiss.

An everlasting kiss.

The trees looked down in silent wonderment, as he tried to revive Rhea.

For three days, he kept her by the coolness of the spiritual river, lowering her into the otherworldly water at preconceived times.

Lying next to her body, he broke the Nazarite instruction *to be removed from a dead body.* Attempting to revive her, he warmed her with his warmth and breathed into her body.

"Wake up, my love." His plea, feint and constant, reverberated over her.

89.4

On the third day, the mighty angel returned. Standing over deKharouf and the still body of Rhea, the cherub waited.

Quietly, deKharouf wept.

Translating away to stand before the Altar of the Eternal Fire, he entreated the Almighty to allow him to raise her up from the dead.

She's gone.

Drawing his head back and lifting his eyes to the moon, deKharouf cried to the stars of the night.

For 145 years, I've loved you, my beloved. I cannot bear life without you.

Chapter 90 Pella

At the site of the ruins overlooking Pella, the angels of the bottomless pit, the prophētai, and the hosioi gathered around the agora to witness the child emerge from the Pythia's womb.

Violent weather filled the sky and lightning bolts exploded across the firmament.

"Spread the legs of the vessel," called out the prophētai into the coolness of the dawn.

Her body held up on the tripod hovering over the chasm, the Pythia appeared to be spiritually drunk.

Gripping her legs, the hosioi pulled back her insides.

Below the swirling clouds, above the violent earth, the child emerged from between the legs of the Pythia.

Lifting the infant to the heavens, the prophētai presented the child to the mighty angels of the perdition. "Oh mighty Zeus! Oh mighty Apollo!" cried out the prophētai.

Unhurriedly the angels—one by one—inspected the man-child.

Satisfied with the child's image, the Macedonian angel handed the baby to the Sybil.

Wrapping the child in a clean blanket, the Sybil smiled lovingly. Gazing up at the mighty angels, she looked down at the child.

"O pai Dios," the Sybil whispered.

Chapter 91 Best Friend

His mouth is most sweet: yea, he is altogether lovely.
This is my beloved, and this is my friend.

—Song of Solomon 5: 16 KJV

He buried her in the guts of the sacred mountain of God.

Years before, in the braveries, gallantries, and heroisms of Mount Yeroham, next to the Temple of the Eternal Fire, he built a sepulcher. Meticulously using the finest treasures, he spent years building the burial chamber.

I had it all worked out, he thought, sorrowfully. "I was supposed to go first, remember?"

He brought her to the mausoleum. Dressing her in her favorite dress—a jubilant ball gown of astounding color—deKharouf rested her before the handcrafted altar.

"You look so beautiful," he whispered in her cold ear. "You were always my dream come true. I never loved another woman, only you."

In the faint light of dawn, he held Rhea's lifeless hand and recalled their great love.

Kissing her hand gently, he placed it over her heart.

For forty days and forty nights, he ate nothing.

For forty days and forty nights, he drank nothing.

In the silence, deKharouf poured out his heart to the Almighty.

I've lost my best friend on this earth.

You are my best friend, Lord God, but she was my sky and my ground. How much I loved her.

The Almighty comforted deKharouf in his misery.

The mighty Fire wept with deKharouf.

On the forty-first day, the morning spread across the earth.

In the next instant, a powerful angel stood to one side of deKharouf.

The angel touched him on the shoulder.

In a flash of divinity, deKharouf translated.

Standing before the Temple of the Eternal Fire, he lamented, "I can't let this go. I'll start again in this quest. I won't lose her for nothing."

In his anger, his tears fell upon the sacred ground of the temple.

"She kept this temple." Somber and cold, deKharouf's calculation persisted. "From this temple, I'll start my quest for vengeance. I'll shake the heavens and search Hell's fires for the enemies who killed her."

Indignation and rage mixed with his tears, as deKharouf announced the declaration of a man. "This'll never be over. I'll never stop fighting against the abomination. I am but a man. But I will stop them."

Chapter 92 Together Forever

In the solitude of a flowing creek, hidden in the *Ihlara Valley*, Uziel tended to Ariella.

Translating back and forth from the Valley and the underground existence of *Cappadocia*, Uziel made supplication for her recovery. In the days and nights of her pain, he discerned the deepness of her spiritual vacuum.

Returning to camp after catching some fish in the nearby brook, Uziel discovered her bed empty. He found her standing in a clearing, in the late afternoon sun.

At the age of ninety-two, to him her beauty surpassed the brilliance of the sunset. The luxury of her hair contained the purity of the waterfall.

Feeling him behind her, she turned and smiled.

"I thought you'd be sleeping."

"I was hungry," Ariella smiled, lightly. "So, I got up."

Uziel held up three large fish he'd caught in the rivulet. "I'm hungry too."

Without delay, they were in each other's arms. Their kiss began and ended slow and gentle.

Pulling back, she asked in astonishment, "How did you save me?"

"I love you. Our love saved us," Uziel managed to whisper in her ear.

In the early evening, Uziel built a fire and cooked the fish.

Afterward, under the stars, they talked.

Ariella cried when she learned of the deaths of the Nazarite high priests and high priestesses. "No," she moaned. "No," she sobbed, tears running down her face. She gripped Uziel tightly. "Those who loved us most are gone. Oh, Uziel." She fell to her knees, the light from the fire casting shadows across the smoothness of her skin.

"Please don't do this, baby," Uziel begged, holding her close. "Be strong."

"Uziel," Ariella called out. "Our nazars... We failed... How can we consider going on when so many have died?"

"I know you hurt. I hurt too," answered Uziel, stroking Ariella's long hair. "But we can't let it be for nothing. They gave their deaths so we could live."

Her tears continued to fall. "I don't know if I can go on."

"You can, baby. Please. I'll help you."

All through the night, Uziel held her. From time to time, he whispered gently to her until they fell asleep in each other's arms.

In the morning, the sun revealed the streaks of tears across Ariella's appearance.

Her hair disheveled and her skin pale, she astonished Uziel. "You're the most beautiful woman I've ever seen."

Ariella blushed. "Thank you, my wonderful, adorable man."

"Ariella, I'll love you forever," he promised solemnly to his treasured best friend, the love of his love.

A playful Ariella rubbed her hand on Uziel's back. "I believe you," she whispered, a woman without doubt of her man's words. "But time is an enemy we can't defeat."

"My love for you is beyond time."

The husband and wife stood at the uppermost heights of *Athirapally Waterfalls*. Far away from the safe overlooks built for the tourists, Uziel and Ariella observed the prevailing sight of the cascades.

"I believe you," she repeated. "You've loved me for this long."

"How long, my treasure?"

"How long, my darling?"

He pressed her to his chest. His hand passed over each wrinkle around her eyes. He still saw her as a young woman.

"Eighty years..." he said, strongly, his flesh unflinching. "I've loved you for more than eighty years."

The torrents and falls enriched their emotions.

"What do the waterfalls tell you?" Ariella asked.

He lifted her head gently and looked into her eyes. "The waterfalls tell the story of our love."

Her eyes twinkled with a young girl's exuberance. She placed her lips close to his ear and said, "But I'm an old woman."

He gently kissed her. "I see you now as I did the first time I laid eyes on you."

"We shouldn't have translated here. We're only supposed to use our spiritual authority for the Kingdom's work."

"Ssshhh," he touched her lips. "We are the Kingdom's things. We are the Kingdom's riches."

After a long while, she said, "I'm ninety-two, you're ninety-six, I don't think we're treasures anymore."

"You'll always be my treasure," Uziel said, lovingly.

Ariella looked adoringly at him. "He remembered us. My dearest Uziel, the Almighty remembered our passions. We are useful to him for more than our sacred oaths."

Uziel squeezed her tightly. "I told you the Almighty wouldn't forget about our love for each other. Now that we've fulfilled our promises, he desires we be husband and wife. He wants us to become one."

"Uziel? We wanted children, a family. How?"

"Remember Abram and Sarai. Never forget when they started their family."

Underneath the stars, Uziel believed he saw the brightness of the galaxies in Ariella's eyes.

Their kisses lifted into the atmosphere and spread across the sky. They held hands and talked to each other like best friends, while starlight fell all around them like rain.

"Come with me, my love," Uziel beckoned to Ariella, leading her gently toward his spirit. "Translate with me into forever."

In a twinkling of an eye, beyond the threshold of life and immortality, Uziel and Ariella translated across earth's horizon like flashes of light and sun.

The End

About the author:

Baltazar Bolado is the author of Publius: Libertas Aut Mors, The Ululant Ache, and numerous short stories. This is his fifth novel. He lives in northern Michigan.

Discover other titles by Author name at Amazon.com

Or connect with Baltazar online @
Website: baltazarbolado.com
Twitter: @Baltazar_Bolado
Facebook: https://www.facebook.com/BaltazarBoladoAuthor

www.ingramcontent.com/pod-product-compliance
Lightning Source LLC
Chambersburg PA
CBHW051408170626
46809CB00006B/2067